THE BIG FED'S THOUGHTS LOCKED ON THE INTERNATIONAL OUTRAGE

It was unthinkable that a rogue or supposed friendly nation was orbiting nuclear satellites, looking to butcher millions for an as yet unknown reason. Beyond the frightening facts, Hal Brognola knew ground zero in the Australian outback wouldn't rate a footnote in history if a nuclear spear was plunged into a major city from above Earth's atmosphere.

He drew a deep breath, let it out and said to the assembled team in the War Room, "The President green-lighted us to do whatever it takes to get to the bottom of what went down in Australia. The Man wants a rapid response, folks, no punches pulled, no mercy to the perpetrators. They go down hard and, if possible, their names and misdeeds are to be buried along with them. That's the good news.

"Unfortunately, he also implied that because of the nature of the crisis, there's a good chance our teams may well be locking horns with any number of operators. CIA. NSA. DOD. DIA. You name it.

"And on this one, it would be best if we kept our backs to the wall."

DON PENDLETON'S

STONY

AMERICA'S ULTRA-COVERT INTELLIGENCE AGENCY

MAN®

STARFIRE

A GOLD EAGLE BOOK FROM

WORLDWIDE®

TORONTO • NEW YORK • LONDON
AMSTERDAM • PARIS • SYDNEY • HAMBURG
STOCKHOLM • ATHENS • TOKYO • MILAN
MADRID • WARSAW • BUDAPEST • AUCKLAND

First edition April 2007

ISBN-13: 978-0-373-61972-6
ISBN-10:   0-373-61972-3

STARFIRE

Special thanks and acknowledgment to
Dan Schmidt for his contribution to this work.

Printed in U.S.A.

STARFIRE

PROLOGUE

Australia

Forty-three minutes and counting, and Chuck Boltmer knew they were cutting it close to the razor's edge. He wasn't even suited up and already he was sweating. If they stuck to training—both mock-up and virtual-reality dry runs—thirty-five minutes and a few more agonizing ticks alone would be devoured just getting set up, more, depending, of course, on the human factor. The low earth orbit satellite was already in position, and Boltmer knew if they were two shakes behind schedule Zenith One wasn't about to hold up the show because the hired help was too slow on the draw from ground zero.

Man, oh, man, what kind of crazy life had he led, he wondered, that would lead him to the brink of suicide like this, and of his own free will?

He knew. A washed-out CIA special op once connected to the Cali Cartel, who loved money more than law and order and was hunted by his own people, broke and down on his luck didn't get to choose which banquet table offered the choicest meat.

Not much more than a street beggar, as far as he was concerned, but those days were fast coming to an end, one way or another.

And in the face of a holocaust that would leave no doubt.

Boltmer killed the Jeep's engine and lights, then stared through the dust- and bug-spattered windscreen. The pub and surrounding area had been chosen as a test site, he knew, and right from the beginning, when his handlers laid out mission parameters and particulars. Remoteness guaranteed limited immediate collateral damage. That, and the handlers figured nobody much cared about a bunch of ex-cons, ex-mercs and other assorted riffraff living off the radar screen, to be used as guinea pigs in what struck him as little more than a ghoul's experiment.

The problem haunting Boltmer was grim knowledge acquired during training. Sure, this stretch of outback fanning away in oceanic dimensions was humped with rocky hills and cut with gorges, all but deserted of human beings, and they were situated well beyond the immediate four- to five-mile incineration radius. Or so said the nameless European principals who had hired him out of obscurity and grinding poverty in Berlin, eighteen months back, but what now seemed another lifetime. What worried him at the moment was all the spinifex grassland, the eucalypt forest to the north and east, subtropical rain forest that would rise up when—if—they managed to extract for the decon site. In other words, the dry countryside was a living hot zone, with enough incendiary flashpoints…

"We will be fine. Show courage. Just remember, we are being paid five million dollars. Apiece."

Boltmer looked over at the big, bullet-head buzz-cut man with black eyes cold and lifeless enough to sub-humanize him as part-reptile in human flesh.

He knew him only as Karlov. Boltmer was certain that wasn't his real name, but judging the accent, slop-ing forehead and high cheekbones, he pegged him as East Euro-trash, maybe Serb or Bulgarian, likewise a gangster, since Karlov had all the greedy, malicious aura of a common street thug, more muscle and ani-mal instinct than good sense. And what made him so confident anyway? he wondered. Did Karlov know something he didn't?

As his partner marked their position on the GPS unit mounted to the dashboard, began punching in the se-ries of cutout numbers on the secured sat phone, then fiddling with the scrambler, Boltmer wondered about his own seeming death wish. The madness he was about to participate in and come out the other side would find those hefty retirement funds plunked down into a numbered Swiss account—or all his hopes, dreams and fears—would be over.

Vaporized, in truth, in less time than it took to blink.

He tried to focus on the positive, such as living. The thermal-insulated, one-piece raid suit he wore was state-of-the-art, similar to the protection tiles that shielded space shuttles upon reentry into Earth's atmo-sphere, only stronger. Same deal for the main protec-tive suit, but with obvious and subtle variations.

Compare 2900 degrees Fahrenheit those astronauts faced to an educated ballpark half-million hellish units he was maybe staring down, what with superheated pressure waves that would come roaring their way at supersonic speed, and both thermal pj's and their black project robot shell better be next to as invincible as any divine armor of heavenly angels against evil.

"This is Vortex to Zenith One. We are at Blast Furnace and moving into position. Repeat…"

Bottom line, Boltmer figured it was all about the spacesuits and their advanced cutting-edge extras, as he heard Karlov confirm transmission. Forget the bush lab rats, the two of them were the real test subjects, once they suited up. He'd been blindfolded and driven from Berlin, he briefly recalled, to the underground complex for training when verbally signing on, he had never been told outright who he'd pledged allegiance to. But he knew enough about the European Space Agency to know it housed the European Space Operation Center in Darmstadt, Germany, and two and two still equaled four, even in the spook world's black hole. Armed now with the latest in supertech armor for astronauts, he knew he was way past the point of hoping the spacesuit to be donned would hold up under heat about as extreme as the core of the sun. At the end of the day, he decided, the principals' main objectives were none of his wonder.

Living to collect five million was his end game.

"Let's do it, my friend," Karlov said.

Boltmer malingered a moment before piling out the door behind his partner, another few seconds lagging before hauling the heavy corpse-size nylon bag out of the back of the Jeep. Hanging the full weight of what would either save or fry his war-grizzled bacon over his shoulder, he felt Karlov's glacier eyes drilling into the side of his head, but ignored the man as he stared east. All the blood on his hands, all the insane schemes by his own machinations he'd lived through in his day than he actually had a right to keep on claiming air, and he was hardly lacking in the guts department. But this?

Pure Hell on Earth.

Oh, but the insanity of it all, no question.

And here he was, Boltmer glancing at the illuminated dial of his Breitling emergency transmitter watch, moving out to fall in behind Karlov. Forty minutes and ticking…

Then, willingly, they would become the first human beings to try to live in the face and fury of a nuclear explosion almost four times as powerful as the one dropped on Hiroshima.

CHAPTER ONE

New Mexico

"We have a problem."

Radic Kytol didn't want to hear about problems at this late stage, but he read the tight expression on Ludjac Muyol's goateed face.

Natural paranoia constant, instinct tried and proved many times during his climb up the ranks in Belgrade to current post as top lieutenant in charge of the Balayko Family's expansion goals, he felt compelled to give the broad vista of scrubland another search through the high-powered military field glasses. Scanning mesas and other outcrops ringing their temporary command post, he mouthed a curse. The sunbaked desert plain appeared one vast heat shimmer, thus creating the mirage that something was always moving, even when there was nothing there. Spooky, he decided, then considered where they were.

Roswell, New Mexico.

They were close to six hundred miles from their final destination east, and the advent of their own extraterrestrial encounter was moments away. It didn't escape him for one second that their safehouse was within an area where wild rumors abounded for decades how alien spacecraft had crashed here, and that the United States Air Force had purportedly recovered the bodies of little gray men in 1947, engineering a subsequent secret cover-up about UFOs and extraterrestrial life that apparently wasn't all that secret. That was, of course, if he chose to submit to the truth as the locals would have him believe when their two minivans passed through town, purchasing necessities there to continue their journey.

Briefly, he recalled the gift shop and diner, all the UFO paraphernalia, meant, he was sure, to further inflame and keep the fantastic alive. But, now that he thought about it, were they not aliens in their own right, invaders, no less? Ah, but considering the mission, they were poised to unleash an invasion of sorts, if not from another world, then just beyond Earth's atmosphere.

Spinning on his heel, he marched for Muyol, handing off the field glasses before plunging into the shadowy bowels of the three-man workstation. He found the computer brains hard at it, earning what was in his mind exorbitant fees, working laptop keyboards in a controlled frenzy. He sensed the tension, torqued up, higher than normal. The living room was barren except for the bank of five computers and the necessary modems that kept them online to their network of contacts, both overseas and in-country. Unfortunately, his knowledge of what they did was rudimentary at best, but he understood enough to know that Milo Serjac's monitor shouldn't be filled with pornography.

"What is that?" Kytol snapped, skidding to a halt behind the trio in their wheeled high-back leather thrones. He noted the constipated look flashing over Serjac's face, as if he—a man who held the power of life and death in his hands—was little more than an irritating mosquito in the geek's ear.

Fingers flying over his keyboard, Serjac declared over his shoulder, "It is a man and woman copulating."

"You get sarcastic with me?" Kytol felt his face flush with hot anger. "I can see that! Why is it on your screen?" he demanded, but feared he knew the answer already.

"Three of our e-mail sites have been bombed," Serjac said. "Melbourne, Tokyo and Barcelona, all compromised."

"By whom?"

Serjac snorted, as if he'd been asked a stupid question. "It could be someone in Butte, Montana, for all I know. Or it could be NORAD or NASA."

"And bombing our supposed secured e-mail with porn?"

"Perhaps a ruse while they attempt to trace us."

"I thought that was impossible. To trace us, that is."

"Nothing is impossible when it comes to computers and hacking into them. Especially when dealing with professionals."

"I want answers, Serjac, not to stand here and suffer your infuriating condescension!"

Serjac moderated his tone. "There are something

like twenty million skilled hackers around the world. There are over thirty thousand Web sites I know of that are set up for the express purpose of stealing information, especially classified information, since they are the most challenging, not to mention the most alluring and profitable. And those are just the amateurs. This would be a first in my experience. All transmissions were supposedly secured by a 128-bit encryption system—I will not burden you by telling you the near infinite number of quadrillion possibilities—but these were firewalls I personally built into our network. Suffice it to say this should not have happened."

"But it has, you insufferable jackass! Change passwords! Create another firewall! Add a more secure antivirus program!"

"That is what I am in the process of doing. That, and trying to discover if other hot sites have been breached. Dear Comrade Kytol, what I am telling you is that whoever is doing this is good, maybe as good as we are. What you are seeing now is comparable to a chess game between masters, but one done in cyberspace."

Kytol ordered Muyol to secure the perimeter, but add another man to help Vishdal watch the cameras, then he barked at Serjac, "NSA? CIA? DOD? Give me your best guess."

Serjac shrugged as a happy face on a stick body and flashing the middle finger jumped onto his screen. "There it is again. London is now compromised. The last access code to put us online with Zenith was being transmitted when this popped on."

"So, you did get the codes?"

Serjac ignored him, his grim stare locked on his

monitor, fingers banging away as the happy-faced stickman mooned him. "This swine—taunt me, will you?"

"Stop playing games and answer me, or I will have your castrated balls sitting on that keyboard!"

Kytol, feeling his blood boil like hot lava in his veins, and who had little patience when it came to finessing a situation, computer or otherwise, wanted nothing more than to whip the .45 Glock from the shoulder rigging beneath his windbreaker and blow the machine into countless pieces all over the room. But the slightly built wiry man, he knew, had been an informal member of the notorious Crna Ruka. The Black Hand was responsible for hacking into the Kosovo Information Center in 1998, and from there it was a short cyberjump to break into NATO databases. For all the good it did, valuable intelligence was stolen from NATO right before the bombs began raining on Yugoslavia. He may not like these men, their superior attitudes, because he didn't understand what they did or how they did it, but they were—in their parlance— super-cyberwarriors. They were the best at what they did, and at the moment he needed them more than the other way around. The days were gone, Kytol knew, when wars were won solely on brute force and overwhelming violence.

Serjac finally deemed him worthy of an answer as he waved at the screen in front of the Russian. "You can see for yourself."

Kytol looked at the digital readout in the top corner of Anatoly Dyvshol's split screen. Forty-two seconds and scrolling down. The Russian worked his keys with a renewed burst of energy, and the solar-winged silver ball enlarged after a flashing series of zoom-ins, the real observation LEO satellite, he knew, now monitoring its orbit. The satellite hung against the endless backdrop of outer space, and Kytol watched as a slender arm on the portside extended from the platform and locked into place, conical nose aimed at the blue planet.

Thirty seconds.

As the Russian began the final countdown at five, Kytol lost the smile. His eyes widened as a cone of fire burst from the rocket's thrusters, instantly swallowed, it seemed, by infinite blackness.

"Three, two…"

It looked to Kytol like a giant silver spear.

"One…"

Then it was hurtling toward Earth, vanishing rapidly for the sea of clouds, a streaking javelin, but packed, Kytol knew, with fifty kilotons of fissionable devastation.

THE SKY WAS FALLING.

And it was all Boltmer could do to pry his eyes off the tumbling numbers on the watch engineered into the wrist of his spacesuit.

Less than a minute to impact.

Boltmer had never felt such pure cold terror. Trajectory, rate of descent, distance and potency of each ring to their observation-monitoring post all calculated—with supposedly no margin for error—it would blow, dead ahead, in their face. Grimly aware he would, in fact, be living just outside a nuclear fission blast—Boltmer could barely concentrate on the final chore.

Lumbering in his robotic-like cocoon, he stepped up and snapped the supersuction cups mounted on the base of the black-tinted diamond shield to the floor with his boot. The list of a hundred-and-one things that could go wrong wanted to scream through his mind. They were on the outer limits of what the principals called the third ring. Instruments to measure wind and radiation levels likewise sewn into the arms of their suits—supposedly impervious to shock waves—with cameras to film the initial blast and its effects shielded inside a classified crystallized carbon composite and meant to bear up under flying debris and searing heat, the winds at this distance would still hammer them at over 200 mph.

Blast. Heat. Radiation.

The three big ones.

The sudden flash jolted Boltmer, a cry of alarm trapped and echoing inside the reinforced bubble of his helmet. It was dazzling, then flared beyond brilliant, like a thousand suns rushing together for one infinite supernova, the burst of light piercing even both sets of protective covering enough he had to squint.

Time seemed suspended, all but immeasurable in this frozen eternity, as Boltmer stood, awed and terrified by the expanding cloud.

The gauges on his arm, he found, were shooting numbers so fast they blurred.

It was coming.

CHAPTER TWO

"What the hell was that?"

They were gasping, all but turned to stone, squinting at the blinding orange-white ball as it roiled across the floor-to-ceiling plasma relay monitor. Swelling until the cloud ran off the twenty-by-twenty-foot screen, the image jumped, then flickered with static as titanic shock waves reached out for the observation satellite. They were too stunned, too late to readjust the ob-sat's altitude and pull it back from the nuke's asteroid-like hammerblows. Gyroscopes, radar, radio, John Ellison knew, the whole computerized nerve center, in short, that could monitor and transmit the situation from those space eyes wiped out.

All systems go, however, from where he stood.

While the twelve-man, three-woman workforce launched into scientific babble all over Control Room Omega, scrambling from bay to bay to check monitors and digital readouts and bark questions into throat mikes, Ellison kept a straight face. Hanging back, he listened as the director demanded to know what in God's name had just happened.

God, the NSA man knew, had nothing to do with it.

What they knew was that the suspicious unidentified low earth orbit satellite their Keyhole and NASA-affiliated observation and military satellites were tracking had just detonated in a measured read of fifty-kiloton self-immolation. The same explosive yield, to their mounting horror and panic, that had just blown a chunk of Western Queensland outback into radioactive dust from a rocket fired from the killer satellite.

Ellison stole another moment to watch their frenzied search for quick answers they weren't about to find anywhere in their computer systems. Director Turner looked torn between the wall monitor's leaping fuzz, firing questions at his scientists and the red phone mounted on his personal command desk in the far corner. NORAD, the Pentagon, the CIA, down to NASA and every American military- and law-enforcement agency in the continental United States and abroad with access to satellites would know by now the United States, its allies, and the world at large was just thrust to the edge of Armageddon. Ellison knew the combined authority of all that clout was scrambling right then to reach the Joint Chiefs, the President, anybody on his staff with a secured cell or sat phone. Only they would flood the White House with SOS to be flung back into this black hole of unfathomable mystery and international menace, the likes of which no power on Earth had yet to face.

Ellison left them to their terror and confusion, looked up at the observation deck. Behind the thick-

glass bubble stood his one and only superior. The man
in charge was casually working on a cigar, looking
down on the workforce like some king on a throne
about to pass judgment on his subjects.

In truth, he just had.

Ellison made eye contact with the man known only
to the others as Sir. It was quick, but Sir lifted a hand
to the blind side of their commotion, long enough to
shoot him a thumbs-up.

THE SKY WAS ON FIRE.

Or so it looked to Boltmer in his flying vortex.

Unless he'd been nailed to the hull of a battleship,
he knew there was nothing he could now do but let
himself get dragged, lifted, dropped and bounced
across the ground. Human tumbleweed. The shimmer-
ing radioactive halo that fanned across the heavens
was the least of his concerns. Round one was punishing enough, as he and Karlov had hurtled in tandem,
sailing west. How far they'd been tossed he couldn't
say, but he was still breathing.

The only good news so far.

He soared, slammed to earth, then was sucked up,
flying on. The raging sea of debris and dust jettisoned
west was now being swept back in the furious clutches
of the afterwinds. The world blurring along in the eye
of this storm appeared little more than a streaking black
whirlwind, all but blinding Boltmer to whatever else
was being vacuumed beyond maybe a yard from his
flight path.

Had he been inclined to pray…

The magnetic tug began losing steam, he sensed, as

the violent slamming of limbs lessened by noticeable jarring degrees. Another fifty feet and he crash-landed, dragged like a tow line, another yard or so.

It was over.

He had survived. For the moment.

He breathed deep through the rubber mask over nose and mouth. Another intake of oxygen and he started to feel he might make it. Despite the Tempur lining in his suit—the special foam material, he knew, that was used to protect astronauts against G-force—Boltmer groaned as he felt the ache and throbbing nonetheless down his battered side, in his joints.

He clambered to his feet.

And found he was just in time to watch the final act. The mushroom cloud kept billowing out, angrier now, if that was possible. Glowing like the blazing maw of some gigantic incinerator—or the pit of Hell—it kept climbing, expanding yet more, rising on for what the principals told them would be its ceiling of five to six miles—or more—toward a sky that all but looked to burn.

Boltmer felt shaken to the core of his being.

He checked his temperature gauge, and froze, eyes bugged as he took a read.

Just over seven thousand degrees Fahrenheit, but dropping now. Then the numbers began falling hard, as they told him would happen, once the brute strength of blast furnace afterwinds sucked themselves back into the rising vortex. The temperature at their own gale-force impact and shortly thereafter was measured and recorded already on a minimodem.

Forget whatever the experiment's goals, Boltmer's

grim concern became extraction. From there, they walked until their tanks redlined. If their contact was late, what with their ride out of the hot zone supposedly constructed with engine parts of classified alloys and which was also a self-contained oxygenated vehicle and decon chamber...

Boltmer was slowly turning when the hairs on his neck bristled. He caught the moaning as it filtered through his helmet, finally pivoted about-face, and gasped.

They came staggering out of the black pall. Boltmer choked down the bile squirting up his chest, cold fear and the unholy sight doing a tap dance on nerves taut as garrote wire.

They were nothing less than a vision of the damned.

What sounded like strangled cries or deep-throated moaning from the zombies grew louder, began pounding his helmet like invisible fists. Clear they were desperate to speak, probably shout, then Boltmer assumed their vocal cords, perhaps their tongues had been fried. They came twitching, convulsing, bridging the gap quick, and straight toward him, as if sensing another living presence.

He stared, paralyzed by horror. Their flesh had been microwaved in the searing winds, with black holes— but like glowing embers, it seemed—where the eyes were burned out, dark red streaks oozing down cheeks where skin was cooked off to the bone. Same for the scalp, hair and flesh gone to expose gleaming patches of skull. Boltmer couldn't tell if they were clothed, if that was flesh or bone or both on down the black-and-red walking cadavers, then felt his senses boggled to another level of numbing repulsion. Nothing but mindless terror or the will to live should have kept them standing. Any oxygen—or most of it, he had to believe—had surely been incinerated out of the immediate vicinity, or turned into living fire, if nothing else.

They collapsed in a boneless heap.

He knew he needed to conserve oxygen, but Boltmer sucked deep from the main tank to calm his racing heart.

Granted, he was all about the money, but after what he had just witnessed, he had to wonder.

Up to ten miles they told him the flash could melt down retina, the initial blast shear away skin to the bone. How many more zombies were left wandering the countryside? he wondered, panning the firestorms, ten to two o'clock. Beyond this night, how many would die a slow, agonizing death from radiation sickness in the weeks, the years, to come? How many babies would be born with grotesque birth defects from mothers suffering from the invisible savaging of fallout?

He stared into the fire, which only seemed to grow more angry and intense in his frozen eternity. Was this but just a taste of Hell on Earth, a microcosm of Fate awaiting humankind? What kind of planet would survivors—the blind, burned and insane—inherit? All water contaminated, the air poisoned by fallout. The sun blotted out by a radioactive shield of dust that would reach around the globe. The only season, then, one winter of eternal subfreezing. No crops, since there would be no arable soil to grow food.

He jumped as Karlov passed by. His partner clambering on without so much as a glance at the dead,

Boltmer followed, but moved as if he was in a trance. He wanted to focus on survival, five million bucks and his own dreams, but wondered if there was any future.

Or one that would be worth sticking around to see if the ultimate madness was unleashed.

CHAPTER THREE

Barbara Price didn't need to read their faces. They knew the threat to their continued existence was grim. The sense of dread was so thick that it seemed to engulf her as she walked into the Computer Room.

But, to a man and woman, they were all seasoned professionals, she knew. They had a job to do, no matter what the odds, mystery or critical mass, and do it they would.

This time the attack was hitting them from cyberspace, which made it equally as lethal. Exposure of their ultracovert Sensitive Operations Group to the world at large would prove a legal catastrophe—possible imprisonment, fines and such—which, of course, would shut them down permanently. Tack on subsequent potential for toppling the White House, impeachment of the President all but guaranteed, and that by itself was no mere aftershock.

It was that bad.

Which meant they needed to go on the attack, and at all due light speed and martial and technical proficiency at their disposal. The problem right now, however, was in determining who was the enemy, where the enemy was hiding, and how to go on the offensive once the enemy was flushed out.

The slim honey-blond beauty stole a moment on the way to their cybercrews' workstations to check the mounted digital wall clocks with major cities marked for each time zone. She noted the time differences on three current flashpoints, mentally juggling day and night disparities. As usual, Father Time was the invisible gathering storm for the cyberwizards here at the Farm in the Shenandoah Valley of the Blue Ridge Mountains in Virginia. The same dire omen, she reflected, could be rolling dark thunderheads over both their field ops, and the entire planet when she considered the situation in Australia.

She was acutely aware that about ninety miles away in Washington, D.C., the best and the brightest of the most powerful country on the planet were scrambling for answers. Answering to only the President of the United States—who green-lighted each black ops for Stony Man and its warriors in the field—Price knew it was always best to let whatever political fallout land wherever it would, devour whoever it would.

Only this time the situation was so grave…

She stopped beside the head of the cyberteam. Aaron "The Bear" Kurtzman acknowledged her presence with a dark glance over his shoulder. His spine had been shattered by a bullet during an attack on the Farm, and the big stocky computer genius was relegated to spending the rest of his life in a wheelchair. He lifted a hand to indicate he needed another few moments, then returned to tapping on his keyboard. A quick look down the line and Price found the main players were hard at it, working in grim silent frenzy. Carmen Delahunt, Huntington Wethers and Akira Tokaido looked like a troupe of master pianists as their fingers flew over keyboards. Satellite images, numerical data and grid maps of AIQs—areas in question— as well as shots with red laser lines around the globe marking satellite orbits, flashed over their monitors. The new crisis was being handled primarily by the team leader and Tokaido. That the Japanese cyberwarrior was without earbuds and MP3 player would have told Price by itself how fearsome the situation, how perilous the yawning black hole that was their immediate future.

What they knew was that an unknown killer satellite had dumped a nuclear missile on Australia from its low earth orbit, vaporizing a six-mile ring in a desolate tract of the Queensland outback, a fifty-kiloton wallop, as previously indicated by the Farm's e-mail and database theft of NASA, DOD and CIA satellite reads of ground zero and contaminated vicinity beyond. The last she heard from her own intelligence sources was woefully limited, since no one knew anything of substance, but that was several hours ago.

That left Hal Brognola in her loop.

The high-ranking Justice Department official, who oversaw the Farm and was liaison to the Man, was off on his own intelligence-hunting expedition, and she silently urged a quick wrap on his end and an even quicker chopper ride back to the Farm. He had taken the three-man commando unit of Able Team along with him for a meet with an unnamed and unknown source he'd intimated to her would either prove highly informative or dangerous to his health.

Make that five crisis fronts, including their phantom attackers in cyberspace.

Mack Bolan, aka the Executioner, was off their radar screen at the moment as he pursued his own campaign in Sri Lanka. They could use all hands, but Phoenix Force had just hit Dagestan in a mission that required their one-hundred-percent iron-clad attention.

"Good news and bad news," Kurtzman suddenly told the mission controller. "The good news is that I've scrubbed our hot e-mail dumps, installed another antivirus and antiworm program in our network. The bad news is that our servers were bombed—a brute force attack that means whoever was trying to track us has put together their own network over the Internet. My best guess is they've created their own supercomputer, with firewall encryption every bit as sophisticated as ours. For all I know, it could be one to a dozen or more hackers."

"And you determined they had broken through our firewalls how?"

"They were either cocky," Tokaido interjected, "or taunting us. They bombed servers we use in emergencies with porn that would make even the dirtiest scumbag blush."

Kurtzman cleared his throat, frowning as he shot Tokaido an admonishing eye for embellished interruption. "Apparently, they've also been busy bombing e-mail from NASA to the CIA and God only knows whoever else."

Tokaido flashed Price a tight grin. "But believe us, the triple-X shenanigans aside, they're good."

They had to be, Price thought. the Farm used encryption software programs that combined elaborate mathematics, symbols and letters that would have sent Einstein screaming into the night. Their crypto texts of substitution, transposition and fractionalization were well beyond the commonly used 56-bit encryption that had seventy-two quadrillion possibilities alone. Only the U.S. government, its military intelligence complex and banks were allowed to use anything above 56-bit encryption. Attempted sale of such encryption programs, home or abroad, was a federal crime.

"We're attempting to backtrack," Kurtzman told her. "But—"

"They can scrub and change handles and create new servers as you run them down."

"I believe I can trace them, however. They're using Old Testament figures as handles—Noah, Cain and Abel and so forth," Tokaido said. "And sticking to the same names. It's almost as if they're daring us to find them."

"So, find them," Price said, and wondered why, if that was true, they seemed so willing to be tracked down and cornered, this invisible enemy being such crack cybercommandos.

Kurtzman's frown was back. "Thing is, Barb, these are most likely civilians. We all know the Pentagon, the DOD, the Air Force and even the CIA have seen their e-mail busted into recently and with frightening ease and regularity. Very few people outside the elite intelligence loop know about that."

"Yeah, embarrassment," Tokaido added, "fear of admitting their own vulnerability. Job security, I imagine, since they don't want public perception of our intelligence and military hierarchy as inept when it comes to guarding national security and its secrets."

"And we hack into their databases all the time," Kurtzman said.

"We're not exactly up for congressional funding, Bear. What's your point?"

"Oh, don't get me wrong, I understand full well the ramifications here. My point is, say we do find them. Statistically most hackers are about fourteen to twenty-five years old. Kids for the most part. Geniuses, without a doubt, but still kids."

Price knew where Kurtzman was headed, but felt annoyed nonetheless that she had to spell it out. "I wasn't planning on offering them a job here at the Farm, Bear."

"But?"

"They're a clear and present danger to our very existence. If information has been stolen from us, or if our location is pinned down and they think it's cute and clever to announce to the world who we are, or they want to serve some mercenary agenda—blackmail for money—then we need to pay them a visit. Retrieve or destroy the information, and give them a stern and fair warning."

Kurtzman nodded. "Give us another hour, give or take, and I can let you know something definite."

"I'll be in the War Room. I want a full package on each front in one hour."

"Will do."

Price left them to their individual tasks. As she headed toward the armored door, she felt her stomach roll over, her jaw tighten. There was no way to spin any positive angle on what they faced. Both the Farm and the world, she knew, had been shoved to the edge of the abyss by unknown enemies with equally unknown objectives. It was too often standard operating procedure to hurl themselves into the fire, armed with little more than questions and sordid hanging riddles, the sum total of which always put countless innocent lives on the scales of life and death. But stomping out flashpoints before mass murder and anarchy could spread to consume entire countries and potentially send the entire world spiraling toward doomsday was what they did best. Only the present critical mass felt more sinister and threatening than at any previous time she could recall during her stint as mission controller. It appeared someone—or some nation—was sending a message they were armed with nukes and could drop them at will from space…

If humankind went the way of the dinosaur, then her worries Stony Man could be exposed by hackers wouldn't matter in the least. All horrible truth be told, if the world went up in a thermonuclear holocaust, then likewise it would be as if the Farm never even existed.

End of game.

End of life on Earth.

Or so far as all of them now knew it.

Maryland

AS MUCH AS Carl Lyons hated ventures through spook snake pits, it struck him that, more often than not, he found himself doing just that. All the slick lies, intrigue and backstabbing, and those spooks who straddled the fence armed with personal agendas, could put any number of politicians on the grease to shame. Not to mention it seemed he was always creeping—or being led—to the doorstep of waiting Death.

Well, it wasn't his place to grumble why, he knew. Just dig in, do it. Nicknamed "Ironman," he was no marshmallow melting in the flames of adversity. And Hal Brognola had handed Able Team its standing orders.

A two-hour-plus jaunt from D.C., for starters, following a web of backcountry roads off the interstate as given to the big Fed by his Shadow Man, and they were guided in by the GPS in the Farm's custom war van. They were here now in the wooded belly of Western Maryland, about thirty miles south of Gettysburg to be more exact. One of Lyons's two teammates had disgorged alongside him into the dark unknown, right in front of the gate with its No Trespassing sign, two klicks and change out from the concrete bunker dug into the hillside where the shadow encounter would go down, and which Stony Man cyberburglars had been fortunate enough to steal a peek at from a passing satellite. Any threat, Brognola warned, wouldn't be overt; it would come sudden and out of nowhere, if personal experience served him right. In other words, Lyons and company knew to trust no one, and to not, under any circumstances, allow the seeming absence of menace to lull them into dropping their guard. These particular wolves in sheep's clothing, he knew— black ops who put themselves above the law and who would execute innocent civilians if it served their twisted ideal of protecting national security—often came bearing smiles and friendly assurances while waving a white flag.

The former Los Angeles detective and current leader of Able Team dropped to a crouch behind a pine tree for quick situation assessment. Given that they knew next to nothing about Brognola's rendezvous with the unknown spook source, they were ready to go tactical at the first double signal transmitted over vibrating pagers fixed to their respective hips. Like Hermann "Gadgets" Schwarz and Rosario "Politician" Blancanales, he was togged in a blacksuit and weighted down with a combat harness and slotted vest stuffed to the gills with grenades, spare clips, on down to a sheathed Ka-Bar fighting knife on his shin. In lieu of his Colt Python .357 Magnum, the Able Team leader's new sidearm of choice was a .50-caliber Desert Eagle, with mounted laser sight. Its clip was filled with fifteen rounds of special "black rhino" hollowpoint pulverizers. Stony Man's resident armorer, John "Cowboy" Kissinger, swore he could now nearly shred Kevlar like foam. Schwarz, he knew, was sitting with the war van, watching thermal screens and monitoring parabolic sensors for any traffic, human or vehicular, while Blancanales was on the move in a perimeter sweep to his deep right flank.

All set, but for what?

Lyons scanned the forested slopes through night-vision goggles, the Heckler & Koch MP-5 submachine gun with attached sound suppressor and laser sight rolling in unison with his visual surveillance. Lyons listened to the dead silence. No matter how hard it tried, no matter the level of skill earned by tough experience, no living creature could advance in total silence through any such terrain. And that went for Blanca-nales, too, despite the fact the man was a Vietnam vet who had been baptized in the blood-soaked jungles of Southeast Asia where there was nothing but armed ghosts who moved silent as the wind. There was brush, twigs, stones to contend with, uneven but hard-packed earth to avoid, that would yield to encroaching weight. The body gave off distinct odors, often through ex-pelled breath. Say a stalking opponent was inclined to smoke, booze, meat, or a splash of yesterday's after-shave, or just so happened to be sweating out any num-ber of toxins...

And Lyons caught a whiff of cigarette residue as a sudden breeze rustled through the woods. As good for-tune had it, he was downwind. The trouble under these circumstances was that he was up against profession-als, bad habits or not. As such they would have night vision, EM scanners—

What the hell was that? Lyons wondered. The fig-ure—if he could call it such—was nearly invisible de-spite his infrared radiation-enhanced eye. It was a specter of human form, but in blurry white outline, al-most perfectly blended with the outcrop beyond a stand of trees. Was it standing or moving, and where did it come from so suddenly? He wasn't even sure he was looking at a living creature, since there was no dis-cernible light-wave read, then he saw a subgun that ap-peared all but suspended in the air. Instinct screamed at Lyons he was marked, dead to rights, whatever the ap-parition, and if he wasn't witness to the Invisible Man, then that was a mounted battery-operated weapon.

And going for broke!

Lyons was dropping for maximum shield behind the fat base of a pine just as the white beam of a laser speared the ghost-murk of night vision and bark flayed his exposed cheek and jaw to the burping retort of muffled subgun.

CHAPTER FOUR

"Extinction Level Event. ELE, if you like."

If he liked. Hell, Hal Brognola didn't like any of it. Not the Shadow Man's flare for the dramatic, nor his vague reasoning of shared interests in national security, certain these meets were also manufactured fishing expeditions. Brognola grew conscious of the Glock 17 stowed beneath his suit jacket, having already noted the hardware tucked at left bicep level under Shadow Man's windbreaker.

"What do you know about the space alerting and defense system?"

He was no astronomy expert by any stretch, but he knew the basics enough to thwart Shadow Man if he was attempting to paint him an ignoramus. Even a small portion of knowledge wielded some power, Brognola thought. He took a few moments to consider his answer, measure the man.

They were nameless sources of intelligence he had used over the years. Sometimes the big Fed went to them, but usually they sought him out through a series of encrypted e-mails they had arranged. Whether to pick his brains or to attempt to confirm suspicions and rumors of the existence of Stony Man Farm, he met them at a mutually agreed-upon time and place. He always seemed to walk away, taking everything, giving nothing, but only insofar as he knew.

They came as the usual clone of buzz cut, dark clothing, chiseled but nondescript faces, a security force of normally two shooters on hand, as was the case now. One mountain of granite with earpiece, throat mike and HK-33 was posted outside the door, the other wraith, Brognola had likewise last seen, was waiting behind the wheel of the black GMC with government plates. There could be more hardmen, likewise snipers buried in the woods for all he knew. But he had come armed with more than foresight and a bad gut feeling. Since nearly being murdered in the past during one such encounter, Brognola had Able Team in tow, more than confident that they had him covered. If the Stony Man commando sensed the slightest threat, the pager on his hip would vibrate to abort, go tactical. Barring that, there was the handheld radio unit clipped to his belt, and Carl Lyons wasn't one to speak softly when it hit the fan.

"SADS," Brognola finally said, deciding he could play the Shadow Man's acronym game. "They are Earth's last insurance policy against NEOs, or near earth objects." He cleared his throat into a long moment of stony silence. "If this is a history on the threat of comets and asteroids, I know about the mile-wide Meteor Crater in Arizona, about Tunguska in Siberia where something like fifteen to twenty miles of forest was leveled by a twenty-megaton blast. I know a one kilometer space rock is considered a 'large impactor.' I know about twenty or thirty billion tons of said space rock hurtling toward Earth and impacting at about ten kilometers a second is what science considers the threshold for an extinction level event, which, I think, would yield something in the area of one million million megatons of TNT. Oh yeah, and a two or three mile rock would create global catastrophe. Earthquakes, firestorms, tidal waves of hundred-foot or more walls if it hit water. Hurricane winds off any chart we now measure them by would ensue and hurl tens of billions of tons of dust and debris into the air. The sun would vanish. A new Ice Age would start."

The Shadow Man snorted.

Brognola felt the guy's penetrating stare, then, annoyed at whatever his act, glanced around the room. The only furniture was four chairs and the steel table at which Brognola sat, all of them bolted to the concrete floor. He suspected there was a cellar, as evidenced by a short, arrow-straight fissure midway across the room. It was barely noticeable to the naked eye, and he would have missed it altogether had it not been for the white light burning from the single bulb hanging over his head. The no-name op remained standing in the outer limits of light in the deep corner, as if deciding what and how much to say. Brognola was reaching for the black folder when a match flared.

The Shadow Man lit his cigarette, flipped the match away and said, "You can get to all that on your own time, Mr. Brognola. I'm here at considerable risk to my own life, which puts you in the same position. Listen carefully to what I'm about to tell you, no matter how tedious you may think me getting to the point." Shadow Man puffed, dug a hand into his pants' pocket. "These SADS and their monitoring of ELEs are kept fairly secret from John Q. Public, other than a passing knowledge they may be out there. In our Milky Way there are two-thousand-some NEOs alone. Most are no larger than your average pebble. Whoever controls space just above Earth, Mr. Brognola, controls the planet. Whoever controls the knowledge of these ELEs alone, why, they can monitor and track them and decide——depending on their trajectory and size—whether to blast or let them pass on by. No warning to us mere mortals here below. Knowledge then being the perfect weapon, or the perfect judgment."

"What's any of this have to do with what happened…"

"Extinction level event, Mr. Brognola. The future belongs to those who can control an ELE. Act of God or man-made."

"So, we watch for the rock that wiped the dinosaurs off the face of the Earth. Hey, you'll have to excuse me if maybe I'm translating for you here, but we—the good guys, I'll assume—need to be the only ones in the neighborhood controlling orbiting satellites with nuclear platforms, whether to blast an ELE into quadrillion golf balls or threaten another nuclear power with a preemptive strike from the stars."

"I wouldn't go on sounding so glib and dismissive."

Brognola pulled out a cigar, stuck it on his lip. "My mistake. I assumed you were in a hurry."

"If most of the human race, say, is destined to go out like the dinosaur, as you put it, then the question facing us, who have the knowledge and foresight, is what kind of world will Man inherit."

"Or *who* will inherit."

The Shadow Man paused, as if Brognola had crossed some line in the sand, then went on. "Because of the coming threat of the cataclysmic impactor, there are nuclear-armed satellites in space, but I'm sure you already know this. Yes, we can safely assume the propaganda will keep pumping it out how such weapons are outlawed. And if they are, by chance, made public knowledge, then they will be deemed defensive measures against the killer asteroid. Lies by omission, we call it. What happened, thus, in Australia, is a result of someone getting the edge on this technology. Our educated suspicion is that a black ops renegade faction of the European Space Agency decided to field test a new toy. But, worse, our side in the space race—that would be NASA who is monitored and provided security by the NSA, which is contracted out on behalf of the Department of Defense—has, as you know, been working for some time with our supposed European space friends to launch any number of shuttles. Mutual-shared space stations for research and development, and so forth. Nobody asks what's really going on up there. Ignorance in this instance is bliss for the majority of common man. Beyond myself, however, only a few in our cloistered intelligence circles are aware that all this rainbow coalition reach for the stars is merely a mask to hide the demon."

Brognola waited for the final grim point, but the Shadow Man fell silent. The big Fed waited him out.

"Washington will keep scrambling to conceal the truth about what we think happened in Australia," the Shadow Man finally said.

"Which is?" Brognola prompted.

"This is where you might come in."

"How come I got the lucky draw? And what makes you think—"

"It is called Galileo. It's a classified NASA complex north of Dallas. They are fronting as a SADS, but the Galileo program is only part of a more sordid truth. One such truth is that behind the scenes they're building RLVs—reusable launch vehicles."

"Space shuttles."

"Not quite." The Shadow Man seemed to vanish behind a dragon's spray of smoke. "The single key difference between a space shuttle and an RLV is that our current shuttles lose their external tank shortly after liftoff. The single-stage-to-orbit RLV, on the other hand, is fully reusable. Winged-configuration will give it fuel tanks…the long and the short is that it has the capacity to become the prototype space plane, requiring little more than ground maintenance, refueling, then it's wheels up once more."

Brognola clenched his jaw at the infuriating silence. "And?"

"Galileo has an RLV long since off the drawing board. We hear it's about six months or so from its maiden voyage. And it's platform is specced to house both a thermonuclear payload and particle laser weapons. But that's not the real problem."

WHEN LYONS FOUND he couldn't clearly mark the shooter in thermal imaging, confusion threatened to freeze his hand. Every yard ever gained in enemy blood to battle the evil that men did, he thought, and he had never seen anything like this! A living ghost was bent on cutting him to ribbons!

Weapons fire strobed in his night vision as he bolted three or four feet, firing his subgun from the hip before he was chased to the broader span of the next available tree armor. The HK subgun it wielded was real enough, but since it was inanimate, meaning no heat generated beyond the muzzle-flash of igniting gases, the weapon was a fuzzy black object in Lyons's night vision, and was considered a "cool area." So if the thing appeared to move like a human being, darting now for its own shield behind the staggered row of trees, jumbled rock and thick scrub, why didn't it give off a white-hot ghost hue that would betray it as living flesh? As far as Lyons could tell, there was little more than the haziest of white shimmer that wanted to frame it as human, like the thinnest chalk outlines of a body at a murder scene.

Lyons went low, flung his HK's muzzle around the edge of a tree base and milked two 3-round bursts, hoping Blancanales was on the way, the thought tearing through his mind that his teammate hadn't paged, but if he was…

The Able Team leader melted back for cover, bearing up under a fusillade of subgun fire as a tempest of bark sliced past his face. He was about to check his handheld thermal imager to determine how many warm bodies were within its thirty-yard proximity when another stuttering volley of weapons fire invaded the Invisible Man's blistering salvo. The ex-L.A. detective was whipping around the opposite edge, HK up and tracking, when the specter came dancing and convulsing out from cover. Its subgun flaying wild bursts left to right, Lyons saw the white mists, the one or two long fingers jet like the slimmest of javelins into his thermal imaging.

Hot blood.

A little more hosing from 9 mm armor-piercing rounds eating it up, the Invisible Man toppled, crunching to a boneless heap. Lyons found ragged white holes up and down its torso, then fading to black as the corpse began to cool and the infrared radiation of its life force fled.

Lyons spotted the haze that was Blancanales, twelve yards north and closing, but checked his thermal imager. Nothing was on the small LCD monitor except his teammate's read, but Lyons did a full 360 sweep to be on the safe side, moving out to link up with Blancanales. His teammate's HK subgun parting the shadows as he advanced with all due caution, Blancanales checked the perimeter, the angry set to his features indicating he was a startled flinch away from unslinging the black-ferrite-painted Multi-Round Projectile Launcher off his shoulder. After what they'd both just seen, the Able Team leader wouldn't fault Pol in the least if he started peppering the forest with 40 mm flesh-shredders.

Lyons toed the body. Close up now, the expression he found on his teammate's face told him Blancanales had the exact same stunned reaction.

"It's the pajama suit that turned him into a ghost,"

Blancanales whispered, then backed away several yards to cover them both, weapon fanning the compass.

That was the only possible answer, as Lyons, one eye and ear on his surroundings, bent to touch the body. The material was some kind of soft fabric, silk maybe, or a silica fiber composite. It was woven in a pattern of scales, hard but flexible, overlapping but meshing together, if he was seeing right, and Lyons wasn't sure what to believe after what he'd witnessed. The black-suit was molded skintight, from hood to customized boots, everything formfitting and blended into one piece except for the night-vision goggles. Had to be some kind of cutting-edge thermal insulation that trapped body heat, Lyons thought, freeing his Ka-Bar fighting knife. The possibilities, he knew, for gaining superior edge in night combat with such a suit were beyond frightening, the hairs on the back of his neck still bristling. There was webbing to Velcro spare clips and grenades, a sheath for a commando dagger—made of the same material—but as Lyons quickly patted down the body that was it. No radio, no ID. A vehicle, then. Where there was one invisible shooter…

Placing the subgun on the ground, Lyons dug the blade into a pant leg, sheared off a strip of material and shoved it down into a slot on his vest. Assuming they all survived the next hour or so and made it back to Wonderland, Brognola had a crack forensics unit at the Justice Department who could give the fabric a thorough exam. He was pretty sure it was pointless to fingerprint the corpse. Most black ops were functioning living ghosts in everyday society, buried so deep and off the books they certainly couldn't risk a social security number. But he took out the inkpad and a slip of paper for just such an occasion anyway, sliced the fabric off one hand. A quick roll and press of dead fingers, and Lyons signaled Blancanales to head out in a due north vector. It was time to abort, and Lyons knew he didn't need to explain the reasons why to Blancanales. What remained to be seen—or not seen—may prove lethal beyond all their combined reason and experience.

And waiting in the night, at the bunker.

SABOTAGE, SUBVERSION and sale of nuclear-platform satellites to the enemies of the Free World were bottom-lined into the Shadow Man's parlay. Whether crafted to finagle Brognola and whoever the op suspected were the big Fed's superiors, the moment suddenly felt all wrong to the Justice Man.

He gnawed on his stogie, perusing the black file despite the nameless op's wishes he hold off. What he saw were standard sat pics and blueprints of the Galileo complex, and what the man informed him were shots of a classified ESA compound in Germany. A CD-ROM was tucked in a corner pouch, and Shadow Man relayed the password. As usual, these sources from what struck Brognola as a bottomless abyss of intrigue and treachery always said a lot but told him little. This time was no different. It was as if a jigsaw puzzle was being dumped in his lap and he was supposed to strain himself into a stroke fitting the pieces together. Factor, though, what he knew about the nuke blast in Australia, the suspect a killer satellite of unknown origins that had self-detonated, the panic now rocketing through the White House...

There was a mission here, no question, or at least a starting point, so it seemed. Brognola hated the feeling that a noose was being dangled over his head. No matter how the intel shook out, he decided this would be the last time he ventured outside his own circle for a face-to-face with spookland, unless, that was, they were an old and trusted acquaintance. He was pondering how many things could go wrong when his pager vibrated.

Brognola gathered up the file, maintained his composure as he set the cigar on the edge of the ashtray. He bobbed his head in rhythm to the man's ongoing spiel about the necessity to hunt down any traitors in place or circling the fort of Galileo. Rising, Brognola whipped out his Glock.

The cigarette fell from the Shadow Man's lips. "What the hell are you—"

"Get on the floor." When he hesitated, the big Fed aimed the Glock at his knee and ordered, "Now. Or I'll give you some help."

Brognola heard the commotion out front. No weapons fire, but he caught coughing and yelling beyond the door. Able Team, he hoped, gassing the shadow guns. The custom-designed Little Bulldozer that Blancanales toted, he knew, had a few armor-piercing impact rounds for the twelve tubes, packed with potent tranquilizer gas. No matter how thick the bulletproof glass on the spook ride, the driver should be down for the count if Pol slammed a 40 mm sleeper home in the GMC. Which left open the grim possibility of hidden shooters in the wooded slopes.

The op stretched out on his stomach. Brognola relieved the Shadow Man of his Beretta M-9. He slipped it inside his waistband, then heard Lyons patching through, the Able Team leader's voice steely but urgent. Satisfied the man was disarmed, Brognola grabbed his handheld radio. "I'm here."

"We're bailing. Your two shadows out front are down, but we may have a problem, I'm not sure."

That didn't sound to Brognola like the take-charge Ironman he knew. "Explain."

"I'll explain when we evac. You're covered. Mr. S will be waiting at the front door."

"Roger."

"I caught that. Brognola, listen to me. I didn't come here to set you up. I've been straight with you. We're on the same team. We want the same thing. There are people I need to flush out, ops I fear who are on the take and ready to pull the plug on Galileo. But I can't do it myself. I'm too close to it, and they'll know. I told you already, my life is in danger, so is yours. Especially after what I just gave you."

Brognola didn't answer as he backpedaled for the armored door.

"Brognola! If you just took out my two men—"

"Not the way you think. The only pain they'll feel is when they wake up with a hangover that will have them screaming for a detox bed. And don't call me, I'll call you." The man was still pleading his case as Brognola tried the steel handle, afraid it was locked. It wasn't.

Two men, Brognola thought, that's what the spook said, as he stepped outside, Glock fanning the Stygian gloom, right and left. Say he told the truth, then who was forcing Lyons to make the call to abort?

The war van, lights out, was already waiting, the side door open, Schwarz at the wheel and confirming a message over his com link. A quick march past the outstretched shadow by the front door, the air still tainted with the after-bite of chemicals, and Brognola was up and in the high-tech belly. A second later, Lyons was bounding in on his heels.

"Go!" Lyons barked at Schwarz.

Brognola landed in one of the seats bolted to the floor. He held on as Schwarz threw the wheel hard left, then whipped the van around, engine snarling as the Stony Man warrior straightened. Lyons looked strange, frightened, if Brognola didn't know better. The white-hot tension thickened yet more as Lyons, crouched in the door, watched the passing wooded hills, HK roving and ready. The Able Team leader growled for Schwarz to slow down as Lyons reached out and helped haul Blancanales aboard.

"What the hell is going on?" Brognola demanded as Lyons slammed the door shut and Blancanales plopped down in front of a console. "If I didn't know better, I'd say something or someone put the fear of God in the both of you."

Blancanales began working the GPS monitor with its grid map of the area, feeding Schwarz new directions other than the front gate they'd come through originally.

Lyons slumped into a chair beside Blancanales. Brognola could almost smell the adrenaline oozing from the Able Team leader's sweat as he tugged a swatch of shredded material from his combat vest, held it out and said, "Something did."

CHAPTER FIVE

"Listen up like you have never listened to anyone in your short miserable lives. Because of this compulsion of yours to prove yourselves divine in comparison to the cybermight of the United States military intelligence industrial complex, we are now officially, young sirs, hot-wired. More to the point, I hope you know what, precisely, that means."

His name was David Rosenberg, but in the cyberworld and to his superhacker comrades in the Force of Truth he was known as Methuselah, and if they were listening, he believed only the Almighty would be able to tell.

He took a few moments in hopes the coming Wrath of God intonations would sink in, as he stood, arms akimbo, in the narrow alcove to the living room of their double-wide mobile home. A former encryption master for the Department of Defense, Rosenberg understood the dilemma staring them all down, as he began to sense they knew they had crossed a line in the sand. Experience, he believed, counted light-years more than raw genius at the moment, a point he needed to hammer home, but subtly, through their thick craniums and Einstein IQs. He scowled and held the command look, nothing less than a father about to sound off with a barrage of much-deserved angry admonishment at rebellious sons. One by one, they finally decided to look away from their laptops, their network of modems and multiple processors. They looked uncertain whether to act sufficiently rebuked or turn smartass. He bet on the latter.

Down the line they were Noah, Job, and Cain and Abel who were, in fact, the brothers Polansky. The skinny youth in the dark shades, working on a fat joint, with stringy hair down to his waist and all of eighteen was tagged the Kid. They were a motley crew, no doubt about it, but no one he knew of could match them when it came to computers and stealing information from cyberspace. He had personally tracked down three of them when they were hot, hauled their ragged bacon out of the frying pan, and maybe from worse than a stint in prison. The trio in question—Cain, Abel and Job—had hacked into classified government databases a few years back. They had stolen secrets they claimed to this day were irrefutable evidence of UFOs and extraterrestrials and a government cover-up, on through to who was behind both Kennedy assassinations to the coming extinction level event. Then thrown opposition networks into meltdown with the all-fearsome worm, a feat so incredible and embarrassing to two famous alphabet-soup agencies that not even a whisper of the crisis made the news. Both virus and worm writers, he knew, faced four years in the federal pen and up to half a million dollars in fines, which naturally no hacker ever caught with his fingers up the other's guy mainframe ever seemed to have handy. Only in their cases Rosenberg suspected they would have been executed on the spot. That was, if he hadn't descended on their doorsteps like manna from Heaven to offer them a job—of sorts—that matched their peculiar but undeniable genius. Saving their lives was an added bonus, his gift to them but one they had never once acknowledged. Genius could also be ungrateful to the extreme.

Cain, whose Aloha shirt was brighter than the sun at noon, took a sip from whiskey-spiked coffee. "What's the beef, Grandpa? It's just another day in Cyber Paradise, us 'young sirs' merely doing what we signed on for."

The smart-ass route, then.

Methuselah had the sudden urge for a cold beer if only to clamp a lid on his rising anger. Instead, he torched a foot-long Havana cigar with a gold-plated lighter engraved with the Star of David. Blowing smoke, he stared at Johnny Polansky, bobbed his gray head. The twenty-six-year-old high school dropout had just come off seven years for manslaughter for stabbing a guy in a bar fight that left him half dead in the process and for which the jury had cut him some years. Going to court with wired-jaw, mashed nose and half of one ear sliced off had also helped pluck a few heartstrings, not to mention the dead man was a notorious three-time loser and suspected pedophile no one in all of Little Rock, Arkansas, would have missed anyway. Having sworn off cocaine, whiskey was the new magic potion the elder Polansky claimed helped him dig deeper into his black hole of creativity. The sad truth was, all of them had their demons. Even Job—what with his computer printout of God First, Fellow Man Second, Cyberspace Third in bold black letters around a crucifix and tacked over his laptop—was a heavy boozer. What could he do? It was most likely warped reasoning on his part, but Rosenberg reckoned he granted them indulgence in the Devil they knew best, if only to keep them steady and walking their highwire act on the tightrope between madness and genius.

With rare exceptions, human beings, he knew, created their own comfort zones, clung like infants to whatever the vice or ill behavior, and God forbid someone should attempt to invade the personal barrier. With this bunch, he figured talent and the extraordinary risks they took to uncover various truths of the ages—but splash them all over their AlphaDataSystems.com— had earned them some slack.

"Despite your best efforts," Rosenberg began anew, "to ghost your trails, I have just learned we have more than piqued the curiosity of the No Such Agency."

Noah swiveled in his leather wingback. The chair was splashed with colored artwork from predatory animals, UFOs, ETs, to tacked-in pics of his favorite film and song queens. "Then we were right. What did I say? If that's a farm in the Shenandoah Valley, then I'm your grandson and I'll go build you an ark right now."

"First and foremost, 'right' has nothing to do with it. And second and last, an ark won't cut it. If what I hear is true—and I have no reason to believe otherwise—then we'll need that Mothership you whiz kids are always ranting about to drop down and take us all away—about a thousand light-years into deep space."

Job piped up. "What are you talking about, oh gray-haired sir? No Such Agency is moving on us? We're civilians, not some gun-packing black ops who are out to sell classified intelligence."

"Besides," Cain said, "you've seen the sat photos, all the thermal imaging from midnight passovers by Big Brother in space. You've read the e-mail that lays out whoever these people masquerading as apple pickers use as hot sites for emergency contacts. Interpol. FBI. Mossad is even in their black bag of vipers. Then we have CIA station chiefs in various embassies from London to Tokyo who are feeding them sitreps through about a dozen back channels we've discovered."

"So bring on the spooks." Abel—Jimmy Polansky—joined in, grinning like a fool as he lit an unfiltered Camel cigarette. "What we have on them, I say we can use as blackmail leverage to keep the wolves at bay."

"Yeah," Cain said. "We'll threaten to go public. I always wanted to be on one of those talking-head shows."

"Armchair expert," Noah chortled, holding up the peace sign. "'Let me make this perfectly clear—I know who shot JFK and why.'"

Rosenberg washed a smoke wave in their faces. "Yuk, yuk. Okay, geniuses, so how are you going to go public if you're all dead?"

That gave them pause.

"Now that I see I have your attention, do you guys have any idea what we've stumbled on to?" Rosenberg pressed. "Have you thought this through? Do you realize the impact of what we suspect we've learned these past three days—and I'm talking beyond the borders of our own country?"

"You're talking about the fifty-kiloton impactor in Australia?" Job asked. "And who we think is behind it?"

"We're just a bunch of geeks," the Kid chimed in, then sucked another huge pull from his doobie, coughing as he choked down the pungent smoke, cheeks ballooning out like a puff adder. "We're American citizens performing a public service." He hacked the words out between toxic palls. "The Force of Truth. People knew about us, we'd be national heroes."

"Yeah," Cain said, "and I wouldn't have to just daydream about my favorite pop star. She'd be banging down the front door to know me. And I'm definitely talking 'know' in the biblical sense."

They started snickering, shaking their heads, the Kid and Cain back to their keyboards.

Comedians. Clueless.

Rosenberg then looked at the one table with its bank of monitors they always seemed to neglect. From across the room he could tell nothing was moving—or at least nothing he was aware of. Their laser webs, motion sensors and cameras were hidden as part of the wooded scenery in this neck of the Hampton Roads Peninsula. They were at the far edge of the trailer park, isolated, their closest neighbor about a quarter mile down the dirt track. But he knew the kind of gizmos ghost ops had at their disposal. Such as cutting edge EM scanners and laser burners a decade or more ahead of their time and which only a handful of people knew existed.

The spooks in question *were* the Mothership.

"Listen up," Rosenberg snapped, then moved to the living-room window. There, as he felt their stares boring into the back of his head, he pulled the curtain two inches aside. As a last resort, they kept two Rottweilers in the chain-linked cage, hidden to the deep front end of their parked vehicles. From inside the trailer Rosenberg could release the gate by radio remote, and Ramses and Apollo would make a meal out of any—

He caught himself. They would chomp down on any "normal" intruder, that was.

"Chill out, old man," Cain said. "Have a few brewskis."

"I want everything you have on hard drive burned to CD," he told them, and ran a hard look down the line.

Abel looked aghast. "Everything? Does that include our SETI—"

"Everything means everything, pipsqueak. Now. I want three copies and however many originals. Shag your smart asses into high gear," he barked.

As they grumbled and shrugged themselves out of neutral, Rosenberg knew it was time to start hedging his bets. He couldn't expect any of them to understand the dire urgency of the situation. With the exception of Abel, violent death had never touched their lives, other than the usual horror stories about broken family life, divorce, alcoholism, child abuse and the ugly like. But he had stared down the barrel of a gun, seen men die for secrets he kept in his head. As good fortune had it, he was still alive to correct that mistake.

He heard them clacking away on their keyboards, but as he went to the steel cabinet, he could feel them going still, looking his way. The cabinet was off limits, and they knew it. The penalty for attempting to crack the code on the keypad was instant expulsion from the Force of Truth. They would be sent packing, shamed before their peers for not honoring the one ultimate request they had pledged a verbal solemn oath to. In their minds, to break their word on that was the military equivalent of death before dishonor.

Rosenberg keyed open the lockbox, switched on the battery-powered keypad and punched in the long series of numbers committed to steely memory. He felt the sudden burning curiosity of his hackers grow into a living force all by itself. None of them knew— and had been warned to not even ask—what was in the cabinet.

The stainless-steel Glock .45, already snugged in shoulder rigging, came out from the arsenal first. He checked the clip, slapped it home, chambered a live one, strapped in. The Uzi submachine gun was hauled out next. Rosenberg was in the process of cocking and locking when he read the stark fear etched on their faces, and said, "Oh… Now you get it."

SINCE LANDING in Turkey to hammer out the present mission parameters, David McCarter believed all along his hunch would either pan out into a mother lode of intelligence and strike a massive blow against global terrorism, or get them all killed.

So, what was new?

A bloody damn lot, the leader of Phoenix Force decided. The relative warm comfort of the special ops base in Kurd country of east Turkey now seemed another lifetime as he scurried for the narrow fissure at the north edge of the rocky shelf, gathering a buzzard's eye view of the hardsite on the fly. His gut instinct quickly amended end game suspicions, and locked him in with laser-guided precision to the grim immediate future.

They were knocking on Hell's door.

A dark truth, no less, was about to be revealed, unless, that was, he missed his guess and the combined wisdom of the CIA, the Justice Department on through to Mossad, Interpol, the Russian SVR and GRU proved nothing more than toxic smoke and shattered mirrors. The way it looked to be shaping up, as he took in the compound's sprawl and number of wandering shooters, there were light-years to go before they bagged any human pythons bent on squeezing the life out of the innocent.

A long way, indeed, before they grabbed the prized trophies. And payback, though it would consume the savages here in fire the likes of which they'd never dared dream in their unholiest nightmare, was on temporary hold.

All indications from assorted spookwork, anywhere from fifty to a hundred or more obstacles stood as barriers to the gates of evil knowledge. The opposition here was heavily armed, well paid by the local Lezgi Mafia chieftain and his Chechen contacts. To a rabid brute they would in all likelihood prove loyal to a fierce fault, determined to win by bloody milestones or go down with their own *Titanic* when the hull had a massive hole punched through it by five black-suited commandos who had come loaded for wolf and bear in predatory human skin. Long odds, no matter how it was blasted, and there would be no winged death from above, which only served to add yet more tension to prebattle jitters over this huge roll of the dice. Beyond the soon-to-be crater in a time and place few sane men had ever heard about and fewer still dare to tread, he knew the daunting shadow of the Russian military and its vaunted special security forces known as Omon were lurking in the vicinity.

First strokes first.

Dropping into the tight little bowl and bringing the HK-33 assault rifle with custom-made 50 mm grenade launcher fixed to the barrel, the ex-SAS commando grabbed a few moments to scan, assess, review. The worst was on the way, make no mistake, he knew, but it felt good nonetheless to stop, breathe and suck down a mouthful of cold water from his canteen.

Review. It seemed to take forever and a day to get it in gear to go wheels-up in the C-130. Part of the problem was verifying intel, double- and triple-checking everything from terrain to enemy players to their own escape hatch, which was flimsy to the point of embracing suicide. But, upon further input from the Farm, McCarter made the call to go when he factored in what he knew, and considered what couldn't be confirmed without the up-close and personal touch of eyeball kills. Cloud cover was the normal maddening order of the day for this unholy eyesore of the world, but there had been enough break in the ceiling twelve hours ago where the CIA ops at their disposal had managed a thorough sat read of the area and handed if off.

Scan. By night the countryside was bleak and gruesome enough to behold as Phoenix Force moved in on foot following their seven-hundred-foot combat jump and subsequent two-mile hike. Not to mention that wandering around this neck of Hell was so dangerous to a foreigner's health that any passports and visas—had they been issued—were as welcome a sight for inspection as a leper's used tissue. By dawn's early light, the Briton now found the lay of the land downright foreboding and desolate, and to the point where the five of them might as well be advancing for battle at an end of the world all but forgotten by man and God. That, he knew, wasn't far from the truth as he considered just where they were.

Dagestan.

Land of the mountains, McCarter thought, which was the literal translation used by its indigenous mixed bag of ethnic descent.

The indigenous bulk were Sunni Muslims, most of whom were fanatical to the extreme as they bowed to the tenets of Wahhabism. The country was no less than a slice of Islamic fundamentalist Hell on Earth, a land that time and most of humankind ignored, if they even knew it existed. Even globe-trotting, battle-hardened commandos like the troops he led, he thought, would be hard-pressed to find this desolate backwater on any globe without some eye strain.

At their present position in the shadow of the towering, snow-capped, cloud-swathed Caucasus Mountains in the southwest corner of the country, what could have been transplanted moonscape fanned out in hills and steppe to the even more ominous empty east and north, until it all eventually dropped off into the vast Caspian Sea. Oil and gas were the country's cash cows, and were the only reason Moscow still humped and bivouacked soldiers to what was loosely billed an autonomous Russian republic. It was no secret that Moscow, McCarter briefly pondered, maintained its iron grip on the spigots of major pipelines to keep pumping black gold and silver vapor north, but the Russians somehow managed to hide from the world that they were about as environmentally conscious as Godzilla stomping through Tokyo. Dagestan was an industrial dungheap, with major ecological contamination.

But tree-hugging was not on Phoenix Force's to-do list, though chemical death, McCarter knew, was one reason they were plunging into an area of the world where its people would just as soon shoot them as look at them.

When he considered a tad more what this part of the world was all about, the Briton really wasn't surprised in the least the fickle hand of black ops had steered them here. In some eerie way he figured it was about time for some scorched justice to find Dagestan's local and imported beasts. Neighboring Chechnya, Georgia and Azerbaijan were always spilling their own legions of rabid terror wolves across the borders. Guns, drugs, weapons of mass destruction, he weighed. Isolated training camps in this scarred mountain land were hidden from even the most stubborn of spy eyes in space. Money and matériel were shipped here en masse to be trained to carry out jihad.

Assess. McCarter raised the small high-powered field glasses to his eyes again. The farmhouse was backed up near a jumbled row of Stegosaurus-armor-like rock at the foot of broken hills that looked equally in part Jurassic. Nobody, including their own in-country Omon and SVR contacts, could swear one way or the other if the opposition could make fast tracks into a suspected latticework of caves and tunnels once the shelling and shooting started. There were three tractors east, parked near wilting apple orchards, pallets heaped with crates and burlap sacks he was reasonably sure didn't require the presence of two heavy DShK machine guns in tow. The main compound, its roof dotted with satellite dishes, was a two-story wooden affair. An attached concrete bunker, an annex to the north where the motor pool drew his eye. There, an armada of vehicles, ranged from Mercedes and ZIL limos, Jeeps, SUVs, Volga minivans and GAZ-66 transports, strewed in a staggered line, west to east. According to the Omon source—and there was a good chance he was buried in the deep pockets of the Lezgi Don—the annex was where the crime boss mixed business with pleasure. Intel had it there were always twenty to thirty imported prostitutes on hand for any visiting VIPs, speaking of which no one could state for certain who or how many big shots would be on hand for this party. Surveillance, or so he was told, was pretty much maintained by roving sentries, with the exception of cameras mounted to roof edges.

Arrogant bastards.

McCarter panned a little farther north and took in ground zero.

He counted twenty-one tankers, flipped an invisible salute that bit of intel hit the bull's-eye on that score. Judging length and girth of those behemoths on wheels the Phoenix Force leader ballparked all that refined petro at…

Call it a quarter-million gallons. And however that number was given or taken, it still dumped the five of them on the potential wrong side of the coming big event.

The truck stop was penned in by basic steel-mesh fencing, for reasons no one was clear on. A spray can of liquid nitrogen would snap off fencing, he knew, and allow two of the team onto the grounds. But with seven—count nine now—assault-rifle-toting guards on the prowl it was touch and go just to light the torch. McCarter framed the sentry in the northwest tower, then saw the smoke cloud hammer the glass booth. The guard then lifted a bottle to his lips, McCarter wanting to scratch him off the worry list, but in his experience there was no such thing as a guarantee in combat. That left three shirkers on the backside, the trio, he'd been informed, apparently more interested in staying warm with a bottle of vodka and hovering near a fire barrel.

And what, pray tell, did all the big shots gathered in front of them need to fear anyway?

Nothing, apparently—or so it seemed.

Truth. A shadow group of Euro-Arab cutouts had finagled deals between Saddam and certain bureaucrats of the United Nations. And McCarter had learned during a CIA brief that a lot of cold, hard currency had been flown via Damascus to Jordan and shipped by diplomatic courier to Western Europe.

McCarter recalled the black op back in Turkey stating the facts of life as he knew them between rumbles of chuckling and obscenity-laden swipes at the French, Germans and Russians. Clear evidence, the op had claimed, had been obtained by electronic intercepts. Enemy agents bagged by the FBI in Manhattan had snitched so loud and fast they had nearly gone hoarse, painting a picture of corruption reeking from New York to Pyongyang. For reasons unknown some marquee names of the upper echelon of the United Nations had fattened Saddam's terror chest way back when. And with not only food but weapons, intelligence and over-size vans stuffed with cash, using East European gangsters for contact. Yet more shadows, McCarter suspected, in a chain of middlemen that only God seemed to know stretched how far and stopped where. The UN jackals would apparently turn around and deliver Iraqi oil to cronies in their own political and business circles who fronted for petrochemical distribution networks. All this rolling flimflam while Saddam hoarded food meant for the starving masses, but to be distributed and sold to whomever he saw fit. Word was the deposed dictator's soldiers—and later, the insurgent rabble—managed to feed themselves like princes.

On more than a few occasions—so the CIA word had it—a second deal was cut by the former regime with another rogue nation in exchange for still more cash and weapons. Yet more rumor connected to the sordid mess had it the Scotch-swilling despot of North Korea and mates were eating pretty good these days, and that alone was enough to have him seeing red what with the tyrannical buffoon in possession of...

McCarter fast-forwarded. Four Iraqis, smoked out by the CIA in Paris, Belgrade and Istanbul as recently as six months previous, were trailed to the Dagestan border before the operatives bailed for reasons undetermined. Here and now, the United Nations moneymen believed on-site felt the heat building, so they had thrown themselves at the mercy of the Lezgi Mob chieftain who had more irons in the fire than the Devil himself it seemed. Finally, Dagestani Don who had free and easy access to move tanker trucks brimmed with gasoline at will told the ex-SAS commando that he was connected to Russian power shadows, and he had more suspicions beyond the UN moneymen on that front. Oh, but McCarter hoped all party animals in question had indulged one last night but good...

He stopped the train of angry thought.

Their mission was two-or-more-pronged, as he warned himself to not project into a future he and the others may never see.

Consequences. Blood was going to run, thick, swift and deep before the sun rose. As he felt the gas mask on his hip, it crossed his mind there was the not-so-little matter of what recently happened in Israel, and yet another savage twist of fate that had urged the five of them to trek to this godforsaken place. VX nerve gas wasn't something any of them tended to gloss over as just a speed bump on the road to Hell. Assuming a cache of weapons of mass destruction was likewise under the roof...

McCarter heard the first voice patch through as T. J. Hawkins told him he was in position.

Showtime.

A hard sweeping scan and McCarter barely spotted the ex-Ranger. With a double take, he caught the top of Hawkins's black-hooded head rising from his sniper's roost, a few dozen meters or so above and due east of the tanker armada, his sound-suppressed Dragunov rifle poised to cover their two-man demo team. Down the line, Rafael Encizo, Gary Manning and Calvin James quickly informed him they were also in position.

Good to go.

Or so it seemed.

McCarter passed the order for James and Manning to get busy planting their ordnance.

A big bang, the ex-SAS commando knew, was in the wings, nothing short of scorched earth about to bring down the roof.

With any blessing whatsoever due them from the gods of black ops, and McCarter figured to live long enough to see the fall of the place of evil in this corner of Hell.

COMPLAINING ABOUT THE MOST adverse conditions of a mission never cut it. In the experience of his line of work, Calvin James knew that moaners and complainers weren't only unreliable under fire, but they were often the first to get cut down in combat. The M and C crowd—of which there were none on his team, and none except for a couple officer types he could recall during his stint as a United States Navy SEAL who were mostly interested in bucking for promotion while the real deal did the fighting and killing for them— floated a mere notch above yellow.

His case in point was made when the two Dag sentries came whining his way.

The black ex-SEAL was through the hole at the base of the fence, liquid nitro spray gun dumped behind on the ground and replaced by the suppressed Beretta 92-F, when they shuffled into view. James didn't know the language, but he could sure read faces and judge bitter tones for what they were. One of them forgot all about his AKM, the muzzle pointing at the ground, as he began jabbing a gloved mitt at the bottle of vodka his comrade didn't seem inclined to share. The bickering decibels rose as the guard gestured angrily at the sky, waved at the line of tanker trucks with a dark scowl on his bearded face, his companion stamping his boot and fuming like a waiter stiffed on a big check. Whether the ongoing gripe was over the cold, boredom with sentry duty or who polished off the rest of the vodka, James didn't know.

But he damn sure cared, since they were in the way of progress.

With a rock-steady, two-fisted grip on his weapon, he ended the argument with two quick taps, as hypersonic 9 mm Parabellum rounds cored their brains.

Two down, and James had a gut feeling it was set to go to Hell. He scanned, left to right, adrenaline practically carrying him to the bodies, despite fifty pounds of plastique added to his combat load. Quickly, he rolled the bodies under the silver beast's tail, ears and eyes tuned to the no-man's land between the fence line and the tankers.

He knew more sentries were in the area. In fact, combat senses shouted they were close. Manning was nowhere to be found, but James took that as a good sign the big Canadian was already making swift tracks.

The tankers were parked, nose-to-tail, in two rows with feet to spare, the odd rig out toward his team-mate's advance from the south. Maybe fifty meters needed to be covered before he met Manning in the middle, and both knew there was no set time to plant and prime the charges, but sooner the better.

James hauled the first shaped charge from his open nylon satchel, stuck it under the back wheel well, speared the priming rod in the middle of the package. It struck him next, checking his six before moving on, that McCarter was holding on to the extra radio remote unit. Backup hellbox, sure, just in case...

THE DRAWING BOARD and spit-balling of finer points for attack strategies always looked and sounded good, like it would all actually work according to plan. The re-ality, T. J. Hawkins knew, equaled the difference between life and death.

Sat images, HUMINT, EM scanners and thermal imaging handhelds and night vision to paint walking infrared radiation of the enemy on the way in was all well and good, and, in truth, solid planning was a must. Those Tomahawk salvos, the F-117 and Spectre strafes were a definite bonus package to soften up the target and shatter the enemy into a senseless slab of jelly, as-suming anybody on the other team was still in one piece to cry the blues. All that and a bag of chips, he thought, but at the end of the smoke and the blood of battle, it all boiled down to the soldier. Skill and ex-perience, a lion's heart in the game all the way, and the capacity for improvising with the mayhem of combat counted far and away the most. All of the above was important, no question, but too often he'd seen that a little smile beamed on the good guys from Lady Luck won the day.

Or, in this instance, the dawn.

The simple fact they were in position and moving in for the kill at that hour was a case in point to tip the hat to Lady Luck, when he considered the agonizing delays on the ground back in Turkey, how bad weather simply wouldn't allow decent satellite pictures. As it stood, sentries had already endured the long, cold night, bored out of their gourds, he knew, on the verge of nodding off as they were anxious to be relieved of duty. Better, whoever the yet-to-be-determined VIP playboys inside the main compound would be sleeping off a tough night of booze and broads. There would be security goons on hand, some of which would either be tasting the goodies on the sly, or sulking in envy and resentment they had to seethe, idle on the sidelines.

Life was tough like that.

The question now moving into the ex-Ranger's scope was who exactly life would get tough for.

Hawkins had sensed the guard in the fur hat with pointed crown and knee-length black-leather coat already knew something was amiss, and before he started barking their names.

"Dhzari! Ghombalj!"

Moments ago, Hawkins caught Calvin James skirting the periphery of his vision, the ex-SEAL a blurring ghost with two kills in his wake. The dead men's comrade was now in search of his buddies, as he stepped out from behind the rear of a tanker, three rigs down from where James had stashed the stiffs. Unless he missed his guess, reading the guard's tight body language, Hawkins was a few moments away from sending him to join his comrades.

The Klieg lights provided ample illumination, so Hawkins didn't need to switch the scope to infrared. He hefted 4.4 kilos of killing power, rose up on a knee, extended the sound-suppressed Dragunov, and tracked his mark with the naked eye for another moment. The Russian piece was a gift from the special ops in Kurdland, and it came complete with a state-of-the-art scope with digital read off the laser sight. The extended detachable box magazine held fifteen 7.62 mm armorpiercing rounds. This time around McCarter had handed him the sniper designation. Hawkins would have preferred a tried-and-proved American highpowered rifle, but he understood McCarter's reasoning that they carry a mixed assortment of weapons into battle. Russian grenades, German assault rifles, U.S. sidearms, and if they went down to a man no one would be the wiser about their origin of allegiance.

As if it would matter.

A quick search of the tankers provided no sighting of his teammates; all was quiet and holding.

But…

The guard spotted the boots under the rig's tail.

Hawkins bit down the curse, hit one of three buttons on the side of his scope. In less than one eye blink the fiber optic scan threw up the virtual reality numbers in the upper left corner where they hung like some ghost script scrawled on a UFO above his field of vision. Distance to target, elevation, down to factoring in wind speed—2.5 knots, and at his back—he read the trajectory data as the guard's expression of shocked anger framed with instant crystal clarity in the crosshairs. The man was reaching for his handheld radio, mouth already opening when Hawkins painted the red laser eye just above his right ear and squeezed the trigger. Muzzling at 830 meters a second, the armor-piercing projectile streaked the eighty-two yard bridge to target in a microsecond, so fast Hawkins had to peer hard before he registered there was, in fact, nothing in his scope but a faint dark mist raining over empty space.

He lowered the rifle, confirmed the decapitated heap of twitching carcass at a glimpse, then began scouring the field. Somewhere to the south—Manning's way— he heard a voice calling out. Another comrade search.

Silently he urged his teammates to hustle.

The clock was ticking, and there was nothing he could do about his kill left out in the open.

Something jumped into the corner of the ex-Ranger's vision. Before he looked, Hawkins already knew what he'd find. Adrenaline kicking his senses into overdrive, the Stony Man warrior confirmed two more hardmen on the move and staring right at the mess he'd just dumped on the ground.

CHAPTER SIX

Azmit Zhuktul always found himself amazed and disgusted by the arrogance of men who willingly sold their souls for money then sought reassurances they had made the correct choice. Yes, he understood how greed knew no limits, how it was never satisfied, how there was never "enough." The men standing in front of him, who had purchased the world they desired, needed to accept the fact they had already charted a one-way course, and that perdition wasn't far off. There were no safety nets, no guarantees. Certainly no going back. There was only the fight to stave off the inevitable—death—and consume and conquer while there was still time. Or be consumed.

One of the three Iraqis, Faisal al-Harqazhdi, began the squawking yet again. "You have been delivered more than a fair price to make arrangements for our safe passage to the Far East. And yet, here we all stand, while you send one of your soldiers to tell us there have been certain sudden changes in plans. Granted, we may well be safe in your country and free of the American CIA, my good Lezgi friend, but there are still many Russians in your country, as I am sure you are aware. Russians who may well be in the wrong places at the wrong time, and beyond the reach of even those who are paid to protect you. Granted, we understand how you have the director general and key staff of the Dagneft oil company at your disposal and that it appears the shipments to our Western European friends will continue as arranged. However, it is our experience that when it all looks too easy, well, quite the opposite could not be far from becoming a most frightening reality." A pause, then, "Are you listening to me?"

Zhuktul made them wait for his reply. They were tiresome creatures. Impatient, weak men who were too unwilling to endure a few days' inconvenience.

Cowards.

He lit a hand-rolled cigarette, then swept aside the bearskin blanket to expose stark nakedness. The VIPs began clearing throats, shuffling from one Italian-loafered foot to the other, frowning away from what he knew they perceived an insult to Islamic tenets regarding modesty. Hypocrites. They paid lip service in public and to unsuspecting peers about the virtues of holiness, yet they were the first in line to get drunk, bed his whores, even snort his heroin. How could a man dare regard himself as a man, Zhuktul wondered, if he didn't live what was truly in his heart? At least he knew he was the very definition of evil, and could willingly accept as much. If there was such a thing as Paradise, then why wait? If God, he believed, wanted man to live as a pillar of virtue, then he would have been created without lust, greed, anger and so forth in the first place. Zhuktul would concern himself with God whenever he met Him in the future. This day, there were many worlds to conquer, too much pleasure to be indulged.

Exhaling the harsh smoke toward the mirrored ceiling, glimpsing ten-thousand-dollar suits and gold jewelry that could have rebuilt any number of cities in their war-torn country, he fished around in the rolling pool of silk pillows and furs until he found a full bottle of vodka. A quick check of the label to make sure it wasn't the brand of paint thinner he served the troops, he uncapped the bottle and took a deep swig. One of the Ukrainian women, sleeping off the night's orgy, suddenly reached out an arm. She was purring for something, most likely heroin to powder her nose with so she could go back to sleep, when Zhuktul slapped her arm away and stood. It was all he could manage to restrain laughter at the sight of their swarthy faces turning red. Where they were soft and flabby from their embassy parties and glad-handing various corrupt UN officials and their aides in midnight meetings, nothing short of war had chiseled his flesh into taut muscle that looked more armor than human skin. He saw them fidget and nervously glance at the sight of old bullet scars, the patches of badly healed and mottled flesh from the razor's end of flying shrapnel. Souvenirs of the lion in the face of jackals.

Slowly, Zhuktul tugged on his trousers, puffing away. "If you profess so much confidence in me," he finally said, slipping into his BDU shirt then strapping himself into the shoulder-holstered 9 mm Tokarev pistol, "then why do you insist on speaking to me out of both sides of your mouth?"

"Excuse me?"

Zhuktul scanned their aghast expressions. He watched their shoulders tighten, one of them glancing back at the soldiers posted around the living room. Evidence of the night's festivities was strewed, he found, end to end. Black and blond hair spilled from beneath wolf or sheepskin blankets, their women stretched out. Ashtrays overflowed with cigarette and cigar butts, empty bottles and trays of powder scattered across massive coffee tables.

Abed Osman cleared his throat, lost his scowl first. "We did not mean to sound…disrespectful. I think at this time we would also wish to thank you for your generous hospitality these past several days."

Zhuktul took another pull from his bottle, dragged on his cigarette, then blew smoke over their heads. "I will accept that as your best effort for an apology."

"Then," Abu Jabayt inquired quietly, "when can we expect to be on our way?"

"Soon."

Zhuktul watched them look at one another, wondering who would be the first to gather enough courage to pose the question.

Al-Harqazhdi spoke up, his voice tight with controlled anger. "My good friend, as has been pointed out when we first arrived, everything you have requested from us has been placed into your capable hands. Money, information, new and numbered and safe accounts that will funnel funds to the appropriate financiers. Any of whom will prove most helpful in advancing your cause here in the Caucasus, as well as the cause of jihad in the name of all our oppressed Islamic brothers."

"Bah! You who have never denied yourselves anything, you who have never fired the first shot in anger, do not insult me with such nonsense how you would care about holy war."

They stiffened visibly, as Jabayt pressed, "Be that as it may, we had an arrangement. Without us you would not have been able to move both your gasoline and what was smuggled out of Iraq. We groomed the contacts. We arranged safe routes for the delivery of men and matériel on both sides."

"I gather this is where I am to tell you four how indebted I am to you?"

Osman stepped in to save their collective face. "We only hope that respect is mutual. However, it was our original understanding that the colonel was to be here to personally greet us, and with a jet fueled and ready to fly out at a moment's notice."

Zhuktul chuckled. There was much that they didn't know.

Al-Harqazhdi trembled, eyes smoldering with fury. "You find our monstrous inconvenience and the potential for a threat to our safety amusing? Now, who is being insulted?"

Zhuktul waved his cigarette, shaking his head. "Gentlemen, gentlemen, please. I need a moment." He shut his eyes, lowering his head. "Ah! The sun has not yet risen and already I fear this day giving me great pause, with a burden, I may add, that threatens to leave me feeling less than charitable." He felt the warm glow spread, but his anger only seemed to build. He opened his eyes, ran a scathing look over their faces. "First of all, let us be clear that it was the four of you who sought out my services."

"No. It was originally the colonel we sent our own people to," Osman said.

Zhuktul felt the blood pressure drum in his ears. Their arrogance and sniveling was more than he could bear to tolerate, but he kept his composure. "So it would seem, I will grant you that. But, the good Colonel Shistoi is indisposed. Like yourselves, shall we say, he is in the process of scrambling to save his own world."

"What you mean to say, and perhaps have neglected to inform us, is that he is either dead, captured by the Russians or hiding in the mountains," Jabayt intoned.

"None of the above. What I am telling you is that the colonel put me in charge of your situation, and my word on that should be more than enough." Zhuktul felt a sudden fierce hatred toward these men who grew rich and fat while placing all the risk in the hands of others. "Let us examine your situation, shall we? Was it not the four of you who fled on your own volition all the creature comforts of Paris and Germany for sanctuary in my humble country? Was it not you who left others to possibly be hanged in your places? Yes, yes, I know all about how the CIA 'stumbled,' as you put it, on to your dealings with the UN. I am aware how you were but a mere few hours away from being arrested like some of your comrades who did business with Saddam and who are now cutting deals with the American authorities in secret to spare their lives."

Scowling, he hit them with a cannonball of smoke, sickened to the point of some murderous rage by their whining as he felt the storm building like hot lava behind his eyes. "But you four…you made it somehow.

And that you are still free men by itself should make you grateful to the point of weeping. Yet you question the very security I have arranged for you, and now when I am in the process of seeing that you can live out your lives and spend all the millions you pilfered from both your own countries and the deal your comrades made with Colonel Shistoi. And that I deal with you at all, considering that it is you who are the ones who could be bringing trouble to my own backyard, should have you on your knees and kissing my feet."

As Osman gasped in outrage, Zhuktul drank, watching them begin to wilt under his icy stare. They knew he was right. He smoked, let them steam in silence. They were breaking eye contact, lips fluttering in impotent rage and frustration, when shouting and shots fired struck the curtained window directly behind the Iraqis. Their panic was instant and infuriating.

"Relax!" Zhuktul barked at the Iraqis, then shouldered through them, ignoring the battery of questions fired at his back. His men were already flying through beaded archways on both ends to investigate. The weapons fire abruptly stopped, then Zhuktul turned on his VIPs and told them, "This happens."

"What happens?" Jabayt nearly shouted.

Raising the bottle to his lips, Zhuktul drank, hard and deep, then grew yet more angry at what he smelled wafting past their perfumed flab—fear, which, he knew, could be contagious. He had a good mind to shoot them all where they stood, but in some as yet undefined way that picked at the back of his thoughts, he decided they could prove more useful to him alive.

Zhuktul listened as they babbled among themselves,

then treated his guests to a scornful eye. "One of my men is simply drunk. Perhaps he mistook a wolf for an intruder. If that is the case, he will be punished. Now. Were there any other complaints?"

THE GUARD WAS LAUNCHED through glass as if shot from a howitzer. The sight of the body sailing from the tower gave McCarter brief pause. Advancing for the line of dreary apple trees, about a hundred meters out and closing on the deep southeast edge of the main building, the ex-SAS commando stole a moment or two to watch the swan dive, his assault rifle extended and ready for live ones. Shattered glass, a dispersing cloud of blood and gore from an obvious head shot and a spinning object he pegged as a handheld radio trailed convulsing acrobatics sixty feet to bone-crunching impact.

They were made.

To the credit of surviving sentries there were no further shouts of alarm, no long bursts of autofire, which meant they were pros, caught napping or not, and were most likely in the process of fanning out to seal a net of lead doom on James and Manning. Somehow McCarter doubted the nine to thirteen or more hardmen were all down and twitching out. As seasoned pros themselves, McCarter knew they would all adapt to the sudden disruption, full bore ahead. Each of them had their own firepoints, tasks to carry out, to be improvised as the need arose.

Aware it all looked and felt too easy on his end, McCarter was scanning the rock-stubbled ground when he spied the tripwire at the last possible second. He stepped over it, scouring all the rotten apples strewed like some slimy morass in front of him, and for improvised explosive devices maybe disguised as produce. Autofire rattled the cold dawn air. A shout, followed by more silence.

How long he could hold off hitting the doomsday button…

Belay that. He would give James and Manning all the time they deemed necessary to clear ground zero, deciding to wait another minute or so before keying his com link.

So the battle had jumped the gun before they were hunkered and blew a hole through the sky.

Sooner was always better than later.

The thought he was eager to turn on the killing heat of hellfire began cranking up his own adrenaline levels, limbs oiled, senses electrified. A few swift but careful meters forward, and McCarter grabbed cover behind the gnarled base of a rotting apple tree.

Hunkered, hidden from more than a passing eye, he was ready to rock.

The HK-33 came up to draw a bead on the large steel door to dead twelve o'clock where he made out muffled bellows beyond. Seconds later, the enemy barged outside, assault rifles swinging in all directions. Four, then six hardmen were trying to get it together as they spilled farther from the building. They were flapping arms and raising a general ruckus on handheld units when the Phoenix Force leader took up slack on the HK's trigger and cut loose.

CHAPTER SEVEN

Stony Man Farm, Virginia

As he claimed his chair at the head of the table in the War Room, Hal Brognola found Barbara Price and Aaron Kurtzman watching him closely. Settling in and leaning back, he took a few moments, conscious suddenly of what seemed to be the ten years he'd just aged in the past twelve hours or so. They had to have read the haggard look and smoldering burn in his eyes for something other than the usual weariness, anger and anxiety when he found the combined power of Stony Man holding up the weight of the world. Since he was in charge of the Sensitive Operations Group, the crushing weight of the ultimate success or failure of any mission was sometimes daunting. But this time he and the Farm weren't alone in shouldering the burden of Atlas. With any number of intelligence and military spooks throwing their weight around, Brognola knew the waters were murkier than he could recall in long memory, chummed fat and wide, with man eaters circling for what may well prove a global feeding frenzy.

Against his will, the big Fed's thoughts remained locked on the cracking ice of international outrage, the possibility that a rogue or supposed friendly nation was orbiting nuclear satellites around the planet and looking for blood. Beyond the stark and frightening facts as Stony Man knew them, Brognola realized ground zero in the Australian outback wouldn't rate a footnote in history if a nuclear spear was plunged into a major city from above Earth's atmosphere.

Sensing the mission controller and the head of the cyberteam were anxious but giving him some time to gather his thoughts, breathe air free of human rot and all its treachery and malice, the big Fed sipped some of the battery acid Kurtzman passed off as coffee. He unwrapped a fresh cigar, stuck it in a corner of his mouth, rolled his shoulders. He took a deep breath, let it out and told them, "In the few brief moments the President could spare me, he green-lighted us to do whatever it takes to get to the bottom of what happened in Australia. Nail it down. The Man wants a rapid response, folks, no punches pulled, no mercy whatsoever to whoever the perpetrators. They go down hard, and, if possible, their names and misdeeds are to be buried along with them. That's the good news. Unfortunately, he also implied that, because of the nature of the crisis, there's a good chance our teams may well be locking horns with any number of operators—CIA, NSA, DOD, DIA. You name it."

"In other words," Kurtzman said, "beware of those bearing free gifts."

Brognola nodded, aware that Kurtzman and Price were apprised of the encounter in upstate Maryland. "The hacker problem is, of course, our situation to deal with, which, needless to say, we're out of business if it hits the *Washington Post*. Now, from what I gather, you two think there are pieces of this whole sordid puzzle that want to fit and that want to tie together the hackers and a nuke slamming into the Australian outback from space?"

Price cleared her throat. "Unfortunately we're not sure of anything at this stage."

"Okay, so we're early in the game, but we're in. Go ahead and give me what you do have. Good news–bad news, what we know and what we don't."

Kurtzman clicked on the wall monitor. "What you're looking at, Hal, is about fifteen to twenty square miles of irradiated earth."

Brognola peered at the image. The screen showed nothing other than an unusual white glow. He frowned at Kurtzman. "Aaron…"

"You see nothing, Hal, because that's what our satellites see as the result of a fission blast more than twice the twenty-two-kilotons that was dropped on Nagasaki. In other words, until some of the heat dissipates our space probes are useless over this tract of Queensland. The good news—if it can be called that—is that there are maybe two human beings per square mile up to fifty to seventy or more square miles in the immediate affected area. My point—I'm thinking there was some method behind the madness of whoever did this, as far, that is, as containing immediate collateral damage."

Brognola chomped on his cigar, trying like hell not to glower. He already knew that electromagnetic pulse had affected Australia as far as Sydney and other east coast cities. He knew that eighty-five percent of the country's population lived along the coasts, which was the only other piece of questionable good news as far as the blast went. He knew prevailing winds would carry fallout and that radiation dosages could reach well beyond the lethal eight hundred. He knew Great Britain's former penal colony was one riot away from declaring martial law, but that a cover story was already being handed to the press by the parliament, everything from a secret nuclear reactor meltdown to an asteroid, though it sounded to him nobody knew which direction to start dancing. He hoped Kurtzman was getting somewhere fast other than a show-and-tell of what he already knew.

"What I'm saying, Hal, and I'm not trying to be a wiseass, is that blank picture is about where we are, at least in regard to whoever is actually behind the incident. The list of countries we know of that have satellites is lengthy. Many of which have covert space programs."

"Black ops."

"Black ops. For some time, the NSA and CIA have believed that China and Russia are dabbling in everything from antigravity devices to reverse engineering of alien spacecraft. The ESA has fifteen members alone, and that doesn't include our friends north of the border."

"So, pick one—that's what you're trying to tell me?"

Price stepped in. "When you transcribed the CD to us from the chopper, it gave us a few nibbles to run with, but…"

Brognola stared at the dark look in Price's eyes as she fell silent.

And there it was.

From the White House, around the world and back to Stony Man, it seemed everyone was at a loss to explain, or begin to find answers. What he knew for certain was the smoke screen to be thrown up between Washington, Great Britain and the prime minister of Australia may or may not hold back the world from collapsing into a tailspin of panic and anarchy.

There was a truth, however, that few outside the elite U.S. intelligence circles knew—Australia had medium-range nukes, and three reactors. It was a covert program, Brognola had learned, agreed upon by the U.S., England and Australia several years back when it was feared North Korea would eventually go nuclear. Since that fear had become reality, the three countries had already scrambled ahead of North Korean timetables to build silos in the Australian outback. The conventional wisdom was nukes in that part of the world would guarantee the shortest, quickest and most undetectable flight path in the event Pyongyang did the unthinkable.

"So, we're nowhere."

"Actually," Kurtzman said, "at this stage, we'd only be feeding back to you a lot of what your source gave you, some of which we were able to verify as accurate through more official channels."

"What about the part of that package related to our hacker woes?" Brognola asked.

"That much we nailed," Kurtzman said. "I agree with Akira that they either aren't as smart as they think or, as we suspect, they're taunting us. They barely bothered to hide their real identities, when you consider they used the same credit card to stay online, one belonging to a former encryption expert by the name of David Rosenberg, who worked for the Department of Defense. They call themselves the Force of Truth. Their Web site is AlphaDataSystems.com. I ran a background check through official and unofficial channels on these guys. There are six of them altogether. The FBI went through with a follow-up surveillance after three of them hacked into their own mainframes, and also dipped their ghost fingers in over at Langley and the NSA a few years back. It's them, no question about it."

"We've already determined as much by my own source," Brognola said, then softened the edge in his voice. "So, just what do you think they're all about? Blackmail? Showing us theirs is bigger than ours?"

"Nuts, brilliant ones," Kurtzman said, "but still nuts. Their Webs read like a conspiracy basket case's textbook manual from A to Z. ETs, ELEs, something called Hangar 13 that's housed in Cheyenne Mountain and that NORAD is guarding the keys to the knowledge of the ages about UFOs. Big Foot, Loch Ness…"

"I've got the picture."

"But they have come up with some juicy facts regarding this Galileo SADS," Kurtzman said. "Whoever they are, these guys are out there in deep space, Hal. Considering their history, the stunt they're pulling now, I'm amazed they haven't been already grabbed by the NSA or the FBI and deep-sixed in the Atlantic."

"But, if we're to believe what's in my source's package, there are official operators who have already gotten the jump, en route, as I speak, to give our basket cases a lesson on the facts of life," Brognola told them.

"Bottom line, we won't really know what they're all about," Price said, "until Able has paid our hacker friends a visit at their Virginia Beach residence. Which brings us to the problem of Able stepping into the crosshairs, figurative or real, of an official operation."

Grunting, Brognola checked his watch, then drew a rough mental map. Factor in miles, and with limited traffic at that hour all the way to Hampton Roads, and whoever was driving certain to tromp a lead foot when and where radar detector allowed...

"When we read between the lines of all the hype and conjecture," Price suddenly said, "the so-called Force of Truth seems to think the European Space Agency is behind what they're referring to as a coming 'litmus test for the dawn of advanced space weapons.' Nuclear test sites in remote areas, human test subjects to measure the effects of fallout and so forth, though they didn't name Queensland."

"And they're putting all this out on their Web sites? These guys know something we don't, or damn well should?"

Price shrugged. "They lay out a list of self-educated theories based on clandestine investigation, which translates to hacking classified government files. Some of it is public knowledge, but some of what they say is backed by truth they had no business learning and that could well undermine national security. Most of what they cite regards a conspiracy on the part of the U.S.

military industrial complex and its loosely affiliated collaborators."

"I'm almost afraid to ask, but I need to know what we're dealing with here. What's the conspiracy?" Brognola asked.

"Bottom line, the common man is a slave to the great economic tyrant," Price said.

"The what?"

"The GET, sometimes referred to as the one world tyrant. This would be the White House, Pentagon, all U.S. military contractors and intelligence agencies. They include the mighty at the top of the heap on Wall Street, the United Nations and its criminal lackeys, and on down to Hollywood and the mass media—all of the aforementioned nothing else but the world's slavedrivers in their craving for more money, more power and dominion and, of course, receiving the homage due them by we, the peasants. According to the Force of Truth, most of us have no hope, no future, no reason to live other than to serve and obey the GET. To roughly paraphrase, we are but chaff to be dispersed into the wind of fate as the GET would see fit, how our passing suffering subhuman existence is only useful where it all better serves the GET. The GET, according to the Force of Truth, is a pale shade of the Antichrist to come," Price reported.

Kurtzman picked up the ball. "I have to tell you, Hal, one even glances at the history of man on this planet you can see where their argument is mighty convincing and carries some weight. To them—and others who subscribe to their philosophy—the average working stiffs are just dupes, pawns."

Brognola grunted. "Right. So. We sit back and wait

to see what Able turns up after they put this Force of Truth under the spotlight and Carl's always-ready diplomatic hammer. And with no word from either Striker," he said, referring to Bolan, "or Phoenix…"

"We wait," Price said.

Brognola felt the tension thicken as he read their dark mood in the silence. "Yeah," the big Fed exhorted. "What can we do, huh? Other than hold tight and keep our fingers crossed that our people turn up answers that could lead them to burning down our European space friends who may or may not be armed with nuclear satellites. Or some renegade black program the ESA may or may not have and who is trying to tell us they're the new bullies on the global block. Last, but hardly least, not to mention locking horns with any number of ops from any alphabet-soup agency, and that our people may be forced to kill operators on the home team."

Kurtzman clenched his jaw and said, "Supposedly on the home team. And yeah, that's about where we stand."

Brognola heaved a breath. He told them to go ahead and rehash what they knew, hoping they'd overlooked some critical detail. No matter how professional, how many past victories under the belt, the day an intelligence operator began thinking he knew it all was the day he should quit, before he got himself or someone else killed. He decided to hold off informing them about the piece of strange material that had rendered a man nearly invisible to night vision. It had been sent on by Justice courier to the FBI forensic specialists in Quantico. This was the second time that someone tried to gain the upper hand by developing a fabric that rendered its wearer nearly invisible.

The big Fed eased farther in his chair and worked at his cigar, but he was hardly relaxed as Kurtzman launched into the rehash.

CHAPTER EIGHT

The pair of Dagestani shooters turned angry looks toward the gasoline jetting from the open valve. They came to a sudden lurching skid, turned to stone, undecided whether to turn off the stream or to search for immediate vent to their outrage and shock for all that liquid cash flooding the ground unchecked.

Too late.

Gary Manning let his HK-33 answer their dilemma. The big Canadian hit them, left to right, a stuttering lightning rod of 5.56 mm doom that ate them up, all but shredding tough fur overcoats as if they'd been shoved through a thresher. A brief epileptic boogey step, and they dropped hard, twitching out in the rapidly spreading lake of volatile fuel.

Manning paused at the tail end of the last rig he just primed to blow, checked the empty stretch to the fence line. Clear, but for not long, he suspected. James had just patched through, informing him of his position and problems in the vicinity, coming from the north and west.

Armed sentries, he knew, were on the prowl but currently invisible to the naked eye, and he and James both knew that the house had been alerted, as he judged all the pandemonium beyond his perch, men shouting in angry and panicked tones, doors opening and slamming. And McCarter would be anxious for a progress report. If the two of them got mired in some extended shooting engagement, pinned down...

Stow it! Time to shake and bake or be vaporized.

"Cal," the big Canadian barked around the edge.

"Right here," James said, poking his hooded head around the end of the next rig over, assault rifle roving for armed opposition, the HK-33 special going left, right and rear.

Manning caught the distant autofire as it lanced through the thundering of heartbeats in his ears. They were short staccato bursts to the deep south and west, he believed. McCarter country.

He glanced at the hole in the base of the fence, gauging the distance about twenty yards. It might as well have been the length of a football field. Hawkins was covering from about his one o'clock up in the foothills.

"I'll take our twelve-six counterclock. Ready?"

"Go!" Manning said, and bolted from cover, his assault rifle fanning their right flank, on back to vacated space, adrenaline racing so hot it felt like lava flowing in his veins. The angry bark of weapons fire was climbing another few decibels from McCarter's zone, when Manning, swinging toward his three o'clock, glimpsed the hardmen wheeling around the rig, their AKSUs already flaming.

Damn it!

Manning's weapon snarled in response, the Stony Man warrior blazing away for all he was worth as the thought seared through his mind he was a done deal. He saw one of them already toppling, half his skull blasted away. But the sound of autofire was perforated as he grunted sharply against the impact of two or maybe three rounds hammering like invisible wrecking balls into his chest, his legs yanked out from under him.

MCCARTER MANAGED about five or so seconds of sustained fire. The HK-33 assault special drilled the first six out of the gate, the big Briton slapping riddled puppets off the wall as he swept stem to stern and back for good scything measure. Number seven guard howled at dark gray sky, his AKM stammering as he fell back into the arms of waiting comrades. Muzzles began starring the gloom from their firehole, then one fool with an obvious death wish actually charged through the doorway. Rounds scorched past McCarter's cheek, way too close, considering the mad attacker was more bent on flailing and screaming out what had to be obscenities rather than focusing on anything remotely close to accurate shooting.

Enough!

The Phoenix force leader dropped lower, edging down and away from a few kissing-close rounds biting off moldy bark, then squeezed the trigger on the customized launcher. The crazed shooter's bellows were competing with his autofire, when the 50 mm HE round impacted on the doorjamb.

No sooner had the fireball ripped apart an undetermined number of shooters then McCarter was keying his com link. Scanning his battlefront, south to north, he veered for the next available cover of one of the tractors.

"Cal! Gary!"

A loud thunderclap rent the air. McCarter glimpsed the rising mushroom cloud above the main annex, wreckage and what looked like mangled toothpick figures riding the fiery crest. That would be Encizo capping off with his 50 mm Multiround Projectile Launcher.

So he hoped.

James checked in first, as McCarter slid into cover behind the tractor, then he heard Manning coughing and gasping for breath. "Status!" McCarter snapped.

The ex-SAS commando dumped another 50 mm HE projectile down the chute, clicked it in. He scanned the billowing smoke, waiting for more armed hostiles to brazen their way into his deathsights.

"We're climbing now!" James shouted, autofire rattling over the link, swelling the air to the north.

"What's wrong with Gary?"

"He took two in the chest," James answered.

"I'm fine," McCarter heard Manning bark in his ear.

McCarter gave a passing silent prayer they'd all opted for the NATO body armor the CIA had on hand. The extra weight lugged into combat proved a lifesaver for Manning, but only for the moment. A few bruises, sore ribs and getting the wind slammed out of any of them as if they'd been kicked by a mule were the least of their concerns.

McCarter needed them clear, and even then he would be guessing on any relative safety margin, once he factored in flying debris, pressure waves. He got their position, did some rough math and told them he'd hold off another thirty seconds, mark it on their timepieces.

As his commandos copied down the line, the Phoenix Force leader watched as two more hardmen raced around the deep southern edge of the farmhouse. They looked more intent on staring, dumbfounded, at the litter of bodies, a second long enough for McCarter to hold back on his HK's trigger and spill them to the earth.

HAWKINS FOUND it necessary to drop one more shooter to an open grave before he joined James and Manning for the hard scramble for higher ground. Their backs were hardly covered, but the fresh kill, he hoped, may give the other three sentries below pause. His best guess was thirty to forty shooters were attempting to seize cover around the motor pool, seeking to bring the fight to them as they swept their spray and pray at everything and nothing. Considering what was on tap, Hawkins knew any pursuit, feeble or otherwise, could only work to their advantage.

The ex-Ranger looked back, Manning's grunts and curses flaying his ears as the big Canadian used raw anger to wash away the brute force of taking a couple of 5.45 mm wallops to the sternum. A few of the heartier souls, he spied, ventured for the gate where one of their comrades had managed to open the way and who was now sprawled with half his face and skull missing. Encizo was drawing fire to the south, but scrambling now for his own cover against the coming conflagration. The Cuban warrior could manage to dump only two 50 mm blasts on the frenzied wolf pack. Three vehicles on the east side of the motor pool, Hawkins saw, were pulped shambles. Some decent-size wreckage was just now floating to earth to bang off the next three or four wheels in line.

Hawkins clung to the hope it was just enough diversion to keep the armed wolves at bay or to send a few of them scurrying back for the relative safety of the wide-open annex doorway.

Bullets began whining off stone to Hawkins's right as James and Manning forgot all about any other earthly concerns beyond grabbing cover. Lead hornets sizzling the air and ricocheting off some of the meanest rock face he'd seen in quite some time, Hawkins risked one last look at his chronometer.

Three seconds.

And the ex-Ranger was in lockstep as he joined James and Manning in their vault over the jumbled bank of stone teeth, beyond which lay the bowl they'd marked on the way in, and now claimed for cover as they tumbled down and rolled up beside one another.

Hawkins—braced for a blast that would light the world around them on fire—poked his head up over the edge, eyelids cracked to the narrowest of slits.

Just in time to see the curtain go up for the big show.

"WHAT'S THAT you say? You wanted 'easy'?"

Zhuktul couldn't restrain himself any longer in the presence of such timidity, and at the expense of other men's lives. He flung a long burst of scornful laughter in their faces. They showed him their patented arrogant scowls, then the four Iraqis fell back to the verge of former hysterics as they flinched and jumped and cried at every burst of autofire and angry shout that echoed down the hall from the front doors. And, yes, one of them had actually blurted out how everything was supposed to have been easy.

He was about to grant them their wish for the easy way out, but with a last effort of gargantuan willpower he kept the AK-74 trained on the grim mystery of the assault raging far beyond them.

"Now what do you intend to do?"

"I will not die or be captured here because of your incompetence!"

"Control yourselves! Are you men or whimpering old hags?" Zhuktul bellowed at the Iraqis, as the prostitutes, some naked, others half-clothed, raced screaming past his guests.

Having already passed out the orders for his lieutenants to take the fight to the unknown enemy, Zhuktul figured discretion was now the better part of valor. Later he could sort through the mystery, once his men had killed or captured the attackers. Right now, he had an empire to save.

There was a tunnel connected to the room where he stashed the steamer trunks of currency, and money could well prove his safety net until he got some answers as to why he was being attacked. Further, an armored ZIL limo was on hand at the end of the tunnel connected to the money room, the getaway vehicle fueled and ready to go for just an occasion as he now found himself faced with.

For a brief moment he was torn between confusion and rage. Had he been too arrogant himself, assuming the money he spread through the ranks of local Russian officers and the rabble that passed itself off as police in the region would let him live in peace, see his empire flourish, and while gladly accepting the table scraps he threw them? Or was this the treacherous work of Gerbaky Shistoi? Had the colonel of the Caucasus Liberation Front been captured, cut a deal to save his own skin and at the expense of the very man who had vowed to see he remain free while he made plans for the colonel's own eventual flight? If so, why? Lack of courage? No faith? Or simple greed? All of the above, most likely, when he considered that wherever vast amounts of money and other contraband were stored, the man the most envied could never be certain his kingdom was guarded well enough, what dark monsters lurked in the hearts of even the most seemingly trustworthy and loyal.

"Down the hall!" Zhuktul shouted at the Iraqis, waving his assault rifle in the direction they should move.

They were shuffling past, gathering speed quickly now that they believed he had their best interests at heart, when Zhuktul caught the distant thunderclap. It wanted to drift his way, another warning bell from the south or the west, he thought, but his ears were too bombarded by the shouts and screams in the immediate vicinity, all but drowning out everything but the tumult renting the air from the motor pool and foyer.

Zhuktul roared at the Iraqis, "Keep moving!"

Then the massive explosion thundered. Rather, it struck him as a series of blasts but melding, building into one titanic upheaval of raging fire.

Like the end of the world.

His world.

Shouts and screams were then either instantly muted by the tremendous peals or switched to the hideous banshee-like wails of human flesh set ablaze. Having witnessed men burned alive during torture, it was a scream unlike any sound of agony known to man.

And Zhuktul knew what was happening, even as his shriek of outrage was swept away by the hellish din spearing his senses.

His trucks had been blown up!

The floor then seemed to ripple in front of Zhuktul, the walls shuddering as pressure waves began to slam the compound. The Iraqis were jerking all over the hall, shouting, cursing, as if the sound of their own pleading voices would assure them salvation. What sounded like comets began to hammer the roof next as the noxious stench of burning gasoline and flesh pummeled Zhuktul's nose.

He was hitting the deck, throwing his hands over his head when the ceiling burst open like a gutted fish. A volcanic spew of dust and a shower of concrete chunks pelted the Iraqis, eliciting more terrified shrieks. Such a maelstrom told Zhuktul the second story roof had all but collapsed, crushing down with any number of tons directly over their heads, cracking the fissure above them like thin ice. Through the swirling pall of grit and shooting meteors, Zhuktul spied two of his VIPs flinging themselves away from the avalanche. A second later a Mercedes limo plunged through the shattered ceiling, a flaming anvil that crushed the other pair to gore-spewing pancake.

GARY MANNING WAS qualified expert enough on explosives to figure he could handle anything short of arming or defusing an ICBM. When the Big Bang was hatched in Turkey, he calculated gas payloads to the topped-out side, proximity of targets, how much plastique each truck would be mined with according to what they lugged in. Matériel varied from country to country, and not sure how thick the steel skin containing the gasoline, he wasn't sure a few pounds of plastique on each hull would create the maximum desired effect, how quickly—or if—they punched through the shell. Thus the open valves to release not only a slick pond of incendiary fuel, but the gas itself would be ignited from the ground, race back to vomit fire through the vents, burst apart the tanks like flimsy tin.

It worked, and better than he had envisioned.

Manning flinched, risking potential retinal burn as another wave of brilliant explosions flared like countless giant Roman candles. The noise alone became a living force of raw anger, spearing deep into his ears as the billows meshed, end to end, to create a screaming and expanding firewall of pure wrath that eviscerated the eighteen-wheeled leviathans.

Time to hold on!

Manning snarled, senses shattered to goo and bubbling nausea. His chest felt sliced open by an invisible surgeon's scalpel where slugs had pounded into his armor to punish his sternum to the point where breathing was still labored and painful. Then he felt pressure waves hurtled their way, superheated winds gathering another force of living fury as he chanced a glimpse at the whirlwind dumping its tidal wave of fire and wreckage over the motor pool and annex.

He was pivoting in a one-eighty along with his teammates as the massive blast furnace began puking out mangled real estate in all directions. Then the big Canadian was eating dirt and rock as the first of many screaming monsters began slashing the air in an angry whoosh, hammering the earth around and just beyond them with nothing less than the thunder of Hell.

Squinting against the fearsome umbrella of firelight, Manning looked up, matching grim stares with James and Hawkins to help keep watch on the falling sky.

CHAPTER NINE

"I still think we should have brought the suits."

Their black van with official U.S. government plates was rolling out of the Hampton Roads Bridge-Tunnel when Roger Zeno was forced to stop admiring the view. He knew he would have to address the concerns of his two operators, questions Nino Nefirelli and Royce Bannon had been kicking around in their minds, he was sure, and since the final brief before they pulled out of Langley Air Force Base about ten miles back. He stole a few seconds, just the same, taking in the sprawl of lighted bank reaching for the U.S. naval base where the James River flowed into the Chesapeake Bay. He had more than a few fond memories from the old SEAL days when he used to tear up Virginia Beach bars with double-fisted drinking and long nights of steamy sport sex with whatever lucky little kitten of his choice. One last look at the behemoth moored down there, and Zeno almost wished he was still the young kickass SEAL of yesteryear, not much more to worry about than waxing bad guys and basking in the glory of the team. Ah, yes, he considered, those days when ships were made of wood, men of iron…

In terms of pure warrior spirit, yesteryear beat working for a so-called living in an "official-unofficial" capacity for the No Such Agency. These days there were too many cybergurus, computer geeks and their feeble spawn, guys at the top of the ladder, he thought, who wanted the glory while their operators did all the grunt work. But even when an operator succeeded in pulling off the impossible, his neck was never far from being shoved onto the chopping block. Superiors were always terrified certain "activities" might find their way to some senator's e-mail address. But whoever was next down in the pecking order could always expect to be offered up as the sacrificial lamb. It was the way of the bureaucratic beast. From where he stood in the trenches, the only difference between the No Such Agency and a pencil pusher was that many shadows behind the scenes had elevated themselves above the working law of the United States Constitution.

But Zeno understood, even embraced the unholy risk he might be called to the mat to make the ultimate accounting.

Screw the powershed. He was a former Navy SEAL. They weren't tough enough to carry his jockstrap.

His two-man unit, with two three-man backup teams, was called the Reprimanders. In their own hallowed intelligence circles they were so covert—and even feared and despised—there wasn't even a whisper of their existence, or what they really did. And when they shipped out to track down a foreign or homegrown threat to national security on American soil, they did far more than spank the offender and send them to bed without milk and cookies.

As if prefacing what he was about to say, Zeno hauled the Beretta M-9 from its shoulder holster hung beneath the black nylon windbreaker. He checked the load, slapped in the clip and chambered a round, then stowed the weapon back in place. Nefirelli's knuckles whitened as he tightened his grip on the wheel, as if sensing the rumbling volcano next to him on the shotgun seat. Bannon, Zeno saw, found time enough to look away from his glowing bank of monitors, frown his confusion and anxiety.

"We don't know what went wrong on Tellier's end," Nefirelli said. "And Mr. Hanson is still in the wind."

"I thought this was ground we already covered," Zeno said, fighting to keep an iron grip on withering patience. "Whoever took out Tellier either bagged Mr. Hanson or the man who knows too much is right now packing his bags for a long vacation somewhere overseas."

"Tellier was left where he fell until Specter Team recovered the body. A message? A taunt? And by whom?"

"Whatever it was, he was minus part of what he was wearing," Zeno told Bannon. "Which tells me whoever Hanson met with now has in their possession not only classified intelligence that could cripple the power beyond us and who we actually work for, but that material is going under the microscope."

"And?"

Zeno bored a cold stare into the side of Nefirelli's

buzz-cut head. "They could have stripped him had they wanted. Maybe they didn't have the time, I don't know. Do I need to spell it out?" He read their constipated looks and stressed, "Should one or all three of us go down, then those suit specials may fall into the wrong hands."

"Assuming, then, whoever met Hanson knows about the geeks," Bannon said.

"And there stands a good chance," Zeno said, "our playing field could get crowded."

"What if the party gets crashed by one of us?" Nefirelli asked.

"The only 'us' is us and our standby," Zeno said. "Anybody else—and I don't give a damn if some White House flunkie aide or the Chairman of the Joint Chiefs—turns up here is a threat to national security. Are we clear?"

There was a hard pause, then Zeno watched Bannon nod at the long slender box on the floor. The young op sounded off a grim chuckle. "You want to talk about something falling into the wrong hands that shouldn't."

Zeno looked Bannon dead in the eye. "That's why you two puppies get the EMP boxes and the HKs and the Flash Gordon toy in that box is my responsibility." He watched as Bannon broke eye contact then melted into the relative safety of the flickering shadows of his monitors. The expression on the young operator's face told Zeno he regarded what was in the lead box as lethal as the combined bite of a thousand cobras. The kid wasn't that far from the truth, Zeno decided, and said, "Any more questions?"

FROM OUT OF THE ROILING black smoke and the hanging bandanna of firelight, McCarter spied some great unidentified object plunging for the compound's roof. Then he decided whatever it was seemed to float down through the expanding billows and the inferno's glazing shield, as the UFO seemed to create its own space on descent. Against his better judgment, he found his mind trying to fully comprehend what he was seeing— risky, he knew, to the point of reckless under the circumstances—but the strange sight threw the ex-SAS commando off track long enough for him to gather a brief spectator's eye of awe and wonder, even as he kept pumping his legs for a penetration point at the shambles that was the side door.

Then he recognized it.

For reasons he figured known only to the Almighty, the gas station on wheels hadn't blown during the initial holocaust. It was, though, covered, stem to stern, in a slick sheet of lapping flames, sloughing off the last tendrils of black pall as it fell. That it still appeared intact, dropping, no less, as straight as if it was riding flat highway, gave McCarter another moment's pause. If he hadn't seen it with his own eyes, the ex-SAS commando would have sworn the behemoth had actually been picked up by a divine force, moved to a point somewhere due east over the roof, and simply let go.

Be it the hand of God or some earthbound touch, the Stony Man warrior found it all both amazing and frightening in its apparent utter defiance of the natural laws of physics.

McCarter, scanning the lay of his own slaughter field, reached the smoking maw just as the titan blew.

Like a thousand lightning bolts ripping off at once, the sky strobed again with the latest massive eruption, McCarter once more figuring why it chose that moment to detonate was a mystery best left to supreme wisdom. Whatever the reason for the phenomenon, the resulting blast and seismic peals left McCarter wondering if what previously remained standing of the main building was simply now tumbling down.

Only one way he knew of to find out.

The earth shaking underfoot, leviathan-size wreckage hammering the grounds and banging off the edge of the roof to the north, McCarter heard distant screams reaching out from beyond the deep end of the smoke-choked corridor.

Now the tough part.

The Stony Man warrior's ears filled with hideous shrieks, autofire and angry shouts, his senses were instantly assaulted by the pungent miasma he knew would only swell every square inch beyond the demolished yawn with every step forward. A final check of his six and flanks, and McCarter, HK-33 fed with a fresh 40-round magazine, plunged into the invisible stream of vile odors, the swirling smoke and grit.

As he stepped over bodies and body parts, the going got tougher right out of the gate. Figuring, though, that if he wanted easy he would have stayed home and gone and sat on a beach somewhere, the Phoenix Force leader caught the groans, spied mauled guards crabbing, mashed spiders from beneath splintered beams or rolling like snakes with broken backs over mounds of stone. They were staggering to rise, three bloody mummies with AK-74s, hacking out grit with eyes bugged into thousand-mile stares, when McCarter blew them off their feet. He glimpsed specters at the far east end, shapeless figures blurring in and out of the drifting smoke wall, but another hardman snared his deadly interest.

The AK-74 was barking in the bloodied demon's mitts, several rounds slashing past McCarter's ears as he lunged to the side, then one round drilled into his chest before the burst moved off-line.

Bloody hell, but that hurt!

The body armor held, as expected, but the breath was vaccumed out of the Stony Man warrior, stars blasting for a near fatal moment in front of his eyes. Already holding back on the HK's trigger, sucking wind, somehow he found he was drilling the guard a figure-eight, crotch up. It was nothing short of pure instinct and lightning reflexes, he knew, that saved his British hide. The hammer blows of 5.56 mm armorpiercing rounds slammed the guard, dancing and flailing, into the wall, down and out next as he trailed a smear of crimson with his topple. There were two more mangled bodies stretched out as he moved ahead, scanning the corridor and its closed doors, the ex-SAS commando dredging up sufficient raw anger to ward off the pain searing through his chest and ribs. McCarter hit them each with a 3-round burst up the spine to be on the smart side.

Good riddance, but more hellhounds were en route, broken free from the chains of mayhem.

The rolling tumult came from around the corner, human traffic hauling scorched or mangled bacon for whatever safety they could find. Moving, he reckoned, on a southerly vector, and straight his way. But, if he read the first sighting correctly, he had to wonder how many and who had already swept past. And if he knew anything about evil, then its only interest was to stay alive to keep on doing what it wanted to do, what it did best. Which was to serve and live for itself, everyone else be damned. That in mind, it was a safe bet the moneymen and the Dagestan Don would either be stepping on stage, or had already made haste for an advance escape hatch.

A delayed explosion rocking the walls and spilling more dust down the corridor, McCarter advanced, the racket of panicked voices growing. Unless his commandos were seriously injured and unable to proceed as planned, radio silence had been ordered.

Swiftly, listening for any sounds of movement behind each wooden door he passed, eyeing one that was already ajar, he was sliding through a thinning patch of smoke when a party of semidressed and buck-naked women flew past. They were a rainbow of imported beauties, and he was hoping the party babes—on-site against their will or simply obliging their role in the world's oldest profession—had the good sense to bolt for the deepest available cover when the fireworks jump-started the mayhem. Factoring collateral damage, he thought, then shrugging it off as just the cost of doing business served no higher purpose when a warrior fought to save innocent life. Sometimes, sadly yes, it was unavoidable.

A pair of hardmen suddenly popped into view, AKs swinging toward the black-suited, hooded intruder. Still more foreign or local prostitutes rushed past, checking McCarter from ripping loose on full-auto. The Stony Man warrior milked a 3-round burst, stitching Sentry One across the chest. The hardman was jigging back, tumbling into the stampede and tripping up a couple of the party gals, when a blistering salvo swept McCarter's position. The Briton hit a knee, threw himself across the hall, squeezing off a short burst as lead wasps buzzed past his face and he rolled on. Somehow, he tagged the goon in the family package.

The enemy's barrage then drilled the floor, hurling out wild ricochets that fought to compete with his screams as he doubled over from agony no man should be forced to endure. Another quick tap of the trigger, aiming up from the floor, and McCarter hit him square in the face, what police sketch artists called the Triangle. The grisly facelift launched the man into an ungainly somersault that swiped through a raining veil of blood and brains.

Adrenaline torquing combat senses to what felt like superhuman levels, McCarter scanned his rear, then hauled himself hard for the edge of the hall, still grunting from a bruised sternum, lungs on fire. He heard weapons chatter and the crunch of more explosions, the clamor of battle coming from the far north and east.

Good.

His mates were in the game, and making progress.

North, maybe forty to fifty meters, McCarter made out a heap of strewed garbage as thick black smoke washed from what appeared three different directions, blanketing the picture of devastation to near obscurity. There was crushed wood, hunks of rubble, bodies, some stretched out and chewed and blackened, others with obvious broken arms and legs, with jagged bone shards glistening in firelight, both from above and in the immediate kill radius. What grabbed his eye a moment longer than it should have was the luxury ride that had crashed through the ceiling to put an end to somebody's running plans with gruesome sudden finality. What looked like an arm was poking out where crumpled hood had flattened the poor sap beneath.

The Dag Don's ship may be sinking, but McCarter was becoming more certain with each passing second that Azmit Zhuktul and his cronies were in the process of bailing.

The fumes of burning gasoline spiking his nose, McCarter figured southbound was his best bet to bag the big sharks. Homed in on the distant voices of men engaged in bitter argument, the Stony Man warrior moved out.

CHAPTER TEN

Johnny Polansky was reasonably certain about one thing.

They were going to die.

And he was a few days shy of his twenty-eighth birthday, no less. Now that he thought about it all, it was nothing short of a miracle he'd made it this far. His nagging suspicion was confirmed as he watched the screens and digital reads on their security monitors zapping out in white squiggle worms. The EMP juice shut down the lights next, as he heard his younger brother and Job gasp from the darkness. From across the room he heard the static shooting out from one of their useless cell phones.

Forget the local cavalry; they were screwed.

And thus, he thought, consider the cold facts of life. These people didn't play games. They didn't read anyone Miranda rights. They didn't believe in handcuffs and smoke-filled Q and A rooms and grim chitchat over coffee. They made people they deemed a clear and present threat to national security disappear without a trace. They had electronic countermeasure high-tech equipment and other gizmos at their disposal that would put any science fiction to shame. Forget thermal imaging, they had X-ray lasers that could scan and paint the human body behind a foot of concrete. Oh, and yes, there were those infamous fabled black helicopters; he and Jimmy had both seen and run from them in Utah and Nevada. And yes, the United States government did, in fact, exercise its authority to execute its own citizens who crossed their imaginary line in the sand regarding their secrets, and that they didn't want the average Joe or Jane Citizen to have in their possession, hard drive, word of mouth or otherwise. He, like the others in the Force of Truth, knew what they did in the name of national security had, in fact, gathered classified intelligence on how they operated above the law of the land, which had been part of their job description all along. They had names, dates, areas of interest and ongoing operations, complete with an A list of assassinations and questionable interrogation techniques by the CIA and special ops, both home and abroad. The reasons were the basic Stars and Stripes nonsense—us and them—but it was still knowledge so dangerous, all of them considered it the next best thing to divine wisdom and all the secrets of the universe.

And their black op version of God had come to cast them out of their Virginia Beach Eden.

"They're here," Cain said, amazed at just how calm he sounded and felt as he marched away from the dead security monitors, Uzi up and ready.

"You think, big brother?" Abel's voice was tight with fear.

"Now what, Johnny? Let 'em walk right in like you said and—"

"Stick to the plan," he told them, then ignored their rising panic, moving toward the curtained window facing west. There, he crouched, cradling the Uzi submachine gun Rosenberg had given him before their leader had departed with the Kid and Noah for North Carolina. He cut the curtain back a few inches with the subgun's muzzle. All dark, quiet and still. Bad, real bad.

Now what, big shot? he wondered. And what plan, other than wing it, brazen it out like some gunslinger walking toward a showdown with the black hats?

It was strange, he suddenly considered as the generator kicked in, casting barely enough light from the emergency bulbs along the base of the floor to sheen the room as little more than shadows, but he felt no hostility, no resentment, no fear. Like the others, if he and his brother had known one full and happy peaceful day in their short lives, then they'd forgotten all about it. Broken or no families, seething incorrigible addiction, pounded from here, there and everywhere by the merciless winds of fate, it seemed the list of sins and miseries was too much to recount without breaking out the sob towels, he figured why bother.

If this was it, then so be it.

Nobody lived forever, not in this world.

The past was but a scourge of memory, the present a fearsome roll of the dice sure to crap them out, and the future…

What future?

If it was true the good died young, then—speaking for himself—he was all but breaking the typecast.

He looked back at his brother and Job, felt his heart growing heavier. Whether out of a sense of some Three Musketeer loyalty to each other or nobility to the greater good, the boys had stood up, nearly clinging to his Aloha shirt when he volunteered to remain behind, both of them appearing willing now to make the ultimate sacrifice. Though they might well be thinking along the lines of salvation in the form of groveling or plea bargain when it hit the fan.

The opposition didn't know the meaning of mercy. Mercy equaled weakness.

Which was why each of them was now armed with Glock .45s, and which he had taken a few minutes after the departure of Rosenberg and the others to show them how to use the weapons. They were cocked and locked, ready to aim for center mass—the chest—and squeeze in a two-handed grip. If it came down to a standing, or a running firefight, then Uzis were laid on vacant desktops, spare clips shoved in waistbands all around. Then there was the surprise package of all hardware. It was stretched out beneath a blanket by his feet. He glanced at the slender bulk. The M-72 antitank, one-shot disposable bazooka was set to lose it 66 mm HE round. Protective caps already removed, inner tube drawn out and locked into place. Aim, squeeze, fire. If it came down to that, the others knew about backblast...

Cain got his head back in the game. At his order, his brother and Job moved to take up positions at the curtain on the far side of the room.

And Cain saw the black van. Lights out, it materialized from the Stygian murk, a ghost ship sailing slowly up the dirt drive. The soft crunch of tire tread over hardpacked earth put everybody on full alert, as Job wanted to know what was happening.

"They're here," Johnny Polansky told them.

"So, why aren't Apollo and Ramses going crazy?" Job asked in a harsh whisper.

"Why do you think?" Cain quietly shot back.

He sensed their fear mount into a heat wave, then watched as the black van stopped a few yards shy of the front stoop. A small, nearly invisible dish on the roof did a slow scan of the house, left to right.

Painting them on thermal imaging. The three of them were rats in a barrel.

A tall, lean figure in black stepped out from behind the driver's wheel.

"Johnny? Say we even appease them and they do take our laptops," Wheeler said. "We're only buying a little time, and with EMP buzzing the air there's no way to activate—"

"Shh. I told you, let me do all the talking. Take it a step at a time."

The buzz-cut black op walked up the steps, attitude cool and superior, pretty much what Cain expected. He was polite, though, about to knock on the door, when Polansky called, "It's open. Come on in."

Polansky aimed the Uzi at the door as it slowly creaked wide on rusty hinges. His shadow filled the doorway for a moment, then he stepped in. The dark specter sniffed the air, parked his wingtips a few steps inside, then looked set to break out in laughter as he spotted his armed competition on the opposite side of the room.

"Boys," he greeted, grinning, acting like a late-night comedian about to launch into his act. "I'll get right to it. In case you don't know who I am…"

"Skip it. We have a good idea what you are," Cain said.

"But, of course. You've been expecting me."

Cain waved his Uzi at the nylon satchel on the floor in front of the first empty workstation. "In that bag are laptops. All our files. Everything you think we might have stolen."

"Where are the other three?"

"They went fishing."

"You mean," the specter said, "they took off with backup files and any other laptops."

Cain felt his pulse speeding up, the first bead of sweat breaking out on his forehead. He licked lips that had suddenly gone dry, peeked out the window. "Here's our offer. Take those laptops. Force of Truth, that's the password. If you're not satisfied, come back and we can talk some more. I know you have others with you, probably have the perimeter sealed. We're not going anywhere. We can't call out to VA Beach's finest, but you already took care of that. You decide to let us live in peace, we'll forget about you killing our dogs."

"Killing, huh. Is that what you think your government is all about? Cruelty to animals? Killing its own citizens?"

Cain went tight in the chest at the tone. He'd walked some mean streets in his short life—been in prison— and he knew the threat of violence when he heard it.

More, he could read between the lines, and know when the other guy was itching to act on it. The specter wanted them dead.

The black op chuckled, a sound of unbridled contempt as he stepped to the bag. He inspected it, bent at the knees, examined its exterior some more, then opened it carefully.

"Hey, goomba, we didn't put any bomb in the damn bag," Abel snarled.

The specter bobbed his head, sneering. "Goomba. That's some pretty tough talk, sonny boy." He opened the satchel, delved inside, fished around, then stood, hefting the weight. He looked around the room, peered at both ends of the trailer, but Cain suspected he already knew it was just the four of them. "Okay, girls, I tell you what. I'll assume you want to cooperate. I'll go take a look at what you have. Then check in with my boss."

"What's your name, spook?" Cain said, not sure why he suddenly felt compelled to ask the question.

He was Mr. Chuckles again, as he rolled for the door. "Barabbas," he said.

"Cute," Job remarked.

"Punks," the specter muttered on his way out.

Polansky felt the adrenaline burn, aware they were only a few moments away from lighting the fuse. What the hell had he done? he wondered as he scoured the night, following the specter as he retraced his steps to the van. The shadow veered around the front, moved past the passenger door and slid open the side panel, vanishing from sight.

"Johnny?"

Cain felt his heart lurch. He detected pure fear in his brother's voice, but he picked up resignation behind the words.

It was Job who then seemed more insistent on voicing the unthinkable. "Johnny?"

Slowly he turned, looked at his brother, then Wheeler. If they were blaming or cursing circumstances beyond their control, he didn't see it. They looked ready to fight, but at the same time they damn near looked like lambs, he thought. Peaceful. Resigned.

Ready for slaughter?

They knew they were no match for what was out there in the night, stone-cold professional killers versus three computer geeks, but he felt reasonably confident they would try.

"They're going to kill us, aren't they?"

Cain nodded, and told Job, "Yeah. They're going to try to kill us."

IT COULD HAVE BEEN hyperadrenalized senses, but Manning would have sworn the bullet cut a slow-mo and very visible path on its trajectory through smoke and fire, parted the glowing pall like it was hung on a line. HK-33 swinging toward the threat, the big Canadian was just about to drop the mutilated sack staggering to rise from the shark's teeth of wreckage when the streaking projectile blasted into the enemy's skull. The walking wounded was all but decapitated from Hawkins's sniper round, picked up and flung into a slab of ZIL limo paneling dug into the earth like a victory lance.

How many more guards about to rise from the dead?

Manning grimaced with the next few steps, bit down the vicious curse, assault rifle sweeping a smoking lake of wreckage and bodies that wanted to brand a vision of the end of the world in his mind. Moments ago, two more rounds had found the armor along his ribs, but pain and adrenaline were working wonders on his combat vision. Unless he chose to drop the gas mask over his face, there was nothing to be done about the combined stench of cooking flesh, pooling guts, body waste and burning fuel.

Love it and dig in or lose it all here and now to mauled enemy.

The smoke was a definite hindrance, thick, black sheets rolling over the demolished motor pool and veiling the annex facade. Every twist and turn through the maze of debris and bodies could be hiding a banged-up rabid possum, laying low and looking to now vent. But the shellacking the enemy had taken from the conflagration looked about as thorough as any of them could have hoped for. Picking up the pace of the walk-through and navigating between two T-rex-size pillars of fire, he found little more than charred and dismembered bodies, broken legs, arms and feet strewed among the litter of vehicles like meat thrown haphazard for scavengers. The heat from scattered firestorms made it even more difficult to breathe, had already so soaked Manning with running sweat he might as well have been doused by a firehose. The mushroom cloud was still rising behind their march, sucking debris past his hooded mug along with most of the air out of the immediate vicinity in a giant vacuum that sounded as if the gates of Hell had opened to consume whatever was left standing. If he wanted easy, then Manning decided he would have bought a condo in Midtown Manhattan and done Broadway every night with ogling women on each arm.

This was what he did, and did best.

Make war on those who would slaughter the innocent.

To call the strike a success, he knew they needed one of two things to happen, preferably both. Intelligence by way of computers or CD-ROMs, or a live songbird or two at the top. One glance at the vast smashed areas where roof and walls had collapsed, it would prove no small feat to turn up anything of value. But there was no such creature as a perfect world in black ops, he knew.

Manning spied an arm twitching to his one o'clock. He pumped a 3-round burst into what he thought was a figure reaching for an assault rifle, pasting the body to a smoking engine block in a sloppy crucifixion.

James was on his left wing, he found, the black ex-SEAL's hood mangled above his left ear where he'd been slashed on the head by raining garbage moments earlier. The sky was still spitting down bits and pieces of metal and human remains, and maybe two full minutes after the last of the tankers had been sent soaring to crash through the roof in some inexplicable event that still boggled the big Canadian's mind. The ex-SEAL's pearly whites, he saw, were bared in pure menace like a neon sign, James fueled by his own white-hot pain and burning desire to mop it up.

Manning began to feel like a deep-space pioneer treading on a distant alien planet as he found a narrow fissure to squeeze through the mountain of rubble, into what appeared a large main living room.

A sprawled groaner was treated to another 3-round burst up the spine by James as the ex-SEAL matched Manning step for step. In the sweeping morass of bodies, partially collapsed ceiling, crumbled walls and beds of smashed furniture the thermal handhelds were of next to no use. He was wending a path of easiest navigation through the carnage when he spied James slide through a thin curtain of smoke, then bend to examine something. Manning strained his hearing, focused in on any noise beyond the crackling fires behind. McCarter had patched through right before they hit the motor pool, detailing his position and what he was up against. They needed speed, but slogging through this mess—

"Gary."

Manning read the look in his teammate's eyes. James had something—or someone—of high value. Swift but cautious, panning the dung heaps of bodies and wafting smoke, he veered to his ten o'clock. Despite the blood he fisted out of his left, James managed a cold smile, pointing his assault rifle at what he'd stumbled across.

Manning couldn't believe it. He watched as James plucked a folded nylon satchel from his belt and unsnapped it. There wasn't much left of the body but pulp and shattered bones jutting from any number of shredded areas. Manning had to look twice to make sure that between pain, smoke and adrenaline his eyes didn't deceive him. Sure enough, that was a notebook computer and a batch of CD-ROMs going into his teammate's hands. Miracle of miracles, there wasn't but a few scratches on any of it.

Sometimes, he thought, the good guys got lucky.

CHAPTER ELEVEN

Royce Bannon was typing in Force of Truth while he relayed the sitrep over his handheld radio with its secured-and-EMP-proof frequency. "Casper to One Phantom. Have made contact. In process of confirm-deny limbo status. Roger that, One Phantom."

He listened with one ear as Zeno copied, the unit standing upright beside the computer like a posted sentry he knew was there but didn't need pay more than passing attention to. The man stated something about holding present position, but Bannon found his thoughts traveling elsewhere.

Sometimes he hated his job, thinking maybe it was time to retire before it was too late. Meaning, may God have mercy if it all came to light what they were prepared to do, because the average U.S. citizen would want nothing short of their scalps on a pike. Placing persons of interest under full surveillance microscope was one matter. Even midnight abductions for a stern warning and leaving the offender stranded in the middle of nowhere and shaking in stained shorts was acceptable. Committing, however, what amounted to nothing more or less than cold-blooded murder against American citizens, sanctioned or not by their superiors...

For some reason the hackles began to rise on the back of his neck. He lifted one end of the laptop, grunting, wondered why his initial suspicion when handling the computer wanted to grab him by the throat again. It might be paranoid imagination, but he'd handled enough computers to think the weight was off a little, unevenly distributed by a few ounces or so to one end.

Chill, he told himself, they were just dweebs in question—or so stamped by Zeno and most likely to salve his own conscience—not devious, malevolent black ops like they were. Then he eased back in the bolted-down wingback as Access Granted flashed onto the monitor.

Their enemy, he thought. Little more than scared kids. They had gotten in way over their heads in some quest to prove themselves smarter than U.S. intelligence, spurred on by a former DOD cyberwizard who had been handed a pink slip for so-called "dereliction of duty," and who should have known better than to try to steal from Uncle Sam's treasure trove of divine wisdom. ET stories—even what he once overheard was housed in deep freeze in at least two different classified installations out west—they could live with, since a few loudmouths from Area 51 and other black project sites had long since gone public, signing book deals, doing the talking-head circuit and so forth. But these young guys had stolen intelligence on past, present and future black ops that could well topple the walls of three different intelligence agencies, and that didn't include what was known about the Australian Ground Zero and their own European friends in a covert space program. Under different circumstances he knew his superiors would hire them on the spot, rolling out the magic carpet, no less, all the booze, dope and women they could only envision in their wildest fantasies. Twenty-something, and they had talent as hackers they'd proved outclassed the best cyberbrains Big Brother had, and by light-years. But what had he once been told by a late field commander on his first Reprimand stint? Something how when mercy was granted, then the enemy saw personal reprieve as a weakness, an opportunity to strike back.

Rubbish.

Out of the mouths of fools...

Sure, he played the part as stone-cold bogeyman well enough, but his heart wasn't really in it.

He had a son, two years old, and someday Josh—God and man willing—would reach an age that none of these three would ever...

He smelled it first, a sickening cloy of melting plastic, then recognized the hiss for what it was.

Bannon jumped to his feet. A picture scalded to mind of the dweebs right then enjoying a belly ripper, as he saw wisps of smoke drift up from the keyboard. He cursed as he caught the matching reptile-like sound from inside the bag at his feet. The sulfuric acid was in full flow now, threatening to paste the laptop to his table when he swept it to the floor, Bannon lurching back from streaming molten lava. Suddenly he realized he'd left the handheld on, as Zeno's bark to know what was going on ripped through the van.

Bannon roared. A running start, and he sent the back doors thundering open with a kick that left no doubt they'd all but been duped—and mocked in the same breath.

THE INVISIBLE FIST of burning fuel and cooked flesh pounding his nose, McCarter spied the carcasses, many of which were still shrouded in flames. What he called the divine wrath had incinerated what had to have been a standing small army of twenty or more, only now littered from a few feet to his left, clear on for dozens of yards to where more blackened mummies were stacked along the demolished east wall. Some gnarled steel poked from around the corner, indisputable evidence of the tanker's landing zone, a dragon's tongue of flames still shooting from down yonder as it ate up fuel and breathed out clouds as black as Satan's heart. Ah, yes, he would gladly accept whatever good fortune Fate deigned to hurl their way anytime, but it was the raging force, dead ahead but hidden from view, that steeled the Stony Man warrior's grim death sights.

They were bellowing a fierce storm from inside the door, women crying out, a gruff voice shouting something above the ruckus as McCarter gave his six a last look. Clear, but his mates were en route.

McCarter wasn't a commando to hot-dog the play, by any stretch of talent and experience. From the briefest of sitreps on the march it sounded as if each of his men had fulfilled his own deadly role, still in the game, bulldozing for the finish line.

The hall came to a dead end, a few yards beyond the screamfest. How many shooters inside was impossible to say, and with the prostitutes...

McCarter plucked a flash-bang from his webbing, armed and hurled it at an angle for the wall running east inside the door. The steel canister ricocheted off concrete, flying out of sight, deep into the lair, as intended. McCarter threw himself against the wall, turned away from the coming peal, mashing hands over ears to spare his senses best he could. The foot-stomping anger and panic seemed to rocket to jumbo-jet decibels a second before the flash-bang shredded all the tumult to muted shock and paralysis.

CAIN RECALLED SOMETHING his brother had recently told him. Each and every single snowflake was unique, different in shape, size, appearance. There was no one human ear or eye like another, even every strand of hair on each human head, he claimed, was different than the other hairs. No two creatures, no two "anything" was like the other. Each was its own brilliant and separate creation, of and unto itself.

Sweet kid, his little brother, he thought, a poet at heart perhaps, but who would never see come to fruition whatever his real talents, hopes and dreams.

The whole point being, he decided—as he saw the steaming pile of what he'd created by his own hand hit the ground beside the van and heard another bellowed curse shatter the silence—there really was an all-powerful, all-wise and infinite creator. No limits, no boundaries to this supreme entity, ever-expanding in creation and wisdom, like the universe itself believed by science infinite but still always and forever reaching and sweeping outward.

Limit and source unknown.

Science and whatever the wisdom of man baffled to explain the unexplainable.

Not that he or any of the others ever doubted any of this, but the bottom line—the Alpha and the Omega—was a few short moments away from being hurled in their collective faces.

And, yes, the three of them were about to be sent from this world to see for themselves what lay beyond.

Red laser beams hit the curtains first, spearing through, front and back of Cain, roving the room in some eerie dance of light. Both Job and Abel were sounding off their alarm when the first waves blasted into the windows. Cain cursed, flinching as glass and shredded fabric sailed overhead. He glanced across the room through slitted eyes and gritted teeth, found his brother and Job hugging the floor. Their shouts were flung away by the relentless barrage of what sounded like a million stuttering weapons, sound-suppressed submachine guns, he reckoned, but unleashing all the infernal racket of the damned freed from Hell to do as they wished on Earth. Fisting his Uzi, Cain looked up and around, the world beyond strobing with muzzle-flashes that seemed to keep on expanding and sweeping like that infinite universe his finite mind had just tried to grasp. Holes began puking through the walls and base in a long steady march from end to end of the main room. Razoring bits and pieces of wood, glass and aluminum swirled and swelled the air, a tempest, it looked, that became a raging entity unto itself, creating a vacuum of noise and debris that only appeared to spiral in on itself for some invisible core where Life met Death.

Cain took the lead. He roared, lunged up and held back on the Uzi's trigger. The specter just beat his tracking line of fire, the black op hurling himself into dense brush as Cain chewed up foliage and ground up earth with his extended fusillade. Hot lead scorched his cheeks, slivers slashing his face. He braved the storm for a few more eternal moments, sweeping his own blistering line of 9 mm Parabellum projectiles down the drive. Floor, walls and ceiling, he saw and felt, began to shudder like some great beast heaving its final few breaths before it collapsed. He heard Abel and Job hurl their own Uzis into the fray, spied bulbs popping off in minidetonations to either side of him, but momentary dark shadows were instantly knifed by the winking veils of muzzle-flash.

Cain burned through the clip, was grabbing a fresh magazine from his waistband when he heard the sharp grunt followed by a brief scream. He was turning when, adrenaline and terror fueling his senses, he saw Job flying away from the sill, slick jets of crimson taking to the air. Job bicycled feet that appeared to levitate off the floor a few inches, his Uzi flaming at the ceiling, hunks of dissected shirt and flesh swirling above, magnetized into the maelstrom as he absorbed yet more hits. He was falling, what looked like a slow-motion spiraling topple, when Cain spotted the slender white beam lance the shadows. He heard his brother shout his name, Abel jumping to his feet, Uzi blazing in epileptic sprays, then the beam painted its bull's-eye on his temple. Even as the din of weapons fire rent the air and the storm gathered a second wind, the split second froze Cain into shock and horror. His mind knew what was happening, but his eyes wanted to lie to him that what he witnessed was impossible. The white beam appeared to core its way out the other side of his brother's skull, floating up wispy tendrils of smoke before vanishing beyond the demolished window, off into dark infinity.

Cain was screaming his brother's name, the air sweet with the stink of burned flesh, his brother crumpling at the knees, when he took the hammer blow from two or three bullets through the ribs. Before he knew it, he was down, flopping around, eating glass and other slivered trash.

Time to go, he heard the voice in his head echo back.

Before he was aware of what he was doing, he pulled the bazooka from beneath the blanket. Grunting, white-hot pain exploding from scalp to toes, he staggered to his feet, hacking out slimy bubbles of blood and other garbage. Rounds kept chewing up the sill and frame, shards vomiting past his face, but he somehow lined the tube up on the black van's grille. He fumbled to find the trigger housing, vaguely aware next the shooting had abruptly stopped. Through the roaring echo in his ears, he heard someone shout, "Give it up, kid!"

He shimmed toward the sill.

"It doesn't have to end this way, kid! We cannot let you leave here, do you understand me!? Just give us your other three buddies and everything you have on—"

Johnny Polansky responded to the black-op monologue, and let the 66 mm warhead fly.

MCCARTER TAGGED three goons with his opening HK barrage. The Phoenix Force leader was angling farther from the door when AKs cut loose with return fire. What the Briton anticipated as a shield of blind counteroffensive autofire was marched up and down the door frame. Four, then five mauled shooters shuffled out of the dust-and-grit showers, still directing weapons fire at their imaginary target. Fear and plain common sense had sent a pack of maybe ten to twelve prostitutes nosediving or bolting for the far corners. A sweet and wide-open field of fire was thus cleared for McCarter to hold back on his HK's trigger. He had a vague impression of Zhuktul and the pair of moneymen pegged by intelligence, with steamer trunks strewed and punched open by the shock wave of the flash-bang, tattered currency floating through the smoky pall. The two standing Iraqis were shrieking, ostensibly for mercy, their silk threads chewed to homeless rags, when McCarter doused his shooting gallery with a long raking of autofire. The last two guards were pitching with their brethren-in-crime-and-terror, crimson stickmen pounding streams of wild rounds into the ceiling, when Zhuktul locked an arm around the neck of a moneyman.

Zhuktul waved the assault rifle, back and forth, unseeing eyes bugged from their sockets, flicking like pinball arms. "Back off! I'll kill him!"

"So kill him," McCarter flung back.

The Dag Don may be deaf and blind still, McCarter

knew, Zhuktul cursing in his native tongue, but the AK he let rip in his free hand was searching for his scalp, powered by nothing less than raw fury and the determination of the damned.

"THE KID'S NOT giving up."

Zeno hung his head, groaned. He couldn't believe it, either. The skinny kid in the dazzling fruit shirt staggered like the bloody wraith he looked, closer to the window ruins, as if to announce his swan song. The double-wide mobile home looked exactly like it should, savaged, top to bottom, end to end by their swarms of steel-jacketed locusts, but like the kid, it was still standing.

Something in the structure groaned, matching the kid's wheezing from a perforated lung, as the roof began to sag. Zeno let the weapon rest on the ground by his boot, a special insulated glove wrapped around what passed for its butt. He wouldn't need it for the finale. The dosimeter's digital read told him the weapon was good for another five seconds of blasting before he had to worry about the thing going hot. Cancer, leukemia, hair loss were the least of his woes at the moment.

Shifting to the other knee, he weighed their options. They were slim and getting slimmer. Thermal imaging painted two down inside, he knew, bodies cooling off on their screens as they gave up the ghost. It was damn near laughable, embarrassing to boot, he considered, as he found the fiery comets still banging to the drive where the last kid standing had just blown about ten million bucks worth of high-tech ride to scrap. Phones, both landline and cell, all radio frequencies had been reduced to whining static, but only up before the kid triggered the LAWs. Now with their EMP screen wiped out…

Zeno came alive as the kid slapped a fresh clip into the Uzi, cocked the bolt with a dramatic flourish, bloody froth spilling off his chin, running slime that seemed to mirror the flames. The kid was a fighter, no question about it, and he was going for the full ride. He then scanned the drive and the wood's edge with a look of contempt, coughing and grunting and weaving around as he clung to life. Zeno heard Nefirelli patch through over his com link, informing him he thought he heard sirens, Bannon wanting to know the play from his firepoint at the north edge of the drive.

What play? Zeno thought. There was a white vintage Chevrolet in mint condition near the pen holding dead canines, and that would be their ride out of here. Beyond clearing cops, they had a lead on the errant geeks. Beyond that…

As a flaming sheet thudded to the driveway, Zeno saw the kid limp out of sight, vanishing behind the home's bullet-riddled paneling. He strained his ears, tuning out the crackle of fire, caught feet crunching debris, the kid kicking through whatever rubbish. He was thinking the kid had another LAWs on hand, then the music blared on.

Zeno fought down the grim chuckle, shook his head. It was little short of a miracle that the stereo hadn't been shot to ruins to begin with. Beyond that, he recognized the tune from both jukebox and video that made a big splash a few years back. Something about a woman burning down the house around her abusive husband.

The kid hobbled back into view, having doubled his Uzi pleasure, and took up a defiant stance.

By God, Zeno couldn't help but begrudge a few moments of respect and admiration. He decided to let the kid shine in his final seconds, the opening chords and lyrics that would take him out of the world on the voice of Martina and "Independence Day."

It was a damn shame, but he found himself really liking this kid.

A PIECE OF DRIFTWOOD tossed about on the waves of raging seas, the waters infested with sharks, and all the way to shore. They smelled blood, these man-eaters growing more frenzied, aware now he was but a few short strokes from reaching the safety of the beach.

That was his life.

That was the living testament to the lives of his brother and Job. The raging sea. The circling sharks. The light burning at him from the shore, and calling him home.

As he searched the glowing tongues of his handiwork, the wavering halos growing distant as blood teared his eyes, Cain briefly wondered why such a vision flamed to mind.

And when it was all he could do to stay on his feet, dredge up the last fiber of fading strength to finish it. Her voice pounding the air from the only thing standing in the whole damn room, the hideous rasp of every burning breath…

Sight and sound began sailing away next, stretching into some warm evanescence, on to infinity.

Cain lifted the Uzis.

ZENO KEYED his com link, and told his men, "Paint him and finish it."

The kid cut loose with both Israeli subguns in near sync, as if on cue, the final act of defiance to his executioners. The red lasers painted him square on the sternum, then Zeno heard them turn their sound-suppressed HK MP-5s loose, scything the kid's chest to ribbons in microseconds flat. He held on for a moment or two that strained Zeno's imagination to the limits, the kid winging out twin lines of fire, twitching with each impact, a puppet being dissected on its strings. Then the Uzis were thrown off mark, fiery lines directed at the ceiling as the kid kept absorbing all they threw at him, jerked some more, spun, then dropped.

Zeno gave the kid a moment of silence.

He was rising with the weapon, watching the smoke drift across the gutted window, when he caught the sound of a twig snapping. He was darting to the side when he heard the brief and familiar burp of a sound-suppressed subgun, then a matching stutter pricked his ears from the east.

Son of a—

He was swinging the weapon around, finger taking up slack on the trigger when the big shadow came rushing out of the blackness on his six.

CHAPTER TWELVE

They were all about the money, and it made McCarter sick with cold anger. He spared neither Don nor Iraqi shield, the Stony Man warrior blasting away with his HK-33. The long hammering barrage pinned them together in a dance of death, the prostitutes shrieking, hugging the floor and plastered to the walls in fetal curls like they wished they could vanish. As the former SAS commando expected, Zhuktul didn't want to give up the ghost, his AK roaring on, his human armor convulsing out of his grasp to crunch at his feet. McCarter took the brute impact of a wild projectile to armor just beneath his left breast, shuffled to the side, forced by the punishing blow into a half pirouette.

Grunting, snarling against the fresh wave of pain, he brought the assault rifle back online, riddled Zhuktul with a rising burst of autofire as rounds hammered the wall beside him. Zhuktul went flailing back, his final spray zipping the last of the moneymen. Fancy Rags was hit by the line of bullets in what looked like a sweeping sword that slashed across the Iraqi's chest, his scarecrow's jig absorbing death that would have otherwise nailed a few women. The Iraqi howled, eyes bulging in what looked to McCarter as shock and terror, then he collapsed into an open trunk. Crimson-soaked bills shot out from beneath his sprawled corpse.

Advancing, HK sweeping the room, McCarter peered through smoke and the ragged flotsam of bloody cloth and currency raining to the floor. Ears ringing like twenty church bells, he strained and made out the faintest sound of shouts, the crunch of explosions and autofire. Cautious, checking the slaughter bed on a rolling compass, the women crying and blubbering in a babble of foreign tongues, the Stony Man warrior slid into position beside the tunnel's open door. Feeding his HK a fresh clip, he keyed his com link. As he received sitreps down the line, Manning and James informing him they were a few short moments away, Encizo shelling what appeared the last of the bad guys to the east with his Multi-Round Projectile Launcher, McCarter gave the abattoir a scathing look.

At least ten trunks, he found, were stuffed with Euros and American hundred-dollar bills, some open, others turned on their sides, spilling loot. How much blood, he wondered, stained all that currency? Money was inanimate, of course, but this particular treasure vault was built in the spirit of evil. The mere sight of so much ill-gotten gain—meant to be used again to keep the evil empire of jihad flourishing and a few fat cats indulging their every whim and vice—made McCarter wonder just how dirty was any single paper note around the planet. At some point or another, every dollar bill, every coin felt the touch of the Seven Deadly Sins, fitted into the next owner's hands, marked by an invisible trail of unknown horror, misery and transgression. Money, he considered, was a useful tool, a necessity of life, but like anything touched by man it was never far from corruption.

End of discussion.

"Do any of you speak English?" McCarter shouted, moving toward the closest trunk.

A blonde raised a trembling arm.

"Myself and my men are not going to hurt you."

She nodded, tears streaming down her cheeks. "*Da*—yes. Okay."

"They are wearing black hoods like myself," he told the woman, and began flipping stacks of rubber-banded currency at their feet. "Take that money and leave this place. How you get to whatever homes you have left is your business, but you are to forget what happened here and that you ever saw me."

"Yes, yes," she said, as the other women came alive, reaching out to haul in their individual pile.

"Can you tell the others what I just said?"

She nodded. "Yes, yes, I speak enough Arabic to make them know."

McCarter pulled a thermite grenade off his webbing. "Good. You have thirty seconds to clear the room, then I burn the rest of the money."

LYONS DIDN'T HAVE the first second to curse for being late to save the Force of Truth, or to lash out at all the other miserable luck that had screwed up this night so far. "Do or die" was hurled straight for his face.

He was twenty yards and closing, trampling all manner of brush in his final bull-charge, when the black op was galvanized out of whatever his morbid reflection, reacting in a lunge to the threat on his rear. As the Able Team leader held back on the trigger of his HK MP-5, he was ducking under the pencil-thin white beam. What the hell! Lyons was threatened with shock in the next eye blink, his thoughts shouting that what he believed just tried to decapitate him was so impossible...

The subgun stammering out its muffled salvo, Lyons hurled himself to the side, his ears tweaked by a strange—

Timber was groaning behind him!

Lyons glimpsed the ragged holes gouted open across the op's torso, dark sprays blossoming the air, telling him the guy had come to kill without body armor. Tough luck. The homegrown enemy was hurling out what sounded like a shredded howl between anger and confusion as Lyons hit the deck and drilled him with enough 9 mm Parabellum rounds to end the fight.

Lyons jumped to his feet, edged toward the body, then glanced over his shoulder just as the tree listed with an angry moan. It fell, bringing down a swath of canopy before it thundered to earth, blasting out dust and brush. The stump, he found, was still smoking from where the beam had sawed through about eighteen inches of lumber. First invisible men, and now this.

He keyed his com link, discovered Gadgets and Pol had just taken down their own ops, in the process of checking their heat-seeking units.

Clear, or so they told him.

Lyons stared at the body, spotted Blancanales step from brush across the drive, his HK subgun panning the area, burning orbs flickering the hot zone from behind the hood. Lyons looked at the weapon, and looked up in utter disbelief.

He had a good idea what it was that chopped down trees quicker than the world's biggest chain saw.

The night, he thought, was fast becoming some lunatic's worst nightmare. A hard ride already, pushing an even 100 mph, and Brognola choppered to the Farm, leaving the three of them with a bag of riddles and in pursuit of vipers. Opposing black op EMP had blanked their own thermal imaging until one of the Force of Truth wizards had apparently hurtled his own middle-finger salute into the van. Only now Lyons was left with nothing but dead bodies and still no answers.

The silver weapon, he found, was shaped something like an M-16, but with a square box for a magazine. There were strange markings, little knobs and dials that Lyons was in no mood to give more than a passing inspection to right then. The barrel was slender, longer than any assault rifle he knew of, no sights, nothing but smooth bore and butt.

Lyons waved his subgun at the bizarre weapon. "Secure that," he told Blancanales, then strode for the mobile home.

Sirens, fire, the shiver of fear and uncertainty dropped Lyons into vertigo as he bounded up the steps. Subgun out, he tramped over the fallen door. He wasn't sure what he expected to find, but at first glance he knew the place had been cleaned of anything worth taking.

A washout, then. Considering the past few hours, it somehow fit.

He looked at the three bodies strewn in front of him, cut to ribbons. He wasn't sure whether he felt anger or pity, or both. They were just kids, never stood a chance against seasoned professionals. The file on them, he recalled, read like a misfit's manual, or a guide on how to avoid all of life's misery and bad luck. The Force of Truth had been touched and battered in one way or another by any number of society's ills, but for these three the plague of their brief existence was over. And what was Rosenberg's game anyway? he wondered. Did the former DOD encryption master fancy himself a savior of the lost and wayward? Teacher and guide? Lyons gave these three credit for stones, though, and way beyond their years, experience and job description. Whether following orders or their own hearts, they took whatever secrets their killers wanted with them to the next world.

One look at the weapons and all the spent brass, and these kids knew all along they were going to die. It was easy enough in his ex-cop's experience to piece together what and how it all went down. Beyond exposure of Stony Man Farm, Lyons wondered just what was so important they had felt compelled to sacrifice their lives here. It made no sense. By all rights, they were just computer geeks, should have thrown down their weapons, hands up, begging for their lives. Then again, he would have done the same thing in their place. Sometimes the lion showed up in sheep's clothing.

He sensed Schwarz watching over his shoulder, told

him to search the trailer, then went and turned off the stereo.

Lyons moved back to stand over the bodies when Schwarz reappeared and told him what he already suspected.

That left three Force of Truth members on the run, or in hiding. With what Brognola had informed him, the Farm had a line on where to look next. By the time they hit North Carolina, Lyons had to wonder if they would again be too late.

He knew Schwarz was itching to go, as he heard the encroaching but still distant sirens. What a waste of life, all this talent, all the potential. Murdered, and for what?

"Carl, we need to make fast tracks outta here, man."

Lyons ignored his teammate's insistent demand. He gave wasted youth another lingering stare, angry at the whole damn world for reasons he wasn't sure of, then turned and walked away.

CHAPTER THIRTEEN

Whatever sun broke through the cloud banks scudding the Caucasus Mountains amounted to little more than fleeting rays, and David McCarter briefly wondered if those racing patches of light were in equal parts to their own hope.

Beyond smashing the house of Zhuktul, freeing a bunch of imported prostitutes to be scattered to the cold and wind, he wasn't sure where the mission stood. Yes, McCarter decided, a chunk of terror pipeline had been partially demolished with the death of the Dag Don, and torching tens of his dirty millions had been an unexpected bonus. But failing to capture a UN middleman or a top Zhuktul lieutenant for interrogation left any number of doors open. Time and circumstance allowed but for only a running cursory sweep of the compound, and considering most of it was nothing but a maze of rubble, the chances of finding any VX were nil from the jump. But, going in, McCarter figured to leave any in-depth tour and possible seizure of nerve gas to the local Russian military or Dag authorities, such as they were, which pretty much meant their hearts and hands were about as clean as the Caspian.

Zhuktul, at any rate, was out of the picture, and McCarter could settle for that much. Gerbaky Shistoi, however, was the big shark in this pond. Unlike Comrade Zhuktul he didn't believe in hiding out in the open, and the renegade colonel had a standing army to match the Don's. It was perhaps stating the obvious, he considered, but the dead took any knowledge on Shistoi's whereabouts with them to Hell, so any solid leads to drop the renegade Dagestani colonel into the net...

Well, McCarter was open to suggestions.

The good news was the late Don's laptop and CDs were in their possession. That, and their own sat-video link with laptop, fax and e-mail supermodems was back in hand, recovered where they'd stashed it all before the strike. Weather and circumstance permitting, McCarter needed to touch base with the Farm. None of them were crack code-breakers, much less fluent in Russian or Arabic. They needed to transmit what was on the CDs and hard drive ASAP.

Taking the slack position, McCarter gave what was pretty much a forced march a hard scour, HK-33 scanning the broken lunarscape. James, their point man and scout, was a dark shadow, perched high on a gnarled ledge of rock, a football field's length or so south. The ex-SEAL was sent ahead to monitor the next available valley, beyond which stretched another fifteen klicks to the border with Azerbaijan. Manning watched the GPS module, its built-in transponder marking their own position and supposedly relayed back to their Russian contacts in lower Dagestan. Encizo was fourth in line, sweeping the rocky crags to both sides of the gorge with his Multi-Round Projectile Launcher, Hawkins picking up the rear, an HK-33 assault rifle with attached custom 50 mm launcher replacing the Dragunov sniper rifle.

According to the few sat pics they got their hands on, their trek would take them across the Samur River. There was an abandoned oil field, then a smattering of villages and two Russian-Omon military outposts to the border, but McCarter was betting they didn't make it that far.

The biggest wild card was their SVR-Omon in-country assistance. McCarter didn't know, nor had even met the men. He hated trusting their hides to the CIA and its shadowy octopus connections, but sometimes it was impossible to move around in the black-op dimension without other intelligence agencies blowing wind into their sails.

Or smoke in their faces.

They moved silent, swift, but as McCarter began climbing he saw James visibly stiffen, then patch through on the com link.

"We've got company, Captain Mac," James informed him, using the Phoenix Force leader's handle. "Three choppers. Two attack birds, one transport. Vector south-by-southwest, heading our way. Three miles out but moving hard."

"Look alive, mates," McCarter ordered down the line. "G-Man, Rufino," he told Manning and Encizo, then pointed at the east ridgeline, what looked the quickest but hardly the easiest climb for a jumble of boulders a few dozen meters up. "T.J., you're with me. Let's hustle up, blokes!"

Easier said than done, McCarter suspected. Round One had punished them all, and literally to within an inch of their lives. Between pulling lead out of their body armor, there were near-death experiences, where flying lead and debris had slashed their blacksuits along the limbs, ragged gashes openly worn and that he was sure James, the team medic, would need to stitch, but for now they had to let it all bleed. Add to that thirty some miles on foot between getting to Zhuktul's compound and now hiking back through some of the meanest terrain he'd seen in some time, loaded down with gear and weapons, no food, sleep…

But they had no choice, and McCarter was more than ready and geared up for the hard way by the time he topped out, hurling himself into a shallow depression, Hawkins dropping beside him. The choppers were less than a mile out by now, bearing down, parting the wispy mist of early morning, and at first sighting it didn't look good. The transport was an old Hip-E, the soaring rustbucket sandwiched between two sleek gunships that grabbed McCarter's grim eye.

Like any good field commander worth his weight in bars and ribbons, the ex-SAS commando kept abreast of the world's premier hardware, large and small arms. The Kamov KA-50 Hokum had replaced the Mi-24 Hind of Afghanistan infamy. Sometimes dubbed the Werewolf, they were considered the world's most formidable attack helicopters. Surpassing even the American Apache in firepower, armor and high-tech tools, the KA-50 was similar in its shark configuration to the famed AH-64 platoon slayer. With contra-rotating rotor, the black skin was heavily armored to withstand anything short of a Tomahawk, chocked with the latest in cutting-edge ECM, heat-seeking and other tracking goodies, right down to ejection seat. It also carried sixteen Vikhr missiles, both air-to-air and air-to-surface, and a 30 mm gun to starboard, which was capable of pounding out a few thousand armor-piercing, HE or incendiary-tipped projectiles per minute.

In other words, McCarter knew they could be blasted off their piece of the rock in the time it took to sneeze.

McCarter keyed his com link. "Mr. Rufino…"

"Way ahead of you, boss," Encizo replied. "Rotors are to go first."

The Briton lined up his assault rifle, finger slipped around the trigger on his rocket launcher, ready to hurl his own warhead into Encizo's mix, when a dark figure began waving a large white towel from the transport's door.

"Hold her easy, mates," McCarter ordered across the com link.

They were painted on their screens anyway, the Stony Man warrior thought, and if those birds wanted them dead they would have already been skewered and cooked.

The black Werewolves hung back, hovering, as the transport shot ahead, then slowed, blasting a whining whirlwind along the ridgeline. As the pilot suspended the Hip-E about ten feet above his head, McCarter took stock of the grinning figure in the doorway. The tall, broad man was swaddled in a knee-length black wool coat and Cossack fur hat, an AK-74 hanging by his side. The black beard reached out in a scraggly web to

cover his cheeks, hair flowed to his shoulders, his
bushy eyebrows knitted together. Finally, noting the
low sloping forehead, and McCarter would have sworn
he was looking at a wolf on two legs.

The Wolfman tossed the white flag to the ground.
"Welcome, comrades, to Mother Russia's humble little republic of Dagestan."

McCarter stood. "We'd rather be sitting on a nude
beach in the French Riviera."

Their contact laughed when McCarter finished the
password given him by the CIA. "I am Rushti. It would
appear you and your men have been very busy, and the
day has hardly begun. Many hungry wolves still await
your hunt. A moment, please, while I throw out some
garbage."

McCarter stiffened at the sound of that, watching as
Wolfman stepped aside and two bodies were dumped
out of the door by a dark goon right behind him. When
they crunched down at a point between himself and Encizo and Manning, McCarter saw clear evidence of torture.

Bloody hell.

There was a time, not long ago, when he had vowed
to never dirty his hands, directly or indirectly, with the
extreme methods used by other intelligence agencies for
extracting information on their enemies, lest he sink to
the level of the animals he and his men were at war with.
It was a tightrope act, no matter how he felt about torture, and he understood all the reasons and rationale. At
times it made sense, playing the devil's advocate, but
any torture hinged solely on dire circumstances, how
many innocent lives were immediately hung in the bal-

ance. When he considered further how those who were caught and forced to give up their murderous brethren under de Sadean or Inquisitionesque techniques and who would, in turn, spare him no agony, and solely for the sake of their sick pleasure...

Dirty war, he knew, meant just that.

If he wanted clean and antiseptic ways to combat terrorism, he'd be sitting in a war-gaming think tank at the Pentagon.

The transport bird touched down, Wolfman still grinning. "Oh, and comrades, I have someone I know you are most interested in meeting."

McCarter was stepping into the tempest of grit and wind when he balked. Comrade Werewolf had that typical flare for Rasputin-type drama that was at once annoying and sinister.

Wolfman reached behind, grabbed a figure, whirled. One look at the bloodied bearded face framed in the hatchway, and McCarter felt renewed hope flame to life.

Wolfman bared his teeth at Phoenix Force in his widest smile yet. "Say hello to Gerbaky Shistoi, comrades." Rushti slapped the back of the renegade colonel's head hard enough to send blood and spittle flying, and growled, "Do not be so rude, Gerbaky. Say hello to your new friends."

North Carolina

"LIGHT AMPLIFICATION by stimulated emission of radiation."

Lyons pinned Blancanales with a fierce glare. "What?"

"It's a laser gun, Carl."

Lyons narrowed a dark gaze on Schwarz. "I know what it is. I'd like to know how the hell such a thing is possible. I know I don't read *Science Digest* nor am I the high-tech wizards you clowns are, but you think I'm that stupid I don't know what laser stands for? Never mind," he growled.

Then Lyons settled back into his seat. He realized he was wired to blow, ears buzzing with anger and adrenaline, but he wasn't in the mood for wisecracks. Schwarz had to have figured now wasn't the time to push the comedy act, so went back to his consoles without a peep. Headset on, Schwarz was in the middle of a conversation with Aaron Kurtzman anyway. Someone needed to add two and two quick, that much Lyons knew. They had just crossed into North Carolina, heading south on Highway 13, and not much more to go on but a hunch Schwarz was playing. Only the electronics wizard seemed to be keeping whatever the pearls of wisdom to himself, which only served to further throw gasoline on the flames of his own agitated state. Or at least the guy was holding back, Lyons figured, until he finished his chitchat with Kurtzman.

Lyons took a deep breath, watched the black wooded country pass for a few more agonizing moments of silence. Invisible men. Laser guns. Black ops sanctioned by someone wrapped in the Stars and Stripes to kill computer hackers—U.S. citizens!—judged guilty and to be executed without trial, on the spot. And now that they had bulled their own lethal play into the unsolved riddle of an ongoing conspiracy it stood to reason the three of them were painted with bull's-eyes on their backs and chests. Oh, but they were being pulled at light speed into a black hole that, just like the space phenomenon, had no end, no discernible scientific dimension, where time was believed to either stand still, shoot into the future, deliver man into the past or some unexplained event that combined all three. He was on edge, no question, his thoughts like shooting stars, flaming off into all directions. Suddenly he sensed Blancanales wanted to say something.

"I hope whatever it is you're about to say, Pol, is at least seminoteworthy enough for you to take your eyes off the road this long."

Blancanales cleared his throat. "Laser weapons are nothing new."

Lyons glanced over his shoulder and looked at the silver weapon laid out on the floorboard, then back at Blancanales. He heaved another breath. "That's a fact, my friend. Uncle Sam has more than a few satellite-mounted laser platforms orbiting the planet they don't want anyone to know about. We have PBWs—particle beam weapons—that use magnets, I believe, to stir up the very particles that make atoms, all but turning guided missiles into useless steel scrap. We have super-lasers that supposedly will drop an ICBM right out of the sky like a stone. Electromagnetic rail guns, which are really giant magnets that will pick up and hurl whatever projectiles available at a target. There's kinetic kill vehicles, there's EMP guns that can shut down the entire communications and defense systems of a hostile country from outer space. We have lasers even meant to drill into a major fault line, produce sonic energy enough to unleash an earthquake on the double-digit Richter scale. I heard where some maniac got hold of one of the latter-type sats, it would take him about fifteen minutes to wind up enough sonic juice into the San Andreas Fault to drop California into the ocean from San Francisco to Los Angeles. About a nine on the Richter, hold it steady and rocking for two minutes straight, and the unthinkable happens. Duration of the earthquake, I understand, is more important than sheer size on the Richter."

"If I didn't know better, it sounds like you learned that from one of your girlfriends."

Lyons shot Schwarz a scowl. "You're right, you don't know any better, and if I did get some live action lately, it beats watching late-night soft porn and the same stinking action flicks over and over like you two. You got something to contribute, Gadgets? Or do I need to come back there and squeeze it out of your brain? And don't ask me again do I need a hug."

Schwarz nodded at the laser. "Light amplification rifle. LAR."

"I bet you're going to tell me," Lyons said, "a laser beam is a powerful coherent light, but very very superhot."

For some reason—call it nerves—Blancanales jumped into the act. "You *have* been reading *Science Digest.*"

Lyons shot Blancanales a scowl. "What can I say? A mind is a hell of a thing to waste."

Schwarz cleared his throat. "While you were turning off the stereo and giving those kids a few moments of silence—well deserved, I may add—I don't know if your trained detective eyes saw the one kid—Abel, I believe his handle was."

"I saw him. So, what did I miss?"

"He had a neat dark hole, about the size of a dime, drilled right through his temple, but it was like the wound had been cauterized."

Lyons frowned, trying to recall what he'd seen, but drew a blank beyond a dead body. "And it wasn't a gunshot?"

Schwarz shook his head. "No ragged edges, no bone fragments, no blood, no grotesque distortion of the face that might come with a bullet blasting through someone's skull and that close to the front."

Lyons breathed a curse. "Yeah, well, we were late, as it stood. But it seems like we're missing a whole lot besides watching someone get zapped by a laser, and we're barely off the launch pad on this one."

"But why just kill one of them with the LAR?" Blancanales said. "Unless to produce that kind of heat…"

"It's either powered by heated gas," Schwarz said, "or that funny-looking magazine is a small nuclear reactor of some type."

"The hell you say," Lyons muttered. "You know how big nuclear reactors are?"

Schwarz nodded. "I know exactly how big they are. What I'm saying, guys, that thing is real, it works. Unlike a flashlight beam the light from a laser does not immediately spread out. It will, given enough distance, but I was looking at thirty, forty yards from where the guy shot the thing to where he dropped the one kid. That's plenty of concentrated superheated light to leave me thinking it's powered by some type of nuclear battery. I ran it by Bear. He concurs that such a thing is quite possible. In fact, he knows that just such a weapon has been on the drawing board for years, and which, Bear suspects, might lead us directly to the mystery source of all our strange close encounters tonight."

"You mean, he knows who and where invisible man suits and laser guns are being produced?" Lyons asked.

"Hal said they'd get back to us on that. The fabric is a lot different from the sample they got from the thugees. Anyway, we won't know more about the LAR until we get it back to the Farm, and Hal still doesn't have any results back from his people in Quantico about our 'invisible man' material. Now, my guess is those knobs and dials are gauges, a dosimeter probably that tells the operator if the thing is getting over-. heated."

"So," Lyons said, as he recalled his near laser-scalping, "we know the thing is good for at least two bursts, call it three, four at the most, then let it cool. By the way, that was quick thinking, Pol, grabbing those gloves of our late *Star Wars* pal."

Blancanales looked at Lyons. "Don't tell me. One of us is going to take that thing into battle?"

"Unless I see some hands raised, I'll take the pleasure of dishing out some payback to any more of our black ops nemesis, and maybe just for those kids they cut down in the prime of their lives. Gadgets, do you think you can read that box?"

Schwarz picked up the weapon. "I'm not sure, but what say we stop first, give it a little field test."

"Sounds good to me. And speaking of battlefronts?" Lyons said, looking back at Schwarz.

"It looks like my hunch paid off about the Force of Truth keeping a main Web dump in North Carolina."

Lyons frowned when Schwarz paused. "You want a round of applause? Out with it."

"The owner is none other than one David Rosenberg. And all indications from Bear's end was that he was written a speeding ticket and sent on his way. And, to play yet another hunch, I bet he's on the way to either visit his Web dump site or is already there, cooling his heels."

Lyons spoke slowly through gritted teeth. "Which would be where?"

"Oh, you're really going to love this." Schwarz grinned. "It's called Dreamland. It's a twenty-four-hour porn palace."

CHAPTER FOURTEEN

"What's that you say? You want details?"

They were in a large stone dwelling that Rushti passed off as his personal command center. Four grim and heavily armed Cossacks manned a bank of computers and other surveillance and tracking monitors, but otherwise McCarter found the C and C base as shabby and desolate as any other square foot of Dagestan. The ex-SAS commando scanned the sheafs of paper, then looked up and scowled at Rushti, who was again wearing his Rasputin grin.

"Tell me you didn't bring us here only to show me some pictures of a space shuttle?"

Shistoi, McCarter spotted, had been dumped like a sack of potatoes in the far corner, sulking but holding up his malevolent front. Manning and James, he knew, were moving into an adjacent room McCarter had requested for privacy, noting that he didn't need to explain the reasons to his Russian contact. Pros that they were, Manning and James would sweep the room thoroughly with their EM and other ECM equipment stowed in the gear bag before trying to reach the Farm.

"Not a space shuttle, but a reusable launch vehicle, my American friend."

McCarter grunted. "From what little I know about them, I believe the single glaring difference is it loses its external tanks once it clears the atmosphere, about a hundred miles up. I thought an RLV was years down the road? Costs, for one thing, then a whole slew of technological headaches, the least of which is getting into space with some massive solid rocket boosters or versions of, then bringing the whole bloody package back down to Earth."

"It is a little more involved than how you stated. But the future, my American friend, has arrived. Expendable launch vehicles discard engines, fuel tanks, their support structures after one flight. What you are looking at is the prototype space plane. One, my American friend, that is right now ready for launch— and is armed with a thermonuclear payload. Those are blueprints, computer schematics, if you will, stolen from a secret base in Siberia."

McCarter stared into Rushti's eyes. There was no smile now, no glint in those black orbs. The Stony Man warrior knew the Russian was getting warmed up to drop a bomb.

Rushti snapped his fingers, one of the Cossacks flying up to him and handing off another stack of papers. He gave them to McCarter. "You may or may not wish to spend a few minutes questioning the criminal. But I suspect you will not learn much more than I did."

"Which would be?"

"He and Zhuktul were hatching some plot, among other criminal endeavors, that involves the prototype RLV, a Russian RLV, I will add, and one that has many technological advances owed to American and European ingenuity. Further, I fear there is some connection between various organized criminals and the European Space Agency. And, I suspect, the ESA is guilty of training and hiring Islamic extremists here in Dagestan and in Russia."

McCarter felt the hackles rise on the back of his neck. He scanned the black-and-white pictures of three men. They were shot moving, separately or in pairs or as a threesome through what looked like an airport, getting out of ZIL limos, or standing in countryside that resembled the scarred terrain of Dagestan, though he knew he was in a part of the world where any number of the "Stan" republics were interchangeable as far as the looks department went.

McCarter's gut warned him he and his troops were suddenly dumped onto some ticking doomsday clock. He clenched his jaw, waiting for Rushti to fill in the blanks.

"Those three men are here in Dagestan."

"And they have answers to some ongoing conspiracy involving what? The hijacking of an RLV armed with nukes?"

"That they might."

"So, why are we standing here?"

Rushti squared his shoulders. "There may be a few details we need to work out first."

"Such as?"

"Such as how we divide the dirty work, the risk, that would be, of even capturing them, for starters."

McCarter worked his jaw. "Let me guess. Assuming we capture them in one piece, we then roll dice for who gets to keep them?"

Rushti cleared his throat, squared his shoulders. "It is not the glory of the capture or necessarily any intelligence they have on any terrorist plot that may strike at my country. Rather…beyond their capture and what we may or may not learn, I have a personal request."

McCarter felt a rising cobra of tension in his belly as he waited for the grim punchline.

"A request, my American comrade, that would involve ultimate sabotage, and that may pit you and your men against the entire military and intelligence wrath of Mother Russia."

DAVID ROSENBERG FOUND using pornography—to both lure followers with visits to Force of Truth sites and attack their enemies—distasteful, to say the least. Filling the human mind with sewage was the lowest common denominator, he thought, no less than a form of pimping, but there they'd been for some time now, feeding a sickness so rampant and widespread throughout Western society that they were actually helping to keep smut seated on its unholy throne as an acceptable form of entertainment. He hated to admit it, but morality and decency were losing, fast and hard, in the media-dubbed Culture Wars. On the other hand, he figured that to win certain battles for the Force of Truth sometimes he had to walk, albeit head bowed in shame, in an uneasy truce with the most undesirable of enemies in his war for the future of humankind. Sad to say, the bottom line was that without the creation of their own porn Webs, the message of the Force of Truth would not be as widespread or accessible as it was, though he hesitated to dismiss the lurid aspects of their work as just another sign of the times when he considered some of the team was barely out of puberty, prone to indulge overactive imaginations anyway, and with God only knew what kind of warped fantasies. The other angle—the key to whatever their success—was that porn had deflected the truth away from their real identity, as irate intelligence operators wondered if the cyberthieves were merely sick and twisted pranksters, or maybe fingers of blame were aimed at some coworker who clearly had too much time on idle hands. In the end, though, the prurient freak show had merely bought them a little more time before the hammer fell.

And the hammer was now falling, as Noah pointed out the obvious.

"That looks like a definite problem, old man."

They were in the back office of the porn mecca, Rosenberg straining to make out the alarm in Noah's voice as the infernal rock music seemed to pound on the door and walls with invisible sledgehammers. Minutes ago, their renegade blogger, the proprietor of Dreamland, had just finished transferring their files to a Web site he had created for them in Del Ray Beach, Florida. Rosenberg was finished shoving the CDs along with the rest of the hundred-dollar bills from his fifty grand rainy day stash at Dreamland inside a small satchel when he shot a look toward the bank of security cameras. Sure enough, it looked as if they were about to be dumped into the frying pan.

They were standard-issue black ops, buzz cuts, as

grim as the Devil's hellhounds, but the telltale signs of bulky weapons beneath their trenchcoats was more than evidence enough to Rosenberg they weren't late-night customers here to peruse the rows of XXX videos, DVDs or hunker down in the slime pits of peep booths.

The war, though, had already begun. Since he couldn't contact the rest of the team, he assumed they had fulfilled their roles as sacrificial lambs. A part of him detested himself for leaving them behind on the gallows in his place, stealing them time, but the older Polansky had volunteered, along with his brother and Job. There was a chance they could have been captured, but Rosenberg doubted just such a scenario that had hung by the flimsiest of threads to begin with. All along the six of them were clear on what could happen if they were found out and tracked down.

It was gut-check time.

"There's a back way out to the lot."

Rosenberg grabbed his Uzi off the desk. He looked at James Flincher, an old DOD friend who still didn't look a day over thirty since their time together in spookland, and said, "Thanks. I apologize for any trouble you might have over us."

"You did that coming in. And I knew what I was getting into from day one."

Rosenberg could well believe that. Flincher had taken no small risk in feeding them access codes to various classified DOD files when Rosenberg had originally come to him with his Force of Truth vision.

"Oh, and which way were you implying was our escape hatch?"

Rosenberg spotted three more men in black rolling up on the back door, one of them working the lock with a slender shiny object. Flincher's curse answered the Kid's question.

Rosenberg was turning to ask his old friend if he had a Plan C when Flincher hauled a stainless-steel .45 ACP from out of the top desk drawer. The Dreamland owner chambered a round, snugged the cannon inside his waistband, left side, along with three spare clips, then draped the tails of his Aloha shirt over the weapon.

"I'll take it this means you assume the worst?"

Moving for the door and thundering wrath of rock and roll, Flincher said, "David, I did that way back when I first starting working for the government."

DREAMLAND.

For one frozen second, Carl Lyons felt as if he'd been transported to the gaudy glitz of Las Vegas. Reminding himself this was no R & R stint, the Able Team leader marched for the winking neon lights, the sign big and bright enough to be seen by the naked eye and clear to outer space, he imagined, a leggy blond nude the size of the Hindenburg perched over the billboard, blinking in places that left no doubt what went on inside the four walls.

For the love of…

Lyons wasn't above a little examination of his own conscience, galled for a moment to think that under different circumstances he might cast his lot among this rabble. He had problems himself in certain areas, he knew, but any man willing to be more than a swine in slop found a way to rise above his base passions.

After their drive around the porn palace, and it looked to the ex-L.A. detective the compound gobbled up a tract of land half of a city block at least, as it squatted in the wooded foothills of the Blue Ridge and Sauratown mountains. No way the three of them could cover it, inside and out. Top that nasty truth with the fact they didn't know the layout...

Good news. Rosenberg's Caddie was parked out back, but the classic with shark's fins and white walls was hardly inconspicuous among all the SUVs, 4WD Jeeps and a smattering of beaten-up older model cars. The first piece of bad news was the two black GMCs with government plates. The next round of dire omens came when they found all four tires on the Caddie shot to flattened tread. But, since Rosenberg was made by whoever and how many the opposition, then Lyons decided the black ops—should they escape—would likewise find themselves stranded and searching for a ride, unless they had eight spare tires on hand. Of course, Lyons knew there was the possibility they had roving backup, and considering they went into Virginia Beach, guns and laser blazing...

Lyons, sandwiched between Schwarz and Blancanales, gave his teammates a scathing look that left no doubt. There had been no concrete plan from the start, so why bother with finesse now?

Just the way Ironman Lyons liked it.

Bulldoze and blast.

He homed in on rock and roll that he figured might just lift the roof off by itself. He marched up the short flight of steps, crossed the porch, grimly aware of the weight he carried beneath the black leather trenchcoat.

Schwarz and Blancanales likewise donned the custom-made "urban war coats." They were slotted with deep pouches, both sides, plenty of room to hold spare clips and grenades. Both of them had mini-Uzis in special webbed rigging, Beretta 93-Rs stowed on the opposite sides.

Lyons's hand slipped through the tailor-made cut in his coat, fisted the LAR, muzzle aimed at the ground, weapon hugged tight to his leg. At a passing glance, they could pass as just a few more lonely pervs, that was, until someone noted the com links snugged over their heads.

Schwarz shot ahead, opened the door to a blast of strobing light and heavy-metal hell.

Lyons strode in, all steel and malice of heart, ears so assaulted by the jumbo-jet decibels of drums and screeching guitar rifts he clung to hope no amount of shooting would be heard beyond these walls. A few long strides over the foyer, he stopped at the edge of the landing, gave the place a long sweeping scan, Schwarz and Blancanales rolling up on his wings and parking.

Row after row of videos and magazines were stacked six feet or more high. To the deep north end he saw the maze of curtained booths, the doors festooned with whatever the aberrant desire of choice. Off to his one o'clock there was a glass and chained-off area that housed every instrument of degradation and then some that would have left the Marquis de Sade wondering at the infernal sickness of it all. That such an abyss could thrive in this Bible belt neck of the woods told Lyons two things. One—the local law and politicians were involved, and with more than just getting their hands greased with cash. Two—there was a whole lot of hypocrisy throughout the land here. Case in point, Lyons spotted fifteen, maybe twenty guys lurking around, perusing titles, shuffling in and out of the peep chambers. More than a few of them were shame-faced, indulging in guilty pleasures when he was fairly certain they should be home with the wife and kids or the girlfriend.

And then Lyons saw them.

Three black-suited clones were rolling past the toy store, and walking with purpose. The dark sunglasses were a bizarre touch, but Lyons figured they didn't care if they were noticed, since they most likely didn't figure on leaving behind any witnesses.

Good enough.

As Lyons followed their hidden stares, he spotted four men to the deep northwest, and moving swift for the first line of peep booths. Beyond the black duffel and Uzi subgun in Rosenberg's hands, their body language told Lyons everything he needed to know.

The surviving Force of Truth was running scared, but ready to shoot their way out of Dreamland.

Lyons gave the nod. Schwarz peeled off to grab the far left flank, Blancanales descending the short flight of steps to seize the middle row.

Then Lyons moved down and out, gathering steam as his ears pulsed with the clamoring noise from Hell and his heart pounded to the beat of his own dark intentions.

CHAPTER FIFTEEN

Stony Man Farm, Virginia

Hal Brognola yanked the chewed stogie out of his mouth, worked the dark expression between Kurtzman, Tokaido and Price. He was pretty sure he'd heard them correctly, which was why the Computer Room suddenly looked and felt as if he were deep-frozen in another dimension of time and space. "Wait a second here, people. What is it exactly you three are trying to tell me? That a Russian black op we know virtually nothing about wants Phoenix to do what exactly?"

"Infiltrate a classified Russian base in Far Eastern Siberia and destroy or hijack a reusable launch vehicle armed with nukes," Price said.

"And that's all?" Brognola threw out behind a grim chuckle, staring at the mission controller as if she had lost her mind. "And just because he suspects Islamic extremists are collaborating with Russian intelligence inside the base and who are about to storm this compound and fly the thing out of there for mission unknown, but which I assume involves some devastation but on a thermonuclear scale?"

"That's about the gist of it."

Kurtzman cleared his throat, jerked a thumb at the series of numbers on his monitor, which made absolutely no sense, the big Fed knew, to anyone but him. "Let me put some pieces of the puzzle together as we so far know them. First, those are numbered accounts in Moscow, Belgrade, Frankfurt and Dallas. Altogether they amount to around two hundred million dollars U.S., but tack on interest, various bearer bonds…"

"I got it. Big money only keeps growing bigger," Brognola stated.

"Anyway, part of what Phoenix took from the late Zhuktul," Kurtzman continued, "was a list that compiled not only banks that were laundering his money and that of Colonel Shistoi, but also had chunks siphoned off into accounts belonging to three men Phoenix is now in pursuit of and who we have identified and who have, we suspect, managed to spread the dirty money to our own shores." Kurtzman hit some keys and split his screen into three faces, pointed at each as he named them. "Beloc Grantkil. Yzoc Luvan. And Heinrich Grumner. The first two are Serb war criminals, presently top lieutenants in the Balayko Family. Along with their boss, Franjo Balayko, they were indicted by the Hague."

"I'm betting the usual sins. Mass murder, torture, rape," Brognola groused.

"And with a few rumors of other atrocities I'll leave to your imagination regarding Muslim women and children and bayonets. The last five years or so, they've been busy eluding the long arm of Interpol and the FBI, but they always manage to slip the net while their crime empire just keeps on flourishing." A dark frown shadowed Kurtzman's face as he went on. "The original war crimes charges were dismissed. Lack of evidence, or that was the word the world at large got, but which really meant they or hired guns either killed witnesses, bought them off or enough dirty money found its way into hands of the right people, all indications being the corrupted powers responsible for their sudden and mysterious absolution were high-echelon UN officials.

"Now, Grumner was a former attaché to the United Nations and is believed to have been a major cog in the oil-for-food scam. How he and the Iraqis we know about—and who are now toast, thanks to Phoenix—worked it out that oil was slipped into Europe from Iraq via Dagestan is still a mystery, but my guess would be the usual greasing of the skids, from top officials at the UN right down to flunkies of the former Iraqi regime. Grumner has been on a CIA watch list, believed to be an enforcer for a covert ESA program that involves some questionable transfers of everything from liquid nitrogen and liquid oxygen to Russia to technicians and special alloys to build a lightweight, hypersonic RLV that can easily take on the added burden of a nuclear payload."

"Questionable transfers?" Brognola inquired.

"Deals negotiated and completed off the books, midnight runs out of Germany and Belgrade and which were videotaped by the CIA," Kurtzman answered.

Brognola chomped on his cigar. "And you're telling me David's Russian contact beat the truth out of Shistoi, that this Dagestani Saddam has these scumbag VIPs in his country as guests. Again, why?"

Price stepped in. "We won't know more until Phoenix grabs them up. But all initial indications are that Shistoi and Zhuktul have created a terror pipeline, one that stretches clear to Moscow."

"And what about this insane 'job offer' David's man in Dagestan put to Phoenix?"

"There may be some frightening legitimacy to the scheme," Tokaido said. "I've cracked a few codes on what Phoenix has sent. The Zenith Project keeps popping up, like the proverbial red flag. The same Zenith Project, I may add, mentioned in NASA mainframes we hacked into and is being currently run out of their sister base, Galileo, just north of Dallas."

"The same Zenith Project mentioned," Kurtzman said, "by Shistoi and by Barb's contacts in the NSA." Kurtzman tapped his keyboard and another face was framed on the monitor. "Radic Kytol. Another top lieutenant of the Balayko Family. He was being watched by the FBI as he danced his way through some shady ESA and UN contacts in Germany and France. Caught a flight out of Paris about a week ago. Slipped through both JFK then LAX under an alias, but has since disappeared. This shot was passed on to Homeland Security from one of their people at Los Angeles International. By the time they realized how asleep at the switch they were, Kytol was long gone."

"So, the question is, why is he here in the country?" Brognola said to no one in particular.

"There was a lot of material," Price said, "on the Force of Truth Webs about their suspicions Galileo had been infiltrated by both homegrown intelligence traitors and foreign gangsters. They even named this Kytol, among a few other high profile bad boys in the Balayko organization and the Vladimir Yoravky Family."

"The Russian Mob?" Brognola queried.

Price nodded. "What we need to happen, Hal, is for both Phoenix and Able to get us some concrete facts, determine for certain if there is a tie between Serb-Russian gangsters, the ESA, Galileo and an impending Muslim extremist plot to hijack a thermo-nuke-armed RLV."

Talk about vertigo, it was a lot for Brognola to digest in a few short moments.

The big Fed took a long moment, chewing over all the riddles. At present, what did they have to show for their effort thus far? he wondered. Hunches and suspicions. A pack's worth of dead hyenas in a country few human beings had ever heard of, and even fewer cared about, which was what actually made the damn place so dangerous in the first place. Add on, then, an unknown number of infernal shadows on the loose with mix and match agendas. Finally, a few strands of pearls from spookland, all of it wanting to add up to dire, nay, apocalyptic scenarios.

In short, they had a hand full of dust.

The big Fed looked at Price, and said, "Speaking of making it happen, what's the status on Able Team?"

LYONS LOST HIS FEAR of the LAR as soon as the black op dug the HK MP-5 submachine gun from out of its Velcroed web-sling. Buzz cuts One and Two were already gone, grabbing point and surging on, ready to practically walk themselves into the lead net Schwarz and Blancanales would drop, when Number Three, hanging back a few feet and spotting the grim trouble on his flank, went for it. The sight of the laser gun that used to be in their possession, but was now swinging up and drawing a bead, turned the homegrown enemy into a statue, long enough for Lyons to squeeze the trigger and end his Medusa trance. It was all Lyons could do next to contain his own shock and awe as the thread-like beam of white-bluish light cored into his adversary's forehead. The HK subgun burped out a wild volley, the black op in full epileptic seizures, as superheated light seared on like the most slender spear of fire through his brain, tendrils of wispy smoke curling above his head from where flesh was getting fried. Wild rounds went slashing down the row of videos and smut rags, the brief tempest of debris washing over a few patrons who were instantly thrown into fits of their own, shouting and cursing and belly-flopping to the deck.

Lyons watched as his kill, brain-dead and bug-eyed, melted at the knees in front of his stunned eyes.

SPECTER TEAMS TWO and Three were the responsibility of Specialist A-2 Phillip Cutler. Whatever happened to Specter One would be sorted out in due course, though it all stood to grim logic his present mission was chained to the mysterious events in Virginia Beach. As sole Reprimand leader now—albeit by default through violent death—he took his task of defending national security with all the seriousness of a shipwrecked man, bleeding and floundering in shark-teemed waters but in search of the first available life raft.

But that was his lot.

Whatever had gone wrong and guided him, indirectly, into this moment—well, he was here to make it right and now, determined to steer it all back on course according to his vision, and, if necessary, by blood and thunder. A man without vision and the will to execute such might as well stay in bed.

Cutler was a warrior, a lion, no less, in human flesh. And if he had to bend the rules, dip his hands in a little blood, then so be it.

These Force of Truth snakes were the worst kind of transgressors in his estimation. They were intelligent, for one thing, talented, perhaps even brilliant in their own right, for another. And last but not least, they simply knew too much that no American John or Jane Citizen had any business knowing, nor much less had the capacity and reason to understand what was really happening in the world, without plunging themselves into blind panic. This knowledge could contaminate, corrupt all the weak out there and thrust the ordinary civilian into rebelling against the powers that be.

By God, not on his watch.

The rows of sordid fantasy, he found, formed a maddening maze of sorts, a half ring that fanned out toward the cubicles, and where he now saw the trio in question. HK subgun freed from its Velcro spiderweb holster, he brushed past some guy who was too busy with his face buried in a porn rag to notice Dreamland was moments away from being turned into a living nightmare.

Something then suddenly felt out of place to Cutler, as if he had blindly walked into a trap. Yes, they had him spotted, marking him, no doubt, for what he was, which was Ultimate Justice about to be delivered, but there was some other danger in the vicinity, wandering quick and deep across his radar screen. Impossible, he decided. It was just them—six lions—and a few treasonous hyenas to be devoured on the spot.

It suddenly flickered through his thoughts there were would be legions of do-gooders who would object to his chosen course of action, whining about constitutional rights, demanding his bloody scalp in retribution, and so forth. He could even hear the collective howl in the back of his mind right then, as he chuckled to himself. What's this about compassion and mercy, understanding and forgiveness?

Not his department.

Time to deliver the wrath of offended national security.

That was his mission, end of discussion.

The ex-DOD hacker, he saw, was already pulling hardware from beneath that Hawaiian shirt, a flaming collage of only God knew what, so loud and dazzling it would have blinded most ordinary men. It made his decision all that much easier, no pang of conscience necessary, but Cutler was good and juiced to go, deciding to bypass any freeze warning or identification of himself as a bona fide U.S. government intelligence agent, and long since before rolling in.

Advancing toward the peep booths, he again sensed empty space behind him, wondering why Doppelganger wasn't practically breathing down his neck, when he heard the familiar burp of an HK subgun.

Just like that, all hell broke loose.

Flincher was banging out .45 rounds, Toteman ripping free a split second behind the ex-DOD target, but turning his HK subgun into a blazing thresher. Magazines and video boxes were being blasted to smithereens beside them from the guy's hand cannon barrage, when Cutler spied the shadow charging up on his left wing from out of nowhere. Something warned him to spare no moves falling back.

He reacted like a wink of lightning.

And just in time.

Cutler lurched back from the first wave of tracking autofire. He caught a glimpse of some guy who looked more like a banker but swarthy in a Latin way, the eyes of a wolf behind the handsome face. And he came bulling ahead, ripping loose with a mini-Uzi, raking the immediate vicinity, every bit as hell-bent and maybe then some as the killing fever that had just gripped him.

Who the hell was this guy? And was he alone?

Before Cutler could fully register his shock and outrage, blood and ragged chunks of cloth flayed the air, all but betraying the fact to him that Toteman was getting cut to ribbons.

ROSARIO BLANCANALES knew he was as jacked up on adrenaline and fear of the unknown as his teammates. It was such a raw sensation, morphing his senses into some electrified force field where sight and sound seemed to lift him off his feet with invisible guiding wires, he was nearly caught off guard, even though he had two of the ops dead to rights.

Or so he thought.

Holding back on the mini-Uzi's trigger, the compact subgun gripped in two hands, Blancanales stitched the leading trenchcoat with a rising burst of 9 mm Parabellum rounds. The torrent of lead sizzlers began to chew up the black op, from lower back to a point between the shoulder blades. Despite the lethal hammering, the enemy turned howling mad, taking what appeared two hits from the Dreamland owner's .45. Red mist blossomed around his spiraling jig, the subgun delivering a long sweeping burst toward a ceiling that up until then Blancanales hadn't noticed was nothing but a vast lake of glass.

And the sky began to rain glass.

Worse still, the other operative hurled himself back into the fray, hardly missing a heartbeat. The hardman's HK subgun stuttering around the corner, the enemy swept out a blanket of steel hornets that left Blancanales no choice.

Glass lava drenching the floor around his compass, a few rounds scorched past his cheeks, parted hair as Blancanales took a short running start, then dived through the standing display of cheap thrills.

THAT THE INFERNAL ROCK CLAMOR switched to a country-gal crooner he would have recognized under different circumstances did little to calm the wrath of Carl Lyons.

Dreamland was getting shot to hell and back. That meant innocent bystanders. That meant cops. That meant everybody was pretty much on their own and the enemy bent on standing their ground or going down with the ship now that it hit the fan.

The Able Team leader was locked in on the direction of the opening barrage, whipping around the corner of the next standing bank of lurid sex images, when the fiend in the trenchcoat suddenly grew eyes in the back of his head. Lyons snatched an eyeful of the point man getting diced from two ends, as his own problem pivoted his direction. Absorbing hits, the hardman was spinning, falling next as he was doused by an avalanche of glass that finished his pounding to the deck. A wave of shards exploded for yards in every direction, but the other clone was already throwing out a burst of subgun fire that sent Lyons scurrying out of the lethal eye of the lead storm. Wild rounds streaked past the ex-L.A. detective's face, kissing close to jaw and earlobe, as Lyons hit the trigger on the LAR. He barely noticed the beam of superheated light flaring on, darting yet more to the side just as the standing display of every degradation known to man was scythed to ragged chunks, bits and pieces of paper and plastic whipping off his face. Lyons was hurling himself farther away from the tracking line of subgun fire when he made out the guy's scream, then spotted the black op plunge through his own rack, leaving in his wake countless images of naked bodies whirling in the cyclone and a thin trace of smoke. As if his senses weren't assaulted enough by the relentless din of weapons fire and country twang amped in at ear-splitting decibels, Lyons whiffed the fresh sickly sweet taint of burned flesh.

The Able Team leader then wondered how good

he'd scored. He tossed his six a check, was plunging a step or two forward when the top row of the rack beside him puked apart against the business end of a subgun.

DAVID ROSENBERG KNEW this dance of death was inevitable, had suspected as much, and probably since the first day the Force of Truth had gone to work. A mere mortal didn't mess with the big guns who guarded national security, much less shame them, and breathe to tell about it.

How many black ops, donning trademark trenchcoats and sunglasses, were swarming the building Rosenberg had no way of telling. For all he knew, it could have been anywhere from a full squad to a platoon or more. Between the piped-in music, the racket of weapons fire and his two adopted sons screaming for answers, it all sounded like the end of the Alamo from where he stood.

That wasn't far from the grim truth.

Somewhere out on the floor the advance team was slugging it out with an unknown party, splitting the unholy racket between weapons fire and guttural animal grunts and bellows. Before he wheeled to bolt down the alley between the first line of peep booths, he glimpsed one—no, make that two shooters now, both wielding mini-Uzis. That their weapons were trained on his lethal dilemma did little, if anything, to calm his fears. One of the two mystery gunmen was racing past the upraised checkout platform at the west edge of the stands. The beefy bald clerk flailed in brief panic, screaming something unintelligible, before common sense and self-preservation took over and he dropped from sight to most likely eat the floor in his walled station.

A microsecond later, Rosenberg ventured a wild guess he was holding on for all he was worth as errant rounds exploded through hanging leather-clad blow-up dolls, vomiting on to shred other adult paraphernalia to swirling rubbish in the next lightning flash of auto-fire. The mystery shooter kept shooting his way forward, both hands now filled with weapons, the compact Israeli subgun and pistol blasting away with double volleys at the three black ops who had crashed the back door and who were now spilling through the archway, armed, angry and letting everyone know about it. A massive auto shotgun, Rosenberg spotted, led their charge, booming out sonic peals, as the black op point man swept the floor with the handheld thresher.

A sharp cry, and Rosenberg saw that Flincher was hit. His ex-DOD pal was reeling back, blood jetting from where half his Aloha shirt was shredded to crimson rags, but whirling and triggering his Colt at the new threat. Another sheared patch of flesh and cloth, and Flincher pitched into the side of a booth where its occupant came flying forth, shrieking and nosediving to the floor.

Flincher hollered, "Go, go!"

Rosenberg didn't need to be told twice.

A few of the heartier souls were now stumbling forth from their dark closets of depraved indulgence, Rosenberg shouting at Noah and the Kid to run. They were jolted out of paralysis just as an invisible hail of bullets began eating up the booths and doors. Sweeping bursts quickly sheared off slews of ads that beckoned whatever the lurid vicarious thrill, and left Rosenberg with little doubt Flincher was no longer available to cover their rear.

The peepers were in full panic, two, maybe three flinging themselves back into their private infernos of lust, but at least two unfortunate patrons were mowed down, screaming out the ghost as they flopped up in front of his flight path.

Sidestepping the bodies, Rosenberg threw himself into a half-pivot, firing back, Uzi jumping around in his one-hand grasp. He was facing front, gathering speed, when he heard Noah scream. Hot blood spraying his face, Rosenberg stumbled over the body and moved on.

LYONS HIT THE TRIGGER on the .50-caliber Desert Eagle Magnum, grimacing into the whirlish dervish of garbage. He was racing ahead, sure he'd missed the black op as the HK subgun flamed on from the other side, not missing a stroke, in fact, as the tracking line of fire to his six only swept forward, turning more mags and videos into detonating mini-minefields of trash. Holding on to the LAR might prove a hindrance to accuracy, Lyons knew, as he cannoned off two more rounds on the swift sidle, but he wasn't about to leave the future of cutting-edge superweaponry lying around for some local yokel to grab up and show off to his deer-hunting buddies.

The stampede was thundering off in the distance anyway, figures blurring past in a mad dash between the aisles ahead, but Lyons dropped into tunnel vision as he went for broke. Sonic boom four rent the air, the massive stainless-steel hand cannon doing a wild bucking bronco in the Able Team leader's gloved hand. Beyond the rain of debris he saw his adversary jerk, the HK still spewing lead but hurled offline and chopping up the display. Lyons knew blood when he smelled it, and so drilled two more armor-piercing high-velocity flesh-shredders through the guy's chest. The subgun blazed on and up at the ceiling, bringing down more sections of glass, falling shrapnel smashing off Lyons's head. With laser-focused vision on the black op, it looked to Lyons as if his opposite number was hit by a runaway freight train, the mangled stickman hurtled and taking a full rack with him in his flight.

"ROSENBERG! GET DOWN!"

He was jolted out of his breakneck pace at the sound of the voice of doom. The sound and fury of combat was shredding his senses, but some deep inner voice warned him to heed the warning. Glimpsing the big guy with the silver rifle and mammoth handgun up and thundering, Rosenberg nosedived. He bellyflopped so hard, he flipped, end over end, a human bowling ball that bounced on, the air punched from his lungs, the Uzi flying away. He spotted two trenchcoats, demon figures hosing the area with subgun fire, howling and snarling from the last bank of peep booths. He was slowing, the floor clawing at his stomach, eyes bulging at the sight of his enemies getting scythed to scarlet ruins. They were slammed into the booths as if hit by wrecking balls, subguns flaming for an eternal second before what appeared converging streams of autofire followed their fall to the floor.

Rosenberg was setting his sights on the Uzi, crabbed ahead a foot or so, clutching the nylon bag, when he felt the presence of pure wrath rolling over him. The cry was locked in his throat, as he looked up, found a face so furious boiling up out of the smoke that for a second he was sure he was dead. He was frozen with pure terror by what he imagined as no less than the avenging wrath of an angel of death descending for him. The hand that stowed the big gun swept down, tore into his shoulder with such force the cry of pain and fear was punched free from its stranglehold.

LYONS SLUNG Rosenberg to the floor of the van. He let his stare of hot rage melt the Force of Truth commander for a long moment, as Schwarz threw the side door shut with a thud and Blancanales grabbed the wheel, fired up the engine.

"Congratulations," Lyons growled at Rosenberg, dropping down into a seat next to Schwarz. "You made it out in one piece."

Rosenberg, torn between watching Schwarz rifle through his bag and Blancanales driving away, asked Lyons, "Who are you guys?"

Lyons let Rosenberg stew in fear. He listened to the shouts beyond the warvan, engines revving to life all over the lot, as peepers kept disgorging from under the neon sign and blinking blonde. Somewhere in the distance, he heard the encroaching sirens. Just in time, Blancanales found a hole between two vehicles charging for the mouth of the lot, slipped through them to a blare of horns. Gently, he swung the van to the right, in the opposite direction of the cavalry, as Lyons spotted the glow strobing over the black hills to the west.

"What do you want?"

Lyons looked at Rosenberg, uncertain how he felt about the man. Five youngbloods were dead, and here Rosenberg was, still breathing, worried about his own future, no less.

"Here's the long and the short, Rosenberg," Lyons began. "My friend here is going to boot up your CD. In the meantime, I want you to tell me everything that's both on that CD and whatever blanks need to be filled in, because I know a smart guy like you has kept a few choice secrets to himself. That's the deal. Yes or no. Do you want to live?"

Rosenberg nodded. "Yes."

"Start talking. And I want it all."

CHAPTER SIXTEEN

"Why are we still wallowing in this rathole of a country?"

It was a good question, one for which Heinrich Grumner didn't have a ready answer. The truth was, the former GSG-9 covert specialist and ex-security attaché for his country's diplomatic corps to the UN didn't know much at all. Or at least anything of note and merit beyond the huge sums of cash that had been sliding through any number of dirty hands the past few years, all of which he believed were designed to pave the way to the future, and which was still an open riddle. Yet the future—whatever it really was—had arrived, those original money shipments having long since evolved into more than just keeping clandestine oil shipments flowing from Dagestan into Europe.

Ah, he considered, how life had changed, forced to wonder if it was all for the better or worse. Those first weeks, after he'd accepted the proposal to help advance a "certain cause" for alleged ESA operatives out of Darmstadt—and where he began personally handling in the area of ten to twenty million dollars—were long gone. The taste of fat easy money was as extinct, he decided, as the abandoned Samur One Refinery he viewed from behind the smudged office window. Yes, the Euros and American currency were still transported in steamer trunks tucked in special compartments cut into the floorboard of SUVs that flew the UN flag. But so many nameless faceless shadows had become involved since he verbally signed on that it was virtually impossible anymore to sift through the web of agendas and intrigue. That, and the milk runs to collect or dispense exorbitant sums of cash were becoming rare, as agendas multiplied and mystery mounted to the point he was considering a permanent retirement, but on his terms.

Exactly why he was lately ordered to cast his lot among gangster and terror rabble he didn't know. There again, more madness, and to what end? These days, he decided, it was much easier to simply accept his role as cash courier and cutout, with information shuttled back and forth between Dagestani contacts and the black ops who ostensibly worked for the European Space Agency. Why complain? He was earning an even one million dollars American with each trip, to be deposited into his Frankfurt account, whether he delivered information, men or matériel to the Serb, Dagestani or Russian connection.

"We should have heard from Colonel Shistoi by now."

That was a good point, and once again Grumner was stymied to deliver an answer. He gave the two Serbs a look, fighting to keep the contempt off his face. They were brute animals, by and large, more interested in grabbing up obscene amounts of money in the long term, while consuming vodka and heaping the ashtray with cigarettes butts in the short haul. They were notorious war criminals who had bought or murdered their way out of extradition, he knew, forever lurching from one crisis to the next, it seemed, while bulling their way into the future. They wanted instant gratification, no matter if it was money, pleasure, information. He knew their cannibal ilk, always placing themselves as the center of the universe. They were very dangerous men. He decided he could give them a little latitude before lashing out to remind them they needed him more than the other way around.

Grumner went back to scanning the towering skeletons of derricks, the rusty latticework of pipelines, the hulking rows of storage bins, noting their armed escort roving the vicinity near their concrete office building, when they should be sticking closer to the main annex. Despite the fact the colonel had provided a standing force of twenty-plus rebels in his curious absence, the nearby quarters packed with a matching number of Islamic fundamentalists who were supposed to be shipped out once the colonel made his overdue grand arrival, Grumner was suddenly grateful he'd had the foresight to bring along both the Makarov pistol and the AK-74, the former holstered while the assault rifle was slung down the side of his knee-length wolfskin coat. He passed on the offered Cossack hat at the border by their security contact. He had no desire to go native that bad.

"I say we demand one of our guards to radio Shistoi and find out why the long delay."

Grumner glanced at Yzoc Luvan, told him, "Patience. Have another drink."

"Patience?" Grantkil retorted. "Have another drink? This is no vacation on the French Riviera, my German friend. We have three hundred kilos of uncut heroin to be delivered to us and for which we have already paid half upfront and for which we have to answer for. Further, the three of us know that Shistoi is not exactly this country's favored son. The truth is, the man's very name is comparable to blasphemy among the Muslims."

"Bah, we should have gone directly to the source himself, Zhuktul," Luvan stormed.

"At the very worst," Grantkil rasped, "we could have passed the time with all the whores I know he keeps at his compound."

"Instead, we sit here, drinking down vodka not fit for a peasant, listening to you espouse to us about the virtues of being patient."

"The longer we remain in this country, and which is not even good enough to be classified a sewer," Grantkil said, "the more at risk we are for even knowing Shistoi's name."

Grumner felt his jaw clench, teeth grinding together. He was about to turn toward them, three or four scathing remarks competing for first place in his mind, when a sudden commotion ripped through Shistoi's men. They were flailing their arms, mouths vented and hurling shouts and screams, other dark scarecrows sliding over pipelines, weapons aimed at something to the south. Grumner was cursing, as he realized what was happening. The Serbs began barking questions just as the walls began to shudder. Then a cyclone of dust descended across a broad swath of hardscrabble earth in front of the window, the Serbs squeezing in on either side of Grumner.

And they were just in time to watch the bulky transport chopper floating down through the hurricane of rotor wash. Grumner made out the distant rattle of autofire next, but his gaze was fixed on the figure forced at gunpoint to his knees in the fuselage doorway of the hovering UFO. One of the Serbs echoed his own rising panic, as he found it necessary to growl out the man's name.

Grumner turned away from the bloodied visage of Colonel Shistoi, the AK-74 up and out and leading his charge across the barren office.

Australia

CHUCK BOLTMER READ the moment, suspected he was about to be rung up. Now that the job was done…

Funny how that worked, he thought, how those who took all the risk, who had all the necessary talent and guts to go where others feared to go suddenly became expendable, destined, what's more, to be so erased not even the memory of their existence survived them.

Life could sure suck like that.

The good news was the old wet-work instincts were soaring to new levels as he fished the Beretta M-9 out of his duffel. Safety off, he checked the clip, chambered a round, slipped the weapon inside his waistband. It was a definite star in the plus column, his bag not being rifled where he left it in the crawlspace, what with the Beretta missing or tampered with while he was off doing their dirty work, but he figured that was just part of them slipping the invisible noose over his head.

Karlov was cool about it, he gave his partner that much, as he found the man looming over the laptop in the corner of the room, grunting and working the keyboard between taking reads off the instruments. Dumping his bag on the bed, Boltmer went to the window, pulled back the curtain, stared out into yet another long bleak night. Yes, sir, he couldn't wait to put the outback and the nightmare he'd lived through behind, but knew he hadn't crossed the finish line yet.

The Eurotrash had increased by two, both of them having shown the same reptilian lifelessness as the automaton he'd ridden the nuclear river with. Those twin dark shadows were now stepping from the Jeep, nylon bags—the body bag kind used by embassies that were meant to pack any number of essentials, valuables and personals in a moment's notice—being lugged along, and bulging. To the east, Boltmer spotted the faint shimmer of firelight where the decon van had been torched, along with their spacesuits.

Cleaning time.

Boltmer weighed his options, quickly rearranging his own travel plans. They were in the original abandoned sheep station in Northern Territory, next door to Queensland, seventy or eighty klicks south of the port city of Darwin. Naturally there would be some hassles getting off of the island continent, considering Karlov had informed him half the free world was apparently trooping in technical and military expertise, though the way he heard it somehow the blow was being softened around the international community as cover stories were handed off to the media, so who could say what would happen when he reached civilization. Money was no problem, though, since Karlov's buddies were bringing payday to the door.

And there was the big tipoff, the sudden change in plans as to how the money was paid. That, and they spoke the same guttural tongue as Karlov, the three of them acting like long-lost brethren, reuniting in hugs and backslaps at the pickup site, while he was viewed as little more than roadkill to be scraped off their boots.

As the cleaning crew stepped through the door, hurling out some comment in their native tongue to Karlov, Boltmer felt his stomach rolling over. He was queasy again, his flesh feeling clammy and hot to the touch. And yet something else to suddenly fear. Was the nausea and fever in his brain the result of radiation sickness? Or high anxiety and searing adrenaline over what he knew was coming?

One of the robots tossed his bag on the bed, grinning. "Payday. Go on, Chuckie. Open it."

Karlov was busy hovering over his laptop, the butt of the Tokarev pistol in plain view, Boltmer detecting the slight shift in stance, shoulders tensing.

This was it.

Boltmer bobbed his head, played along with a fool's smile, their sacrificial stooge. Out of the corner of his eye, while reaching for the bag, Boltmer saw their hands vanishing inside their windbreakers for the machine pistols hung in special webbing, Karlov reaching for his weapon. Whether it was pure anger, adrenaline or fear he'd never get to spend a dime of five million he'd earned in a manner no sane human being would even dream to attempt, the Beretta was in his hand, his body swinging toward them, so fast, he was nearly shocked by his own speed. Before he knew it, the Beretta was chugging away, two, maybe three rounds ending it all before they cleared their weapons. Robots One and Two were in full spiral, blood and brain matter splattering the wall behind them from what Boltmer believed were head shots, but he was too busy giving Karlov some much-needed extra attention. The man was snarling something as he absorbed two then three hits to the chest, his pistol barking, spewing rounds all over the room. Boltmer painted a third eye on the bastard's forehead, dropped him like a stone.

For a long moment, he held his ground, nose filled with cordite and blood. That end-of-the-world vertigo he experienced in the face of the nuke grabbed him again. He forced himself out of his trance, the shock and awe at how quickly he'd just snuffed out three lives. Now what? he wondered. He was out in the middle of nowhere, the skies were swarming with military aircraft…

At least he had money, he thought. But what was this dread slowly creeping over him? He hesitated another second or so, terrified to look inside the body bag, then unzipped it—and cursed. The Eurotrash had stuffed it to the gills with rubber-banded newspaper clippings, no small labor by itself when he considered the time and effort necessary to create the obscene joke. And, oh, yes, that was supposed to have been the big moment when they gunned him down, flinging shock and outrage back in his face at being duped, but proof he'd been way more ready—and better—was stretched out at his feet.

Heart thundering in his ears, Boltmer flew to the other bag, paused, then nearly tore off the zipper in a maddened sweep. He lurched back, hands shaking.

Bingo.

They were American hundreds, a beautiful winning lottery to behold indeed, his heart bursting with joy. Judging the depth and width of stacks, hefting the weight, it was easily five million, maybe more. But why stab him in the back? Why couldn't men honor their word, even among the jackals and sharks? He had willingly agreed to their terms, but he understood the piranha mind-set of paymasters who devoured human beings like so much raw bloody meat then discarded the gristle and bones.

Their world, their rules.

In this case, they had just tried to burn the wrong guy.

Quickly he piled their weapons into his travel bag, then took the computer, the strange instruments, the cutting-edge modems the likes of which few intelligence agencies outside the United States had at their disposal. In they all went, as a new plan formed in his mind. The hanging question was whether to blackmail the pack of hyenas on the other end for more money or…

Boltmer smiled as the lightbulb flared on in his head.

Oh, he knew exactly what to do with the treasure trove Karlov had on hard drive and CDs. There was a rogue Web site he knew of that had been putting more fear into the hearts of his ex-employers at Langley than any foamy-mouth tribe of self-righteous senators hauling them in to Capitol Hill for a full scalping. Truth Squad, or the Flaming Pillar of Virtue, or something like that. It would come to him in time.

Try to punch his ticket, would they? Boltmer chuckled, grabbing the money bag and heading for the door.

He just needed some quick breathing room, then he'd splash the truth about what he knew happened in Australia and its connection to the ESA all over the World Wide Web.

RAFAEL ENCIZO GROANED. The world wanted to blink out, and it was all he could manage to haul himself back to angry life. He coughed, touched his vest. His chest and ribs seemed like one skewered slab of throbbing fire, the pain grinding all the way back to a spine that felt as if it had been pummeled with tire irons by cracked-out gang-bangers. That he was still in agony from taking two, maybe three or four rounds, though, was a good thing, he decided. Better still that the shooter was erased from his list of woes. And where the hell had that guy come from anyway? he briefly reflected. One second he was descending what appeared a clear but rock-stubbled path after being dropped off by the Hip-E to grab his firepoint on the south edge of the oil field, the next thing he knew the AK-74 was blazing away, the shooter looking as if he'd just grown out of the earth in one lightning leap.

The distant shout and crunch of explosions stirred the fire in the Stony Man warrior's belly some more.

The curtain was up, he knew, certain to reveal a

bloody stage of utter pandemonium and dead men running.

His HK-33 still smoking, Encizo shimmied to his feet, raking the assault rifle around the compass. One look at the shredded corpse a few yards downrange, and he figured he had to have burned through half a clip.

McCarter and teammates, he found, were working their way hard and fast to the back end of the office building where Rushti's hillside spotter claimed the VIPs were holed up. Clear to him they were unaware of his personal plight, not that it mattered in the bigger picture anyway. Attached to what would become a bunker for the targets inside the main office, there was another squat concrete block, its back wall knocked down to grant easy access to a motor pool that consisted of two transport trucks and a ZIL limo. McCarter and gang were laser-focused and rolling swift and mean.

Man, oh, man, he thought, sighting the two Werewolf gunships as they began winging missiles around a mapped target area, the former worker quarters going up in climbing pillars of fire and rubble. He was most definitely feeling a little worse for wear, but grateful to still be in the fight.

And geared to rock and roll.

Encizo unslung his custom-made Steamroller. He settled into a craggy fish bowl, filled his hand with the Multi-Round Projectile Launcher. There was a mixed assortment of incendiary, armor-piercing HE and fléschettes rounds in 50 mm ready to rip. Targets were no problem, as he found thirty to forty shooters racing pell-mell all over the designated hot zone. Armed figures were stumbling away from wreckage floating down from the demolished work quarters, other shooters directing autofire at the Werewolves. He gave the lay of his fire point another quick but hard scouring, trusting his instincts next that all hands were needed below.

Time to go to work.

Encizo joined the Werewolf turkey shoot, began blanketing the enemy with fireballs that marched a thundering point east to west. Four quick thunderclaps, and Encizo was hurling his own volatile mix of slaughter into the hellish scenario.

Between the rolling sea of fire and whirlwinds of razoring shrapnel, the Phoenix Force warrior dumped a dozen shredded bodies and counting on his bloody scorecard, as they were hurtled away from shattered pipelines, bounced in mangled bits and pieces off the titanic storage drums or went sailing on flaming cones of fiery ruin.

WHEN THE GOING GOT TOUGH, the Serbs showed they fit Grumner's bill of contempt, in fact proved themselves marquee names of cowardice and loathsome self-centeredness.

It was a small consolation that Grumner could still read the hearts of men like some all-knowing oracle. He led the dash into the makeshift carport. His ears were lashed by the sound and wrath of Hell being dumped on the oil field and the bleating wails of the Serb gangsters like a thousand and one bullwhips, when he spotted two, then three dark-clad armed invaders scurrying down the hillside. Wondering, by chance, if he'd misread his comrades, he flung a look over his shoulder, but only found the Serbs more concerned in wrestling with their oversize money bags than handling Skorpion machine pistols and concentrating on the enemy advance. In fact, one of them began cursing and beating on the ZIL's roof when the door didn't open at his first yank.

The childish and unforgivable display of such selfish madness!

A volcanic rage suddenly erupted in Grumner, spiking his senses into an incendiary core of utter defiance and murderous resolve. Shistoi was in the bag, which meant Zhuktul was either history or on the verge of getting impaled. The sum total of which meant he would either fight his way out of Dagestan, or die in this wretched country.

The hell with the Serbs, he decided, he'd handle the crisis his own damn self. If this was it, he'd rather go out like a lion than live with the shame of knowing he'd been one of the first to bail, instead of standing his ground and fighting with all the warrior skill and grim determination he could command.

The Serbs were still pounding the limo with kicks and punches and cursing like the damned they were when Grumner roared.

And he surged forward, cutting loose with his assault rifle just as the black-garbed invaders spewed the first wave of bullets into the carport.

THE GERMAN WAS clearly hell-bent on going out in his own blaze of glory and defiance.

McCarter intended to grant him complete ruin, but gave the enemy all due credit for courage and tenacity in the face of overwhelming odds, just the same. But Grumner, he knew, was some type of deep shadow op on the fringes of the vaunted GSG-9, one of the world's premier counterterrorist commando units. As such, the big Briton wasn't surprised when the man came charging the guns, about twenty yards down and out, his AK-74 assault rifle flaming like the long sword of Thor. Figure, though, that superb training, strict Herculean conditioning over the years and pure Teutonic arrogance of unflinching belief in his skills and superiority had seized him in these final moments to go for the full ride.

Why not indulge the man's insane death wish?

For a second, McCarter was surprised, however, that the Serbs showed no more willingness to do anything other than find instant safe haven inside the limo, bolt like whipped, frightened pups as fast and far from the battle as they could. So much for tough-guy gangsters. Then again, they were war criminals, which meant they thrived only on the giving, and when all odds were stacked in their favor. Receiving all due punishment and pain for their transgressions and atrocities committed against their fellow man when their marker was called in was as far from the nature of evil as…

Well, Heaven to Hell.

The Phoenix Force leader held back on the trigger of his HK-33, Hawkins, James and Manning spread out on his right wing and hitting the German with what should have amounted to a combined knockout punch of 5.56 mm sledgehammer blows. Instead, Grumner held on, bellowing like a tribe of Viking berserkers hitting the shores for invasion and conquest, his assault rifle raking the hillside, even as he jerked and twitched with every flesh-shredding round. McCarter heard one of his teammates shout a vicious curse as stone was flayed into a shrapnel hurricane, slivers of rock detonating down the line, cutting short their fusillade.

McCarter keyed his com link as autofire slashed the air and ground up more earth to his side. "Eat some Dag dirt, mates! Cover your eyes and ears!"

Grumner, chest pumping out blood, was sidling for a concrete pillar when McCarter dumped a 50 mm flash-bang down his grenade launcher, cocked, locked and sent the projectile streaking on. The Serbs had the limo's back door open when the 50 mm missile plowed into the trunk. McCarter gave it a full second for the sense-shattering flash and thunder to cleave them hard and deep before he took in the damage.

The Serbs were staggering slabs of jelly, he found, crying out and reeling away from the ZIL, empty hands grabbing at eyes and ears. Grumner, though, shimmied around the corner of the post, cracking home a fresh magazine. He cocked the arming bolt then snaked a pistol from beneath his longcoat to double his suicidal frenzy. He began firing, blind and wild, when McCarter and teammates chewed the fur off his hide with a barrage of autofire that drove him back into the boiling smoke.

Feeding his HK a fresh clip, with Grumner plunging into a slow topple backward to a withering burst of autofire, McCarter waved his men out, indicating Manning and James flank either end of the carport while Hawkins watched their rear.

Before he reached level ground, McCarter took a

sitrep from Encizo, scanned the field of slaughter around the derricks, drums and pipelines. Bodies were still being torn asunder as the Werewolves scissored, east to west, devouring huge tracts of earth, metal and flesh with 30 mm salvos in pure lightning sweeps. If the industrial wasteland was an eyesore before this, it was a vision of Hell on Earth now, McCarter decided.

Weapon out and fanning the carport, the ex-SAS commando advanced, homed in on the pitiful groans and whimpering curses of two vipers about to be dumped in his personal intelligence bag. As the smoke thinned, McCarter spied the rain of paper flotsam, allowed himself a tight smile. Two songbirds squawking at his feet, and on top of that it would be sweet frosting, he decided, to throw some loose change into the War on Terror coffers.

THE SUDDEN AND UNEXPLAINED acceleration of what was supposed to have been a strict timetable wanted to alarm Radic Kytol. He wasn't sure what to make of it all, since the original plan called for them to stay in their suite at the Dallas Hyatt Regency for another forty-eight hours. But the call to arms had come through just after dawn, the metallic voice over the scrambled line of his secured sat phone informing him of the change in plans, how to proceed. It seemed their Russian counterparts were already inside the base, ostensibly cleared by NASA and their NSA contact to act as technical assistants on behalf of their country's pledge of cooperation on the new international space station and sister RLV project. That was a stretch all by itself, when he considered cold-blooded killers of the Yoravky Family were masquerading as top-notch aerospace engineers. He could only imagine the tap-dancing, bluffing and dodging of the real experts that had gone on the second they were let inside Galileo, though he was sure that particular aspect had already been thought through enough the high-wire act could be maintained.

The more he thought about it, the more he found a thousand reasons why they should stick to what they knew and did best. Which was expand the organization's business of basic vice. Drugs, prostitution, pornography—film and Internet—money laundering through various legitimate ventures and murder for hire, even the trade in WMD was something vastly more simple and suited to his skills. Industrial espionage, the theft of high-tech secrets, was beyond both his patience and understanding. Fortunately or not, he knew the bottom line wasn't his to question orders from back home.

He was paid to obey and execute.

As his lead vehicle rolled toward the main gate and the guard in white security uniform stepped from his booth, Kytol gave the Galileo complex a hard scan, running down numbers, area to be covered, the vaults where he knew the high-value intelligence and schematics were stored.

It was a one-story rectangular building, taking up about two city blocks on the dusty prairie near the Oklahoma border. But he knew the nerve centers where special projects were in progress were either underground or in the massive white hangar looming at the west edge of the parking lot. Black-tinted glass hurled diamond sparkles off the facade, forcing Kytol to adjust the dark shades higher up the bridge of his nose, thinking it all didn't look like much more than an innocuous office complex off the beaten path. What fairly gave it away was the network of runways, the military VIP jets and Black Hawk helicopters, all the liquid oxygen and liquid hydrogen, labeled and stored in the tankers penned around the north side of the hangar. All that, and the launch pad to the south, but which was still in the early stages of construction, betrayed deceptive appearances.

Then there were the batteries of antiaircraft guns his own intelligence sources stated were housed in concrete bunkers beneath the edges of the hangar, below and to the sides of the runways, with two more big guns that could rise on remote-controlled vaulted platforms beneath the roof. Hidden surveillance cameras were also blended in as part of the dreary landscape around the compass, or so he'd been told. If they had been marked on their way down the only paved road, as he was told they would be by their man on the inside, then Kytol wondered why the pager on his hip hadn't yet vibrated.

As the guard opened the gate from the booth, Kytol decided to give it a few more moments before succumbing to panic, aborting the mission.

Zumij flashed the tall guard a smile, pointed at the VIP badge clipped to his jacket. The American was wary, as he bent and looked inside the van, then examined the photo ID. He stood, began checking his clipboard when Kytol felt the pager vibrate. Kytol gave the parking lot one last look. At that hour all personnel would be inside, at their posts. As he'd been informed, there wasn't a soul wandering the lot.

Kytol slid the Beretta 92-F from his shoulder holster, called, "Sir?"

As the guard leaned down, Kytol drew a bead on the face framed in the window and squeezed the trigger.

Stony Man Farm, Virginia

"CHARLES BOLTMER," Akira Tokaido announced, wide-eyed in awe and with a beatific smile as if he'd just found the Holy Grail. "He checks out with our own composite watch list of suspected or known dirty U.S. intelligence agents."

Barbara Price again noted the look and tone from the young Japanese American. She saw a ray of hope, but contained her own sudden excitement.

"I was going back over the Force of Truth Webs on a lark," Tokaido said as Kurtzman wheeled around in his chair, looking from his teammate's monitor to the mission controller and back. "I was sifting through all the info Able sent along from Rosenberg, matching it all up with the Force of Truth X Files, if you will, with Rosenberg confirming their substance, while adding a few choice tidbits of his own under Carl's tender loving care."

"And Boltmer is bombing the Force of Truth Webs with what he says are absolute concrete facts about all we have before now only suspected?" Kurtzman growled.

"You sound like you know this Boltmer," Price said.

Kurtzman grunted. "I know of him. He's been near the top of Striker's to-do list for some time. He was part of the CIA's Sphinx Program when the Cali Cartel lifted off the cocaine launch pad after their Medellín rivals sank to the bottom of the cesspool. The idea was to infiltrate the Cali Cartel with Company black ops, either as importers of major weight with ironclad smuggling routes and distribution pipelines, or as pilots or security analysts in computers, money laundering or good old-fashioned kidnapping, torture and murder. Boltmer made huge inroads into the cartel, but his only interest was looking out for number one. Word had it, the CIA found and froze various bank accounts he had, left him flat broke and desperate for work, put out a contract on him, chased him into limbo, the last I looked."

"So, if he's involved in the nuclear explosion in Queensland," Price said, "and claims he's part of a covert ESA project—"

"The Zenith Project," Tokaido interrupted.

"Right. Then why suddenly chomp off the hand that feeds?"

"Because it's no longer feeding," Tokaido said. "What I gather, his ESA principals tried to kill him after he completed his task."

"So he's leaked their conspiracy—"

"And naming names, dates and places, mentioning high-tech goodies such as that laser gun, and which no one but someone on the inside like Boltmer would know about," Tokaido cut in.

"Okay. So what's his angle?" Price wanted to know. "Revenge? Blackmail? Confession?"

Tokaido shrugged. "Maybe all of the above. But it

only turns all those straws we were grasping at into a big fat solid whipping rod."

"Or a pile of dung," Kurtzman observed. "What if this is a smoke screen to deflect attention off him?"

Tokaido shook his head. "I don't think so. There are too many details tying all the loose threads between Galileo, the ESA, a Serb-Russian mafia connection and what Phoenix has bulldozed their way into in Dagestan. And that's just the A list of rotten apples in the whole cart."

Price knew they had actionable intelligence to take to Brognola who was in the War Room and waiting to give something solid, in turn, to the White House. "Print everything you have," the mission controller told Tokaido. "A list and B."

CHAPTER SEVENTEEN

"We go in hard."

Carl Lyons half expected minor resistance from his teammates, a question or two at least, as he turned away from the cockpit. Instead, he found Schwarz and Blancanales picking it up another notch, hauling out hardware from footlockers, restocking combat vests, webbing fitted with spare clips and grenades. The Able Team leader armed the bolt on his HK MP-5, unscrewed the Gem-Tech sound suppressor and chucked it on one of the Gulfstream's seats. Going in hard meant kicking down doors and making lots of noise. And Lyons, feeling like a five-hundred-pound chained lion that hadn't eaten in months, couldn't wait to do just that.

The former L.A. detective went to a portside cabin window, lifted the field glasses to his eyes. He hit the small red button on the side, which brought the lens into instant focus as the high-powered fiber optics were fed by the battery-operated digital read minimodem fixed to the hard plastic frame. Wherever he panned, no matter what the distance, the optic read made the necessary adjustments in a nanosecond.

Only a few hours earlier it seemed they were handing Rosenberg off to some Farm blacksuits in western North Carolina. Since then, they'd been poring over cyberstolen computer blueprints on what Lyons strongly suspected would become their next battleground, chewing over the facts as they knew them, but aware before they headed out from a private airfield secured by Brognola east of the Smoky Mountains a few malignant questions were about to be excised the hard way.

They were three or four miles out from Galileo, the customized Justice Department military jet soaring over the prairie from about three thousand feet up, speed cut back to about two hundred mph, but both altitude and speed dropping. Bearing down on the classified NASA sister compound from the northeast, he took in the main office building. It looked like a squat black block, baking under the late-morning sun, plopped down in the middle of the prairie. Lyons couldn't find the first sign of life around the perimeter, nor beyond to the runways. Even at a distance, and even though his Farm blacksuit pilots hadn't been able to reach Project Director Harvey Turner by radio—or anyone else for that matter—it all felt wrong to Lyons.

As they closed to about two miles, Lyons began to trust his instincts still more that it was wise to scrap the original plan. Plan A had called for a simple face-to-face with the project director, putting it to him straight, shake some trees and see what fell out. Brognola had pulled some heavy strings to get the three of them—

Special Agents Lemon, Schweeney and Blanco—on the ground and inside Galileo, but since Dreamland and subsequent Q and A of Rosenberg, he canned any fleeting ideas of dropping in to spread some sunshine.

"What do you have?" Lyons called into the cockpit.

"Static," the pilot answered.

"What? Why?"

"It doesn't make any sense, but all of a sudden our computer navigational systems look like they want to blink out on us."

Lyons felt the hackles rise on the back of his neck. "Which means what exactly? You going to be able to land us in one piece or do we get bounced clear down to Dallas in a ball of fire?"

"Fear not. I dropped the wheels right when the whole schlamozzel started to go hinky."

"The 'schla'—what?"

"I'll get us down in one piece."

Lyons could believe as much. The Farm hired out only the best from all branches of U.S. military elite forces. He didn't need to scour the fine print on the track record on either flyboy, certain they'd flown under the worst conditions, such as enemy fire, lights out, seat of the pants. Still, his gut was knotted with mounting tension and anxiety, grimly aware they were dealing with people, places and things that should have defied all reason and rationale. The Able Team leader turned, as visions of invisible men and laser guns seared to mind. He found Schwarz working their own communications and tracking monitors.

Schwarz looked grim as he told Lyons, "You want the bad news or the very bad news first?"

Patience may work for saints, but Lyons was in no mood as he gritted his teeth, fire in his stare. "What?"

"This might be a wild guess, but somebody sure as hell doesn't want us to land. They're throwing out an EMP shield. That's why all our instruments are going haywire. They'll only get worse after we land."

"Is that the bad news or the very bad news?" Blancanales asked.

"Once we're inside…"

"It means," Lyons growled, "no contact with our guys here."

"Worse than that," Schwarz said, "it makes our com links, our transponders and thermal handhelds useless."

"So, we stick close the whole time." Lyons looked at Blancanales and told him, "Grab your Little Bulldozer. And, Gadgets, make sure you pack some C-4, just in case we have to make our grand entrance even more grand."

"Why blow down doors, big guy?" Schwarz said, and thrust his HK MP-5 at the LAR laid out on the floor toward the back of the cabin.

Lyons bared his teeth like a white shark ready to pounce on a bleeding seal. "Two reasons. One—the damn thing makes me nervous. Two—I want my hands filled with something more earthbound I know works and when and how I want it to. Any more questions?"

"Yeah. Now that you ask, what about the antiaircraft batteries?" Blancanales said.

Lyons started to frown, realizing in his adrenalized state to cave in doors and slap some bad guys around, he had forgotten all about that not-so-insignificant problem. "That's a good question. Okay, two things the way I see it—and don't hold back, ladies, if you disagree. One, the EMP screen should knock out any computerized or battery-operated platforms."

"Should—maybe," Schwarz said. "But, considering the *Star Trek* convention we've seen so far, are you willing to bet our lives they may or may not have some type of internal antishield to deflect their own EMP?"

"Well, my Number Two snappy answer is we're on public property, covert base or not. Whatever they're in process of doing inside, knowing what we now know, I'm betting they don't want to blast us out of the sky or off the runway in a mushroom cloud they might see all the way to George W.'s ranch in Crawford or have one of those missiles skip on past us and plow into downtown Dallas. Did you catch all that?" Lyons barked into the cockpit.

"You're the boss."

"Just the same, if it looks to you like we're painted…"

The pilot bobbed his helmet. "Emergency evasive maneuvers. Roger."

"Here's what else I want you to do once we're dumped off…"

JOHN ELLISON LONG AGO thrust himself under what he believed was a granite-encased impression that he would be fully and unflinchingly prepared for the Day. Shortly after he had agreed to a plot that was no more, no less than treason and mass murder, he dangled several glorious mental banners over the moment, certain he could prepare himself well in advance.

Day of Reckoning. Day of Truth. Day of the Future. Sounded good, noble, righteous.

But the reality—now that the Day was here—was no comparison to any flights of fantasy meant to fairly stitch up what he knew all along was an open wound of bleeding conscience. One look at the small bank of monitors, white lab coats chewed to crimson rags, bodies flailing across the screens while the subguns of their black-clad executioners flamed on in muted butchery...

What could he do now? No sense whining, looking back or straying off a course he'd chosen on his own free will. No, sir, he was along for the full ride, and wherever the roller coaster took him next he needed to maintain the heart of a lion.

He took a moment for himself, just the same, thinking if he tried hard enough he could rationalize the madness besieging Galileo. Naturally, there was a ton of cold, hard cash involved in his final decision, eighty million dollars U.S. to be exact, to be split any number of ways—which rankled him more than a little—but accidents were sure to happen between now and then that would beef up his take. Beyond sealing the gilded doors shut to the plight of the human race, securing his own retirement of comfort and pleasure, there was a whopping fat syringe of cynicism and cold indifference to his fellow man plunged into the bottom line. America, for one, was under siege by any number of political, social and moral ills that were so growing—nay, multiplying at a phenomenal rate. And there was no going back. No redemption.

He figured if he couldn't beat them, then bail. No

way did he want to look back at the end of his days and swallow regret like bitter gall. He wanted to live, and live large. As far as that went, the sky was the limit when they were handed their cut on the other side of the Atlantic. Truth be told, he would find himself so flush with cash he wouldn't know what to do first. Sure, there would be his personal island nirvana to maintain, lavish toys and such, like speedboats and a Jacuzzi and a private jet to purchase. Then decorate his tropical palace with all sultry manner of imported women.

Just in case wretched excess wore thin, there would be plenty of glitzy hot spots around the globe he could turn into his personal playground.

He'd live large, like the king he was.

And damn right, he was owed, considering all the years and risks he'd undertaken for an increasingly ungrateful, narcissistic country that was swirling the bowl anyway. Take a look around, he thought, the dike had too many holes to plug up, and he was only one man— granted, he was a warrior—but standing against a mounting, raging tide of barbarians storming the gates of democracy. Nothing less than the threat of nuclear annihilation would hurl the savage unwashed masses back in their place.

Time to fly, tough guy.

He wanted to stand around and justify himself a little more, mentally submerge himself neck-deep in the golden sea of the future, but the action was heating up, demanding all of his grim focus. He figured half of the Russian team was just then hitting the Omega Control Room, hard at work, sweeping the work force with their on-screen silent dance of death, while the other Muscovite pack was spreading some more joy around Alpha Hangar.

Smoke, he found, was still curling out of the Gem-Tech sound suppressor fixed to his HK MP SD-3 sub-machine gun where he'd riddled the guy with what he figured was half a clip. He rated the project manager a last look, if only to make certain the man was dead. Harvey Turner was finally twitching out, he saw, the leather wingback creaking under deadweight and swinging some to the right. The PD's office was Spartan except for a desk with its smorgasbord of family pics, American flag, some shots of the guy mugging with the President and other Washington notables, awards and medals of service and valor that didn't mean squat anymore. But the Omega Main Terminal, where two of the computer wizards on the invading force were now burning CDs, was the star of the Galileo show.

Then the big man rolled in, three raid-suited operators with HK MP-5s in tow. A broken wisp of cigar smoke flying away in his wake, Sir hefted the black suitcase, swept the desk clear of Turner's blood-tainted nostalgia, hurling memorabilia to the floor like so much refuse. Ellison felt his skin grow clammy, as Sir keyed open the case, then powered up the battery. As the bodyguards peeled off and shot the security monitors, the big man used another key to turn on the digital readout, began tapping in a series of numbers on the keypad. A twist of the small metal key to the far right, removing it and dumping into his pants' pocket, and Ellison watched the slender box flare on with the red numbers to doomsday.

Sixty minutes and counting.

From somewhere down the hall the cries of agony and shouts of terror and panic seemed to mount to a shrill crescendo. Ellison found an odd smile on the big man's face as the guy turned his way.

"Is there something you wish to say, Mr. Ellison?"

There was, in fact, but he wondered how wise it would be to ask what might sound stupid questions, thus betray a lack of faith and courage when he was reasonably sure Sir had all the bases covered. Still, the one-kiloton package would turn Galileo into a radio-active tomb, and that didn't included God only knew how much liquid oxygen and liquid hydrogen that would be touched off, but that was part of the ruse, he knew. By the time anybody of self-crowned importance combed through the rubble they'd be long gone. Three Cessna Super Citations were parked near the runway, fueled and ready to fly, but Ellison wondered about the sanity of detonating such a powerful explosive. In other words, did they have enough time to lift off and clear the shock wave and resulting EMP? And, if the compound was raided by the authorities, what with Justice Department agents already on the ground, why leave the package out in the open like that?

"Sir? They're here. Bearing in from Runway Alpha, south, and closing on Portal L."

Ellison followed Sir's laughing stare to the monitors. Three supposed Justice Department agents were barreling toward the door in question. Armed and clearly weighted down with tools of war, one of them lugging a fat Multi-Round Projectile Launcher across his shoulder, it was a reasonable conclusion they hadn't come

to Galileo to serve search warrants. They either knew
the score, or suspected Galileo, Ellison thought, was up
for grabs by a conspiracy that reached clear to Russia,
which was why Sir ordered the sudden acceleration of
their original timetable in the first place. One of the alleged G-men was checking the door frame, when one
of the operators said, "All doors are locked, as ordered,
Sir."

"Yes, but they don't look the types to be dissuaded
by such a minor inconvenience. Why make it difficult
on them?" Sir said. "Unlock it and let them in."

LYONS WASN'T TWO STEPS inside the reinforced glass
door when right away he knew what was going down.
Likewise, he knew they were marked, let in with no initial resistance, which told the Able Team leader the
enemy believed they were walking them into an ambush. He'd be struck deaf, dumb and blind before he
could say for certain whether they were being monitored and tracked by high-tech cameras so cutting edge
he knew they could be blended in as part of the walls,
ceiling, floor.

So be it. The three of them were bringing it on blind
anyway, no fix on numbers, no faces even to match the
opposition, but Lyons had a simple ironclad rule as far
as that went.

If it was armed and angry, it went down hard and
bloody.

HK subgun out as he scanned and advanced, Lyons
locked in on the long burping retorts, the pandemonium
of shouts and pleas for mercy flaying the corridor from
what sounded the only open door before the floor met

the east-to-west bisecting hall. Lyons felt his blood boil over this mass murder, like bubbling lava in his veins, as he hugged whitewashed concrete wall, hustling even harder with each forward step on his north vector for what were the aboveground think tanks. Schwarz and Blancanales, on the other side, were crouched, with Pol keeping on eye on their six.

Good to go? Only one way to test it all now, the Able Team leader knew.

Lyons slowed, creeping to the edge of the open door, the muffled subgun fire and screams so loud it seemed they wanted to bowl him off his feet. He hand-signaled Blancanales to lag behind and watch the corridor, indicated to Schwarz he should follow second and peel to the left.

Then Lyons bulled into the slaughterhouse.

RADIC KYTOL HOSED DOWN three more workers with a sustained burst from his HK submachine gun as they went lurching and shrieking back for their small offices. Others were attempting to slam doors to their cubicles, only the emergency lock system, he knew, had already been bypassed through the project director's main computer and security terminal.

Nowhere to run, nowhere to hide. Kytol moved down the narrow hall, sweeping them alone or in pairs as they huddled in the tight quarters of their cubicles, kicking in doors where necessary, spraying occupants with short or long bursts, depending on the number of victims or if they were squeezing into a cubbyhole that required a few more skewering rounds.

Maybe fourteen kills to his credit so far, Kytol began

to find it so ridiculously easy, mowing them down like so many fattened calves where they stood, sat, screamed for mercy or tried to squeeze themselves beneath their desks, that a dark cloud of suspicion wanted to intrude his concentration.

And what was this nonsense all about? Doubt? Fear? Overconfidence?

The hell with all that feeble noise, they were mostly men, engineers and scientists and such, but a few women in lab coats had been scythed in his marching execution thus far, and he couldn't help but indulge a fleeting fantasy how he would have liked a few minutes alone with the females before blowing them away. It was messy work, killing them in such close proximity to his subgun bursts, that each office—most of which were not much larger than a walk-in closet—was practically demolished and left in blood-streaked, flesh-dappled ruins. Bodies thrashed and spun, as he surged into each doorway, spraying the cubicles, victims taking with them to the floor sparking, smoking computers and shattered desktop photos of family and friends, flesh, cloth and blood spattering walls like grotesque modern art where a mad drunken painter just threw his brush all over the place.

As he found a man on his knees at the last cubicle, hands up as if they would ward off the inevitable and screaming something unintelligible, Kytol, feeding his subgun a fresh 40-round extended magazine, listened to the brief stutters of muffled HKs and cries from the hallway where he knew two of his comrades were wrapping up their own death march, sticking to their vector.

Briefly hovering in the doorway, vaguely aware of his next victim pleading in front of him, he crunched numbers. Over one hundred Galileo employees, including security staff, maintenance and kitchen personnel, were being gunned down while their own computer wizards seized all critical data on present and future classified space projects. A lot of bodies between one full squad. And for what? And so what? He didn't have all the particulars, but Boss Franjo had irons in the fire with a Russian Family that had convinced him the future was in supertech space stations and RLVs that could house nuclear platforms, only he suspected beyond the huge sums of money to be earned from this nasty business in America, there was another agenda that involved their people's recent investments in Dagestan.

Not his immediate concern. He was just a soldier, carrying out orders.

Kytol riddled his last victim with a sustained burst, flinging him to the wall, the brutal impact seeming to pin him there like a giant bug before he crumpled in a sideways topple.

Easy work, Kytol thought to himself. Just another day at the office.

He was falling back, reaching for his handheld radio when a man-shape blurred into the corner of his eye. He was thinking it was Vidan or Luvan but a warning blared in his brain, instinct forcing his hand as he swung the subgun toward the armed figure that came charging like a gored bull. He was holding back on the trigger, spewing out 9 mm Parabellum rounds, nearly had the HK online when the first lances of hot lead tore into his chest.

CHAPTER EIGHTEEN

"Ironman! Do you copy?"

It took several seconds before Lyons realized he was hearing Blancanales over his com link. He was amazed that it worked after all. Schwarz, he saw, toed each of the two executioners he had chopped down, but drilled a 3-round burst into each skull for good measure, then began a cursory sweep of the cubicles, HK subgun extended and smoking as he peered into what Lyons knew would be individual chambers of murder.

Lyons looked into the first cubicle on the deep east end. And felt his heart thundering on with new hot rage at the sight of a woman splayed over her workstation. She was facedown in a growing stream of blood, vacant eyes staring back at the Able Team leader, as if wondering why.

She was all of maybe thirty, Lyons figured, picture frames of her with what had to be two young sons and husband knocked over on her desk, their smiling images splattered with blood.

Sons of bitches.

If he stood there too long, gripped in the pulsing heat of his own mounting anger while other murdering savages were on the loose…

Lyons keyed his com link. "Yeah?"

"I nailed two of the bastards on my end. I'm looking at maybe twenty, twenty-five bodies in the northeast wing alone. We can do a walk-through of the first floor, but something tells me—"

"I'm way ahead of you," Lyons rasped as he found Schwarz stepping toward him, checking his personal digital assistant, scrolling through the list of Galileo blueprints he had programmed into the state-of-the-art minicomputer with the help of Kurtzman. Opposition tactic—the enemy had let them in, free and unmolested as the breeze, Lyons reasoned, because their own butcher's work was nearly finished. Figure they had left behind a slack team, and the advance party was looking to retreat. "We'll check below, but you get to the runway pronto. I counted three military VIPs and some Black Hawks on the way in. Do whatever you have to, but if it's set to fly…"

"I copy. Turn it scrap."

"Then we're on the same page. If there's any prisoners to bag, you let me and Gadgets worry about it."

Lyons looked up and saw Schwarz indicating a door directly behind him. He spun on his heel, sick to his stomach with anger, but knew he had to get a grip. He nearly thundered the door open with a bootheel to let off steam, then caught himself in time and tried the latch.

It was open, and Lyons found the way into the bow-

els of Galileo clear. As he edged toward the stairwell
landing he listened hard for any sound of life. It was
silent from down below, too, and that only served to further twist his guts into a white-hot ball of simmering
fury as Lyons became fairly certain of what they would
find.

NOT THAT BLANCANALES doubted that the opposition's
ploy was to maneuver them into the complex while they
slipped out the back door, but the three big hardmen he
found moving fast and hard from Alpha Hangar burned
away the Able Team commando's last specter of wonder.

That, and the ladder ramp was down on the last of three
Cessna Citations, a figure squeezed into the hatch and
barking out what sounded like orders, and in Russian. The
turbofans on the military VIP wheels were whining, loud
and angry, Numbers One and Two already taxiing farther
from the small aircraft hangars to the west while Three
hung back to gather in the rest of the execution team.

With Little Bulldozer filling the Able Team
commando's hands, Blancanales gauged distance to
the birds—about eight hundred yards out, plenty
enough within the four-hundred-yard range of his pla-
toon-slayer. He decided to let the Russian trio cut it
close enough to their ride where he could both blow
up hope in their face, and maybe bag a wounded snake
in the devastating process.

If he didn't bring a prisoner home to Ironman, then
life was tough like that.

If they had spotted him, as he veered on an angle toward the two Black Hawks grounded on the helipad to

his three o'clock, they made no sign of it, Blancanales thinking he might just pull off a clean sweep before the birds hit one of the two runways that stretched north to south. With Lyons having passed on the order for their own bird to stray the edges of the compound's northern perimeter to avoid any potential SAMs, wait on word to pick them up…

He was hefting the Multi-Round Projectile Launcher, ten yards and closing on what would be his firepoint, when the shouter spotted him. He was gone next into the cabin, flailing arms and muffled shouts betraying his intentions.

So much for his back door sneak attack. Blancanales opted for Plan B.

VIP Birds One and Two, he found, began swinging onto the closest runway, noses aimed south, when Blancanales decided to rip a page from Ironman's tactical playbook.

Little Bulldozer up and ready to blast, Blancanales bolted away from the Black Hawks and went for straight up the gut as he bounded onto the runway.

"YOU KNOW WHAT THAT IS, don't you?"

Indeed, Lyons did.

Why it was open and set in full view on the desk, perched, what's more, in front of the late project director's body was only mere speculation. But now, after finding another forty or so dead personnel scattered down the halls, heaped where they were gunned down in the main control room, Lyons believed the enemy was looking to rub acid into open wounds that only seemed to gape wider and deeper with each new round.

Lyons clenched his jaw, a buzz of hot anger in his ears. Each door they kicked down only seemed to fly back in their faces. Too late once again, this time to stop the massacre of unarmed civilians, the seizing of whatever the enemy stole off the Galileo computers, and now too slow on the trigger to keep the whole compound from being blasted clear into the next county. Other than a few enemy dead, the opposition was looking like a winner. They would leave behind ashes and rubble, at best, to cover what they'd done here, contaminate the air clear down to Dallas-Fort Worth with radioactive fallout, at worst.

Lyons came out of his angry trance as Schwarz went to the desk, began examining the small suitcase. He saw the digital read, noted the numbers that were tumbling fast.

Schwarz cursed. "We've got twenty-nine minutes and counting, Carl, to get up top and get on our bird, and fly fast and far."

"I suppose you're going to tell me there's no way to shut it down."

Schwarz gestured with his subgun at the empty key slot. "Not without the arming key. And then you're talking about a series of access codes that even then won't reverse the process unless they're put in ten to fifteen minutes from when our fission bullet strikes."

"What's your best guess on the yield?"

Schwarz lifted one end of the suitcase. "I couldn't tell you with anything close to absolute certainty, but as you know, these usually come in at anywhere from a five- to ten-kiloton wallop. Call it half to two-thirds of Hiroshima."

It was the Able Team leader's turn to curse.

"This one's a little smaller, a little lighter than our standard eighty-pound Green Beret package," Schwarz said.

"Meaning?"

"The Special Forces and the CIA have these at their disposal in the half- to one-kiloton yield," Schwarz told him.

"So, I've heard. They've used two in Afghanistan already to do a little cave excavation."

"It's hard to tell just by looking at it, or picking up one end...." Schwarz trailed off.

"But we're hoping best case is one kiloton."

"Carl, there's no way I can deactivate it."

"And it isn't like we have time to take it with us, fly the damn thing way out into the desert and dump it," Lyons stated.

"We'll be lucky if we make our own jet and get enough bare-bones clearance when this blows. If it's a five or more..."

"We're blackened toast," Lyons growled.

"We're no toast. Look!"

Lyons swung toward the line of security cameras as Schwarz ran to the terminal. Two steps closer, and he made out the familiar shape of the Multi-Round Projectile Launcher, with Blancanales sprinting down the runway like he was going for the gold.

Lyons whirled and raced for the door.

ELLISON ABRUPTLY STOPPED counting naked island girls and humming country tunes when he saw the bastard with the big weapon in his mitts charging down the runway like a speeding locomotive.

The guy raised what may well prove to be, Ellison suspected, his personal paradise annihilator meant to blast him clear off the runway to El frigging Paso!

Ellison pressed his face into a portside cabin window, the HK subgun suddenly growing heavy in his sweaty grasp. The way Bazooka Man swung that anvil of doomsday, it looked like the Russian crew was marked first for total obliteration. In that case there was a chance, albeit slim...

Ellison knew that bird was topped out with enough high-octane fuel, what with the reserve tank stuffed to the gills. Factor that, and the distance wasn't much more than a stinking thirty or forty yards and that Super Citation was gaining on them instead of them putting much-needed desperate frigging clearance to the coming ground zero those doomed occupants were slated to be incinerated by. Worse, the flyboys were either unaware of the threat or the big man in the lead aircraft was too busy working on his first or fourth whiskey by now, patting himself up and down the back and puffing up a storm, his flunkies chuckling all around...

In other words, all the lollygagging was holding up the whole freaking bloody parade! Damn it, he knew it! Twenty minutes or more alone had been eaten up just getting aboveground, as they'd been forced to root out and shoot down a few more personnel on the way out who'd been hiding and blubbering for their lives.

The clock was running!

No! Time was up!

Ignoring the angry questions from two of Sir's vaunted black ops, Ellison charged the cockpit. "Get us up in the air!"

"Sir, I can't move us any faster…"

Ellison could see that, even as his vision filmed over with rage and terror. "Give them a shove then, damn it! Fly over them, but do something and fast!"

"What? Are you crazy!"

"We've got some lunatic on our ass about ready to blast us to buzzard meat!"

"The hell you say!"

It looked like Sir's jet was suddenly gathering a little speed now, but Ellison…

He ran to the cabin door, hammered the release button, sobs and curses choked in his throat. At that range, his HK was about as useless as a water pistol but he had to do something, anything…

He was thrusting the weapon around the edge when he heard the first sonic boom, the searing flash of light that told him the bastard had just hung paradise over the edge of perdition to all but fry.

They were bellowing out the panic now, then the shouts of horror ripped to new ear-piercing decibels as Ellison felt some titanic force slam into the tail section. He was tumbling to the floor, subgun flying from his grasp, when the back end was sheared off like rotten wood under a giant chain saw and the jet was pounded into a bouncing slide off the runway.

A HUMAN PHOENIX SHRIEKED out from the roiling fireball to their one o'clock, roughly thirty yards out. It was minus an arm just above the elbow, but the subgun in the screaming demon's good hand was tracking and spewing lead, breaching way too close inside Lyons's comfort zone. Advancing down the runway at a loping gait, Lyons joined Schwarz in a double stream of sub-gun fire that doused the infernal creature and sent it dancing back into the fiery rubbish from whence it came.

Lyons swept the fruits of Blancanales's first two harvests of ruin with his HK, searching for walking wounded, but had to believe anything inside those fireballs was microwaved stew and on the way to Hell. Sheets of mangled wing and burning cabin were still sailing away in all directions, chunks of smoking garbage, the size of small cars, floating to earth, banging off Omega Runway, as Lyons watched Blancanales adjust his aim.

The first two or three rounds, Lyons saw, had streaked past the lead VIP jet, black smoke billowing twenty yards or so farther down the runway from the getaway bird evidence that Pol needed to right his aim, and quick. Blancanales stole a critical second, dropped to a knee as the lead bird torqued it all the way, gathering steam and on the verge of turning itself into a streaking arrow, the flyboy bent on bounding them through craters and wreckage, risking instant immolation, but the guy knew he was left with no choice.

Balls to the wall, and on both sides.

Lyons gave Blancanales some silent mental encouragement, then checked the sky behind them. He found their own ride dropping down over what was nothing other than a silent dark tomb, and soon to be vaporized, but he was coming in for the emergency evac.

Correcting the trajectory, aiming higher as if the hardware itself implored an act of divine assistance, Blancanales was giving the jet some more lead, then popped out two rapid 40 mm projectiles. Lyons watched as the first of two Hail Mary rounds slammed down, erupted in a fiery cloud, yards behind the bird, instead of out front, and he knew at that point nothing short of a miracle…

The miracle happened.

Number two warhead arced down at the near farthest reach of the launcher's range and plowed into the port wing. As the main blast ignited fuel and puked the whole nest of vultures apart, Lyons shouted at Blancanales, pointing at their ride. Schwarz, he found, was already charging for Omega Runway, the sleek Gulfstream touching down, out of nowhere, it seemed, screeching tread pluming out the smoke as tires clawed at concrete. It was a welcome sight, but Lyons felt hope waver some as their jet raced on, the sky raining fire and brimstone as it just barely streaked under the hammerblows of three or four raining meteors.

"Gadgets!" Lyons hollered as he fell in behind his teammate. "How much time?"

"TEN SECONDS… Nine…"

"We got it!" Lyons growled, jumped out of his seat, beating Schwarz and Blancanales to the starboard windows.

They were climbing, maybe three thousand feet and soaring up and away at top 631 mph. Lyons was just about to get his air legs under him, when they started to level out and began heading northeast of the doomed compound. He took in the hot zone, two miles back and shrinking fast, the Able Team leader clinging to hope that…

To the distant south, he could just make out the hazy skyline of Dallas-Fort Worth as it baked in the blistering sun. Closer in, the vast mottled and gleaming lakes of suburbs began to stake claim to the prairie, the interstate maybe three miles or more due east of the blast site, and clogged with vehicles for as far as he could see in both directions. The Galileo compound was ringed by cyclone fencing, Lyons figuring the perimeter enclosing ground zero circling three to four miles around the compass. There was flat and empty brown prairie fanning out beyond the fence line, what he believed were heads of cattle to the far southwest...

"You might want to look away, guys," Schwarz said. "I can't guarantee there won't be retinal burn..."

They were gaining distance like a streaking bullet, but Lyons would have sworn he saw the earth on both sides of the runways ripple, swell, the whole flatland collapse, with the diminishing black block that was the main building looking to sink some, then the upheaval shot the whole works straight for the sky, a massive erupting volcano, but one that blew a nuclear lid. Squinting, Lyons looked away, not sure if the blinding flash was due to all the liquid hydrogen and liquid oxygen being ignited, the blast itself or a meshing combo of both.

He peeked back as the mushroom cloud began to rise, then looked at the grim faces of his teammates. The screens in their personal comm center jumped and flickered some, but EMP, he knew, was something not even the most brilliant of scientists could accurately predict. And since they didn't know the yield that was lighting up the prairie back yonder...

The flaring supernova glowed against the cabin windows, seemed to want to call him back for one last look, but Lyons had seen more than enough.

He knew the hanging question now was as elusive as the entire mission had so far proved.

Where did they go from here?

CHAPTER NINETEEN

Stony Man Farm, Virginia

"Where are we exactly? Big picture, little picture and every nook and cranny you can think of in between needs to be filled. Start with Able," Brognola suggested.

"The Galileo crisis," Price began, "is being contained, at least for the immediate future. Both the Army and Air Force have stepped in with what I'm hearing are 'special emergency units,' and the FBI and FEMA are both sorting through the mess and erecting what I'm also hearing is a barricade of damage control. Because of the undisclosed nature of NASA's Zenith Project, the press is being fed a story about an accident that involved enough liquid hydrogen and liquid oxygen that an explosion in what Carmen and Hunt learned was measured at almost two kilotons can sound plausible to the public. The fact that the compound is at least a known launch pad—or was perceived to be under early construction—for space shuttles and RLVs may be enough to calm public fears."

Kurtzman cleared his throat. "As for fallout, Hal, long-term effects, cancer and so forth, and on top of that there is a definite air of panic spreading, and beyond the Texas borders. Considering what the world is already being told about the crisis in Australia…"

Brognola grunted. "No one knows what to believe. For that matter, I'm not sure I do, either. We've got one laser gun, which is about fifty years ahead of anything I've ever heard of that's currently on the drawing board in any classified base across this country. We've got some material that renders a man near invisible but which the best forensic scientists down at the FBI lab in Quantico can only determine is made of some flexible ceramic, the likes of which they've never seen and can only guess at its properties. We've got black ops—DOD, NSA, DIA or maybe something none of us has ever heard of coming out of Homeland Security—but that no one knows for sure which black hole of whatever intelligence agency they crawled out of. We've got a two-kiloton burial of any evidence that might have been obtained for all this super-technology, stolen classified files from what Able's telling us and which jibes with the Force of Truth's diatribes, and not to mention over one hundred murdered civilian employees. Tell me. Am I wrong in thinking we're never going to get to the bottom of this?"

Price took a deep breath, her nostrils flaring as determination hardened her face. "It's called PetroBal. And I cut Able Team loose on them."

"The Serb-Russian mafia connection to the UN?" Brognola responded.

"Thanks to Phoenix," Price said, "we've learned from Shistoi and the two Serbs they have in custody that Franjo Balayko had—and this is still unclear how—groomed United Nations big shots who were in bed with the former Iraqi regime."

"The Serbs drew up an informal contract," Kurtzman interrupted, "between the Iraqis and a petrochemical company that is tied to Balayko but is run by various European businessmen."

"A front for his other unsavory ventures," Brognola said.

"Which includes his strange alliance with Muslim terrorists," Price said. "Or, rather, what appears a sideshow venture where he recruits fanatics through various cutouts and has them shipped to Dagestan for training to carry out operations—like the suicide bombers strapped down with nerve gas in Israel."

"Yeah," Brognola agreed. "And when you consider how Balayko and his thugs purportedly have enough Muslim blood on their hands to have made the Crusaders genuflect before them…"

"Money is still money," Kurtzman said.

"Right," Brognola groused. "Sharks don't care what's out there bleeding, as long as they get their chunk of choice meat."

"To answer your original question," Price said, "it's dubious whether we will know with anything that resembles concrete fact about who and how far this whole hydra reaches. I can say this, Hal," the mission controller said with a sudden hard note in her tone.

"Whether or not we simply stumbled into this particular conspiracy because of forces beyond our control, or some quirk of fate guided us here, there's no telling what could have happened, how many innocent lives would be hung out there if it weren't for both Able and Phoenix. We didn't call this one. It called us."

"I hear you," Brognola said. "A little gratitude, I suppose, goes a long way. Problem is—and I'm sure I'm stating the obvious here—our people seem to be lurching into each crisis either as it happens or as the smoke is thinning around the dead bodies."

"What we have," Price said, "is actionable intelligence for Able to take down Franjo Balayko."

"And my own inquiring on that front," Brognola said, "has informed me the FBI in Belgrade have enough solid evidence on Balayko to clip his wings."

"That depends," Price said, "on your definition of 'clipping.'"

Brognola chuckled. "This is just a fantasy, folks, but it would be nice if for once we could take care of business the nice clean way. But we'll never have to worry about falling into the bad habit of offering sweetheart deals with lifetime all-expenses-paid witness protection at whatever the bad guy of the day's favorite playboy resort."

"Just the same," Kurtzman said. "If Able can bag a few big crocs over there, we might be able to drive a few more hyenas out of the bush."

Brognola worked on his cigar. "At this point, Bear, I'm neither counting on that happening, nor do I care how Balayko goes down. Before you two came in, the Man called to emphasize that it's open season.

Whoever is regarded as even loosely connected to what happened in Australia, and now Texas, is fair game."

"And what about the Russians?" Price wanted to know. "Political considerations, fireworks between Moscow and Washington. That's not our quagmire, I understand, but if he's prepared to launch a covert war on the Russians...what I'm saying, where there's one snake in the woodpile—well, if and when this turns nasty, it could root out some corruption in the Russian hierarchy that could turn the whole country upside down. All but trample what are presently brittle relations between Moscow and Washington. The bottom line—I'm worried about getting Phoenix out of Russia. And I'm wondering if the White House will just let them sink if the waters get too deep and the sharks look like they'll start swimming toward the Oval Office."

"I hear that. All I can tell you is that the Man danced around some on any fallout, the blame game and like that. But I read in between the lines enough where I can assume he's pretty much washed his hands of whatever loose cannons Phoenix Force turns up in Siberia. And he's offered me the direct assistance of all available U.S. military and CIA personnel in that part of the world, which includes three carriers, two battleships and two nuclear-powered submarines and whatever else I can think of we might need for swift and safe extraction. Speaking of Phoenix, what's their status?"

Price turned a darker shade of grim as she told Brognola, "That's where Bear and I have both drawn the same conclusion."

Brognola didn't like the sound of that at all. "Which would be what?"

Kurtzman cleared his throat. "If we give them the go-ahead, Hal, there's better than a fifty-fifty chance it's one of two things. An ambush. Or a suicide mission."

Brognola scoured their faces. "I take it you've both been anxiously waiting for me to make the call?" He paused, then said, "Let's back up for a minute. Do you have an exact location on this Russian base?"

"The general neighborhood, but we're working on a satellite pass-over of the area," Kurtzman said. "But getting any good imagery is contingent on the weather in that part of the world. From what we've gotten from David, and this via Rushti, it's in Far East Siberia, southeast of the Lena River. Frozen tundra country. Mountains, too. Mist. Low cloud cover from initial weather reports. Fronts. Snow. It doesn't look promising on getting an accurate lay of the Zenith base."

Brognola scowled. "Forget the weather report for now, the logistics alone are going to be a nightmare. First of all, the Russian Federation is—what?—seven million square miles and eleven time zones, I believe?"

"A little over six-and-a-half million, with Siberia gobbling up five million of those square miles…"

"But who's counting?" Brognola offered.

"Eight time zones," Kurtzman said, "from where Phoenix took off in Dagestan to the Russian Zenith."

"And you're talking about breaching Russian airspace, MiGs maybe shooting them down," Brognola said.

"The way David made it sound," Price said, "Rushti has a plan."

"He'd damn well better," Brognola growled. "A C-130 transport rumbling across Russian skies is a big fat slug of a target."

"The Russian special ops," Price said, "are called the Czars."

"The Czars?" Brognola repeated. "And this would be Rushti and his comrades?"

"David's new comrade practically bragged about it," Price answered.

"Did he now? Why is that just more gasoline to throw on the fire, I fear? And why is it I've never heard of these Czars before?"

"Not even the CIA knew about them until about three years back," Price said. "They came to the CIA's attention when they were aiding Russian special ops in tracking down and dismantling Chechen terrorist pipelines that were busy setting off bombs in Moscow and slaughtering schoolchildren. Ostensibly, the Czars are former Spetsnaz commandos, and they have presidential carte blanche to do as they see fit in the field."

"In other words, they're a Russian version of our own people," Brognola said.

"The word is," Price said, "they're not very discriminating when it comes to collateral damage. They're strictly wet-work specialists. Terrorists. Homegrown traitors. They specialize in internal security problems, also."

"Which is what's really bugging me about this Rushti and now his Czars," Brognola said. "We all know we've sent our people into Russia before, either at their request or in joint cooperation to clean up one of their messes. What's the catch this time? Or do we even have a clue?"

"According to Rushti," Bear said, "there is no catch. Phoenix helps them. Phoenix gets to walk away with super-technology that was stolen by the Russian collaborators from the ESA and NASA."

"An olive branch?"

Kurtzman shrugged. "As we speak, David is supposedly getting the particulars on the mission parameters to move against the Russian Zenith."

"And do what? Blow up their state-of-the-art space shuttle? Hijack it and fly it back to the States?"

"It was more an internal threat," Price said, "from Islamic fundamentalists who Rushti believes have either already infiltrated the base or are mounting an attack."

"And they're going to hijack this RLV?"

"Stranger things have happened, Hal," Kurtzman said.

"You're right, Bear, and worse," Brognola admitted, thinking that very few even in the U.S. intelligence loop would have believed 9/11 was possible until it happened. "It's one thing to learn to fly a jumbo jet. I have to imagine it's a light-year leap from that to operating an RLV, which, I'm assuming, works on the same aerodynamics and operational principles as a space shuttle."

"From what little information Rushti gave David on their RLV," Price said, "it's run by computers, nearly Alpha to Omega. Everything requires access codes. Once it's up in the air, there's virtually nothing left for ground control to do but track and monitor its flight and check in with the crew."

"Implying what? That if suspected fanatics did hijack the thing they could program it for autopilot? And with stolen control and access codes could arm the thermonuclear payload? Then just sit back on the flight deck and watch whichever city or cities of their choosing go up in a thermonuclear cloud?"

"From the fanatic's point of view, that would be a reasonable conclusion," Price said.

Brognola fought back visions of an impending holocaust a hundred thousand times or more worse than 9/11. "I'm thinking Phoenix is going to need backup."

"Well, that would be a definite problem, unless you want to go further still outside our own circle," Price said. "With Striker so deep under and Able Team on the way to pay Balayko a visit…"

"It could be anywhere from twenty-four to forty-eight hours before Phoenix moves on the Russian Zenith, right?"

"That depends on what I hear next from David," Price answered.

"And I'm counting on Able to take Balayko down fast, since the FBI has him under a microscope and knows exactly where he is."

"Then we have the logistic problem again," Price said. "If you're thinking about attaching Able to Phoenix."

"Well," Brognola said, "I told you how serious the Man is about nailing this one down, whatever it takes. He has put at my disposal an aircraft that is housed in a hangar at the American air base in Incirlik. He went into a few details, I guess to put my mind at ease that anything we need is ours. This is a prototype superbird, straight out of the Lockheed Skunk Works, part of our VentureStar black program. Mach 5. Stealth technology that will make it invisible. One-hundred-thousand-foot-plus ceiling. The way I heard it, it's straight off the assembly line out of Groom Lake, and has already flown two missions over Afghanistan. One pilot. And a special cargo hold for bunker busters, fuel air explosives and nukes, but that also doubles as a six-seater cabin for special ops who can be dropped for a HALO."

"So," Price said, "we can take it you were already planning ahead?"

"Not up until about thirty minutes ago. But yeah, despite everything on our plates, I was looking into my own crystal ball."

"This is just a thorn that's been nagging me," Kurtzman suddenly said, "but I went ahead and had Akira do something regarding a loose cannon by the name of Boltmer."

"Do tell."

"He's zapping all the Force of Truth Webs, but he's keeping open one line of communication in particular with Boltmer, letting him know about it, sort of, uh, steering things, just in case the man wants to do some more whistle-blowing at his leisure. And for a nice little fee of a quarter-million for any more juicy tidbits, a lump sum, which, Akira, of course, does not have."

Brognola nodded. "Let me guess. You're looking to reel in the big fish that thinks it's going to slip the net?" Brognola asked, and watched as the wicked grin spread over Kurtzman's face.

CHAPTER TWENTY

"Comrades. I will do one more round with you, then I must retire to, how would you say, tie up some loose ends?"

David McCarter felt the grim smile tighten his lips. Loose ends? The Russian had a sense of humor, he'd give him that much, he thought as he stared out through the bulletproof, wire-mesh glass at the runway of the Czar-CIA special ops base with no name. They had been in the air most of the night before touching down at this remote base at the far northeast edge of Kazakhstan, McCarter wondering occasionally, between then and now, just how crazy he was to give his nod of approval and cooperation to the Russian black op. As he looked at the six MiGs that had escorted them to base, grounded near the row of hangars, dark figures armed with assault rifles plunging through the white swirl of snow-driven wind, a strange and unsettling revelation began to flare through his dark, troubled thoughts.

This mission was far from over or being settled,

one way or another, on any account. What had started
out as a hunt for Islamic fundamentalists responsible
for the mass murder of Israeli civilians and with the five
of them chasing the ghosts of corruption that howled
around a vast conspiracy between the UN, some Serb-
Russian-Dagestani gangsters and ESA covert ops who
were bankrolling the theft of RLV technology now had
them standing on the eve of infiltrating a covert Russian space program that was believed by Rushti to soon
be under attack. Both from within the Zenith compound by national traitors, and beyond its walls by
armed Muslim fanatics who were supposedly going to
hijack his country's prototype RLV for a thermonuclear
joyride. What briefly disturbed the Phoenix Force
leader was the fact they would have never blundered
into what was a certain doomsday scenario if not for
Zhuktul and Shistoi, who simply couldn't confine their
greed and blind ambitions to the usual plunder known
to common gangsters. They had sought to go high-
tech, in search of bigger money yet, their own arrogance and pride swollen so great it was beyond their
control, and in the process the mighty had brought
down the walls of their own respective kingdoms, and
thanks, in no small part, to their own devouring ava-
rice. Funny how that worked. One dead. One now in
the custody of the CIA after McCarter had thoroughly
scrubbed Shistoi's brains clean of information.

"Will you and your men join me, Commander
Mac?"

McCarter turned slowly, looked at each of his men.
They were grouped around a large metal table, poring
over all satellite pics, blueprints of the Zenith base.

Rushti was holding up the half-empty bottle of vodka, the Rasputin grin pasted on his lips.

"It will be four to five hours before we are in the air in my country's version of one of your own military VIP jets," Rushti said. "Plenty of time to catch your sleep, clean weapons, check gear."

"I'll pass, but any of you blokes care to join the good comrade, feel free."

Rushti lost the grin, shrugging when the Phoenix Force commandos declined another round, which didn't stop him from killing one then two quick shots.

McCarter walked up to the table as Rushti poured another drink. He scanned the photos and sat imagery and said, "Your RLV covert compound sure doesn't look like much to make such a big fuss over, Comrade Rushti. What do we have here? A few rows of propellant tanks. What look like two movable hangars, a launch mount and two runways."

Rushti made some noise that resembled something between a chuckle or a long grunt. "There is a saying about appearances being deceptive."

McCarter saw that one draw a few looks from his mates. "Exactly what I'm thinking."

"My American comrade, I have explained. The nerve center, the ground control, is below ground."

"Along with enough hardware," Hawkins said, "to hold back an invasion by China."

"T-72 main battle tanks, BMPs, batteries of your new radar-optical fire control ZSU-23-4M cannons with targeting computers around the compass," Manning added.

"And," James said, "mobile SA-4 Ganefs with command homing guidance systems."

"A squad of MiGs and enough of your new Hokum attack helicopters and Hind-24s," Encizo threw in, "to cover every rebel-held piece of square yard in all your Stan republics put together."

"But you exaggerate."

"But we don't. What my men are saying, Comrade Rushti," McCarter said, "is that all indications are this is an elaborate military base, an underground city, in fact, to house that kind of firepower you indicated they have at their disposal."

"And, as I have already explained, most of it is there merely in the event of an emergency. Fifty troops presently stationed. Three officers I can say beyond any doubt are loyal to me."

James snorted. "You don't classify a bunch of Islamic terrorists working in collusion with some of your own people under the Zenith roof and who are going to seize a thermonuclear-armed space shuttle as an emergency?"

"A containable crisis, shall we call it, and that is why we are going in."

"As ESA middlemen," Manning huffed, "with phony ID badges and duffels stuffed to the gills with weapons? Who will be delivering some special load of rocket fuel?"

"What is this? Are you saying you are all getting cold feet?"

"We know what you've told us, comrade," McCarter said. "What we would now like to know is what you haven't told us."

Rushti heaved a dramatic sigh, straightened, ramrod-stiff, clasped his hands behind his back. "Very well. There is corruption beyond the highest levels of our space program, and which we are trying to root out by this counterattack on Zenith. Unless it is dealt with in swift, certain fashion, my superiors fear that our joint spacelab station program could be jeopardized, if not permanently damaged."

"You're telling us," Hawkins said, "that maybe you've known for some time the marquee players and what they were up to?"

"Yes. More or less."

"But, we just happened along to lend a helping hand?" Encizo said.

"More or less," James added.

"Comrades, I have heard it said that timing is everything in life. Perhaps this is merely Fate steering you to me to aid the few good men of my country in thwarting what could be a monstrous agenda, one that could see hundreds of thousands perish in a nuclear holocaust."

"Which leaves us wondering still," McCarter said. "Are you holding out?"

Rushti fell silent, then bobbed his head, McCarter watching him closely as a strange fire lit his eyes. The Czar black op filled another shot, killed it, heaved a dramatic breath. "Comrades, where is your faith?" he said, as if so exasperated he verged on despair. Another nod, and Rushti hurled the glass. It missiled, inches past McCarter's face, shattering against the window, but the ex-SAS commando didn't flinch, though he read the sudden anger and confusion in the eyes of his teammates.

"What the hell," Encizo growled.

"Call it coincidence, call it Fate, call it justice about to be meted out by whatever God you pray to," Rushti said, squaring his shoulders as if defying any of them to physically attack. "Yes, I knew you were coming to Dagestan, as you knew that I knew, though you did not know who I was until we met. I do not, and will not stand here and justify myself to any of you, nor will I implore you to believe me at my word, which, I tell you now on my blood is better than gold. The world in which we live and deal is one of traitors with many hidden skeletons, as I am sure you are aware of. They want money. They wish to perpetuate twisted ideology through the mass murder of countless innocents. Or they want both. And to achieve their aims they will go so far as to eat their own like a child to be sacrificed on their personal altars of greed and ambition. I learn what I now know because I thrust my very capable hands into these nests of serpents and withdraw them to squeeze the life out of them until they give me the truth.

"Should you proceed with me to Zenith, I can assure you it will not be easy, and I cannot and will not guarantee the outcome, whether success or failure or the ultimate sacrifice of your own lives. Men are going to die, bad men who have deceived my country and brought in Muslim extremists to hijack a prototype space plane. How, precisely, it will be done, what they intend to do with it, where they intend to strike with thermonuclear weapons, I do not know. It could be Moscow. It could be Iraq. It could be Hawaii or any city or cities on your continental United States. My personal source inside Zenith tells me the supreme hour of the conspiracy has already begun. That was the loose end I mentioned. Final details, last-minute intelligence.

"Now. In exchange for your help, for you disabling this space plane by, yes, blowing it up and helping me and my men to smuggle out the thermonuclear payload—assuming, that is, it is not already on board—you will receive all schematics, all critical intelligence and prisoners, anything that was stolen by these traitors from the ESA and your own NASA. This base will be shut down, permanently. And, should that happen, the world at large will never need to know how close it was pushed to the brink of World War Three. Now. I have spoken my mind, and from the heart. Are you in or out?"

McCarter kept his composure as he wandered a look over the faces of his commandos, none of whom appeared to know what to make of the Russian's outburst. He found Rushti staring at him, waiting for his final answer. McCarter could never be positive of anything in their world of murder, sabotage and mayhem but he believed Rushti was sincere. May God help him, the ex-SAS commando decided, if he wasn't shooting straight. If his will be perverse, if his intentions were crooked, McCarter would have no problem straightening him out.

The Phoenix Force leader showed Rushti an easy smile, held his arms out, and said, "We're in. Was there ever any doubt?"

THE MERE SIGHT of the ostentatious playboy mansion, perched high like some gilded eagle's nest to overlord the Adriatic Sea and the beach crowd far below, was enough to make Carl Lyons want to throttle the arrogant life right out of the guy. For just one nasty little tidbit, the pedigree on the Serb boss read like a nightmare straight out of Hell, one for which Dante would have created a whole new circle. Between his suspected track record as a war criminal and his career as a major crime figure in charge of an enterprise that stretched from Moscow to, apparently, Dallas, Texas, there was enough murder, torture, rape and every abomination in between this Serb bloodsucker would have made the Romanian prince known as Vlad the Impaler look like a teetotaling, wispy fop by comparison. The bottom line to all the madness, thanks to his underworld endeavors, his connection to the UN oil scam and rogue contacts in the European Space Agency, the FBI believed the Serb was one of the richest men in Europe.

But that was just the way of the world, Lyons thought. Sad to say there were few greater axioms on Earth than crime did pay.

The bad guys never believed it, Lyons knew, but there was a heavy price tag attached to that sordid truth for those who would become king of an illegitimate empire at the expense of untold suffering humanity.

And Franjo Balayko's tab was long overdue.

Lyons clenched his jaw so hard he felt his heart beating through his teeth as he shoved down murderous fantasies of what he'd like to do to the guy, but lived in hope he might just get the chance to act it all out, and in short order.

According to the FBI, the Serb's main pleasure palace was two stories and had thirty bedrooms. The facade and roofline were all hung and trimmed in marble and cedar, with hand-tooled carvings of Greek and Roman gods jutting up from a gold-tiled roof that reflected the afternoon sun like divine light. Looked about right to Lyons, and yet he was faced with the not-so-little problem of covering all that ground when they crashed the gate. Then the pool, custom-designed, no less, in female statuesque, legs and all, Lyons observed, with breasts reaching out as giant melons for the Jacuzzi crowd. Another hard scan through his field glasses, and Lyons gave up counting all the beauties strutting or lounging about pool and barside. Innocent, or maybe not-so-innocent bystanders. Well, Lyons decided, they'd better duck or hit the water and hold their breath until the storm blew over. He wasn't a fan of collateral damage, but he hadn't come all this way to get tripped up from bagging the big man-eating sharks because a few guppies didn't know when to get out of the way.

The good news was that the security force in black tux, dark shades and wielding stubby machine pistols—five in all—was having some well-understood difficulty concentrating on watching the store. In fact, two of them were busy chatting it up with the girls, with another hardman taking a long time out to rub oil over two of the sunbathing kittens while number four appeared more interested in helping himself to the boss's liquor in one of three thatch-roofed bars. Grunting, not quite sure it was contempt and disgust he felt, Lyons could only imagine what was going on inside where the boss and his VIP entourage were stashed away, but if the hardforce under the roof was as sloppy and lackadaisical as this bunch of gun-toting playboy wannabes…

Lyons heaved a breath, then glanced at Schwarz and Blancanales, his commandos flanking him, but taking the time all of a sudden to throw him a look that told him they suspected what he was thinking.

"No," Lyons rebuffed, "I'm not jealous."

Schwarz grinned. "You sure could have fooled me."

"That would be no major accomplishment, my friend," Lyons said.

If he judged his teammates by how he felt—weary from more than just jet lag but with fresh reserves of adrenaline and pure malice of heart now kicking in— then it was a safe bet they were good to go. The question was how, exactly, to proceed? Or did they even bother to shift tactics, other than a full rampage straight down Broadway?

Their surveillance roost was a boulder-studded bowl, swaddled by pine trees, a few hundred yards southeast and up from the gangster's getaway from the trials and tribulations of Belgrade. Those woes currently plaguing Franjo Balayko and threatening to crash his 24/7 party were the FBI. Two of the Serb Don's headaches were right then squeezed in behind, and practically breathing down Lyons's neck with a sickening mix of cologne, cigarette smoke residue and a lunch that was heavy on garlic, onions and sausage. They were wearing flak vests, and sweating like lambs over the fire, Beretta M-9s in shoulder holsters beneath windbreakers, tactical radios hooked to their belts. Lyons flashed them a look—both of them scowling but pulling back a few inches—before he went back to scanning the lay of the land in search of a battle strategy. Special Agent in Charge Feodor Jomanski, he noted, looked especially eager to start putting his HK-33 assault rifle with scope to good use. In fact, the word from Brognola was the guy liked to kick down doors and go in shooting. His kind of agent, a little rogue and a lot of gung-ho, but Lyons had fairly informed them they were backup.

"You boys really hit the jackpot," Jomanski said, raking the compound with a sweep of his field glasses.

"That's the third time you've said that," Lyons observed, "since you picked us up and flew us here by chopper from Belgrade. Why don't you just come right out and say what's on your mind?"

Jomanski lowered the glasses, looked at Lyons with a narrowed gaze. "I'm just saying your timing couldn't have been better. According to my agent watching the Zruna Dtiva airfield, the Russian Don just landed. Congratulations. You've got all the fat cats about to be gathered under the same roof."

Lyons already knew as much from Brognola's personal team assigned to watch the private airfield. Six shooters were coming in with Vladimir Yoravky. But they were merely bit players in what Lyons knew was a freak show who's who of the European Space Agency and the United Nations already partaking of whatever the Serb boss was offering. What galled Lyons even more was that the savages didn't even bother to hide who they were, as he looked again to the Russian Mi-26 parked on the helipad to the north. It was a big gray transport beast, and even at a distance Lyons could read UN on the belly, with United Nations painted out on the tail. Yet another hassle. Lyons knew they were raw human sewage, would most likely bluster in outrage when he put the facts of life to them, but in the eyes of their so-called legitimate diplomatic world they were aboveboard, untouchable. What the hell, he figured, they could play with the poisonous snakes, feed at the same trough as criminal swine, why should he suffer some crisis of conscience when the lead started to fly?

The Able Team leader sensed the original bitterness from the SAC bristle even more, now that the showtime was upon them, with Special Agent Don Myers not doing much to give Lyons a good old feeling that mutual cooperation was the order of the day, as the shorter of the two agents seemed hell-bent on maintaining the same sour expression since they'd all been introduced back in the big city. One of the advantages, though, of working for America's premier ultracovert intelligence agency, Lyons knew, was its close but secret ties to the President of the United States. Then there was, of course, Hal Brognola with his own special run of the Justice Department, and which the FBI's operations around the world fell under his command and control whenever the crisis demanded. And woe be unto the agents, Lyons thought, who didn't stand up, salute and obey and with a smile of peaceful resignation on his face when Brognola came knocking.

"What my partner's saying," Agent Myers suddenly attested, "is that we're kind of hoping the FBI is more than just a taxi and intel service for you three cowboys. I mean, it isn't like we don't have anything invested in this. What would you say, Big Jo? About twenty thousand hours of surveillance? Listening to wiretaps all day and night, seven days a week, watching the Serb Don living high off the hog for how many years now? Going on five?"

"Yeah, something like that."

Lyons kept the smart remark in check. He wasn't here to coddle the FBI, take them in his arms and pat them on the heads and apologize for stealing their thunder and hurling up a barricade to any personal career advancement with the show he had waiting just offstage. Still, if there were any live ones left worth taking prisoner he would gladly dump them into the FBI's lap. Paperwork wasn't his bag anyway.

Lyons spent a few long moments scouring the vast motor pool, raking the dense tree line that flanked the long cobbled driveway. Between all the Mercedes limos, Rolls-Royces, Cadillacs, what looked like custom-made Hummers, Lyons certain every ride was armored and with windows bulletproof enough to stop anything just this side of a cruise missile...

Figure there was money enough on cars alone to buy the multiethnic mess of centuries-old festering hate and strife of whatever they called the former Yugoslavia these days, and twice over.

Lyons could feel both FBI men now boring looks into the twin .50-caliber Desert Eagle Magnums he was openly sporting, and with the SPAS-12 autoshotgun stretched out at his feet he was sure it was all they could do to keep from asking questions about who they really were. Plus, he was reasonably certain they would like nothing better than to unzip one of the two nylon body bags within Schwarz's reach. Soon enough, they'd see just what the three of them were all about.

"You know what really bugs me?" Lyons suddenly rasped.

"Uh-oh," Blancanales muttered, with Schwarz throwing in a loud groan.

"These guys are little more than pigs and jackals and plain insufferable jackasses, and are the worst of criminal scum, without the first shred of character, without the first scintilla of heart and guts and balls. No halfway decent-looking woman in her right mind would look even the first time at if they didn't have cash enough to buy them their every little whim of the day. The boats, the mansions, the furs, the money. Take all that away and you have a walking bag of punk-loser those women down there wouldn't let drink their bathwater."

"Whoa," Schwarz said. "I thought you said you weren't—"

"Shuddup."

"Maybe God in His Infinite Wisdom denied you all your heart's sick desires and burning lust to spare you from eternal ruin."

Lyons slowly turned and looked at Jomanski. The guy was serious, but Lyons had to wonder if maybe the guy wasn't on to something.

"So, what's the plan?" Myers asked in a voice that fairly demanded to know the play.

"I'm thinking," Lyons said, his eyes drawn back to the motor pool. "It's going to be, what? Maybe an hour, ninety minutes before those Russians get here?"

"Around that," Jomanski answered.

"Okay," Lyons said. "I figure let them get settled in, pop a few drinks, do some glad-handing with the hyenas, but more like a whole bunch of grab-assing with the poolside talent, I'm sure. By then, the sun will be down."

Jomanski gritted his teeth. "But, what are you going to do?"

Lyons was wondering about that himself, then the lightbulb flashed on in his mind. Why didn't he think of this before? he wondered, then turned and smiled at the agents. "What's this, you ask, O, ye of little patience? Why, I'm going to walk right up to the front door and arrest the dirty SOBs. Serbs, Russians, UN scoundrels, the hired help and anybody else I don't like the looks of. What do you think of that?"

CHAPTER TWENTY-ONE

The big lights swept the sea of frozen tundra, and for the life of him, T. J. Hawkins couldn't tell from which direction. At first they appeared like giant hovering stars, he thought, or maybe small dirigibles of fire, floating, it looked, toward their tanker truck convoy, and from some great way yonder to the east, splitting the vortex of snow as if...

Hold on, soldier, he warned himself. Zero hour was at hand, but there was no sense in getting carried away. Sure, the old nerves were talking to him now—precombat jitters, all but perfectly understandable—but what was this invading nonsense of the mind? Why was his imagination all aflame, a distant voice whispering to him that what he maybe saw was a swarm of UFOs descending on what was certainly some of the most remote and desolate stretch of Earth and which he figured not even the worst of criminals should be exiled to.

Hawkins shrugged off the bizarre balls of light. They had to be beams that were hung, he figured, from slender poles invisible to the naked eye, the mere sight wishing to infiltrate all reason with wandering figments of his imagination, but fairly certain that was the intent and purpose to start with.

A deep breath, and the Phoenix Force commando looked into the sideview mirror. The load—or so they were told—was a special rocket propellant—liquid hydrogen, oxygen and a nitrogen compound, supposedly, and he was no rocket scientist but that sure sounded like a strange and volatile brew—and which, worse, was primed with plastique to blow in the event Rushti needed to seize back the edge under what he claimed would be certain opposition fire. Behind his rig, four more mammoth tankers—likewise juiced with an even hundred pounds of plastique—chugged along on what was the only paved road for about a hundred miles through snow-drenched endless steppe, McCarter and his other teammates claiming shotgun seats, with Czars as wheelmen.

Hawkins glanced over at his own driver. He knew the big man in black only as Fyodor D. Since landing at yet another clandestine base about sixty miles due east of Zenith, his Russian black ops counterpart hadn't said the first word, his AK-47 canted against the seat, muzzle up. The ex-Ranger, likewise keeping his own assault rifle within lightning pickup and resting on the seat between them, figured the Czar's stony silence was just part and parcel of what he was sure would be a mission that may well thrust all of them to the brink of extinction. If that happened, he could just see the world headlines screaming about rogue U.S. commandos invading friendly Mother Russia and—

Belay all that rubbish. If they were dead nothing else mattered.

Speaking of jumping into the frying pan, Hawkins figured the way it was all laid out smacked of hidden agendas, despite Rushti's tirade that was meant, he was sure, to win them over with confidence bolstered fat enough they were all certain to pledge undying loyalty, no matter what the odds, the crazy scheme, the skeletons in whoever's closet. Hawkins was positive he could speak for the rest of his teammates regarding the surgical strike and heist of the thermo nukes, considering they'd spent a long session covering the merits of watching their own asses. What they wanted were answers and solid facts on adversary numbers, key enemy players, from Russian personnel down to alleged Muslim terrorists.

What they would like to know was how four nukes, each with a yield of five megatons, could be so carelessly managed that they were suspected of even right then being loaded onto what was nothing short of the biggest flying bomb humankind had seen to date. In short, what they wanted was to wash their hands of this insanity, let the Czars go blasting into Zenith while they hung back on the sidelines and watched the Russians devour one another, then step in and settle the matter about the RLV and four thermo-nukes on their terms.

The facts of life in their world, though, were more often than not the simple but plain ugly truth, which was, by itself, hard to swallow. Especially when the wielders of such truth were faceless specters on the fringes of the shadows, and ever-ready to blast away with little or no warning. In other words, what they wanted was not what they would get, that much the five of them could bank on.

Again, Hawkins knew he could speak for the others as he determined he would be prepared for the worst-case setup.

The weapons they carried had been delivered by Rushti. Under his loose-fitting black-leather trench-coat, Hawkins toted what the head Czar called a Tokarev Bear submachine pistol. It resembled an American Beretta 93-R, complete with foregrip, 20-round magazine with 9 mm Parabellum rounds and selector mode for single and 3-shot auto. The assault rifles were basic AK-47s, but so clean and even freshly oiled Hawkins figured they had to have come straight from someone's untouched stash. Webbing and combat vests were fitted and slotted with a mixed assortment of flash-bang, incendiary and HE grenades and snugged around their body-armored torsos. Hawkins didn't need mental telepathy to know all of them clung to the hope there were plenty of spare clips and grenades to tackle come what may. Pros that they were, they had spent time enough to strip down, reassemble the small arms, test them back in Kazakhstan, along with lobbing a few grenades to determine—one—if they worked—two—their kill radius. The grenades looked like the standard Russian RGD-5, only bigger, which made perfect sense, each one being packed with 200 grams of TNT, nearly twice the payload of the normal defensive hand grenade for that part of the world.

How it all played out…

It remained to be seen. And, if it was true what waited at the end of this ride…

They materialized out of the near-blinding light and swirling snow, and Hawkins had to blink and refocus on the pair of illuminated shadows just to be sure that what he saw was men brandishing AK-74s and now stepping up to the windows.

Fyodor D. grunted he should roll down the window. Sticking to the plan, Hawkins produced his security clearance access card with magnetic ID strip. He hand-cranked the window down and held out his pass. The granite face inside the hooded-parka stared back at what became to Hawkins a long uncomfortable moment, before a black-gloved hand shot out and plucked it away. The sentry then used a small rectangular device to scan the card. A red light blinked, and Hawkins felt his heart lurch, wondering if that was menace hardening the face of the Russian guard. Apparently he was good to go, however, as the Russian handed him back the card, then stepped away to wave in the next rig in line, which would be McCarter and Rushti. Fyodor D. was a little heavy-handed on the clutch, grinding gears and jolting them ahead, Hawkins thinking he spotted a grin ghosting the black op's lips as he thrust a hand out and braced himself against the dashboard.

As they lumbered on at about 5 mph, the lights grew brighter. Hawkins squinted, unsettled by both the eerie brilliance of light that had no visible source and combat instincts that were razor-wired in his guts and twisting harder with each eternal second. McCarter, then James, were waved through next, he spotted, as Fyodor D. headed them for one of the two titanic white hangars.

Fyodor D. tapped brakes that squealed loud enough

to make Hawkins wonder about the last time they were checked, but he was grateful, just the same, that they were at the end of the line.

Or at least that the easy part was over.

Hawkins watched as Rushti parked a few yards behind them, then the ex-Ranger scanned the open ground of Zenith. Supposedly the closest hangar was where the RLV was either housed, or sitting on a massive hydraulic platform-ramp about fifty feet below ground—Rushti couldn't say which. The runway, Hawkins saw, was cleared of snow, as two giant plows chugged in toward the blind side of the hangar. What little snow now drifted down, Rushti had stated during his brief, would be melted away by a network of heating tubes built into the concrete, piped to the surface through vents, as Hawkins noted the steam rising off the runway. It made Hawkins wonder why the man had found it necessary to inform them of that fact. Was he covering a contingency for some dire emergency, and one that he was keeping to himself?

Hawkins heard about a dozen angry questions roiling in his mind when the earth about thirty yards out parted in a straight line. The beams of white light that speared through the widening fissure did little to calm the ex-Ranger's raw nerves, but he'd been told what to expect.

They were going below.

Into the belly of Zenith.

Fyodor D. ground the clutch and lurched the tanker ahead. His heart pounding like a jackhammer against his chest, Hawkins cracked his eyelids to mere slits against the glaring white veil, as the front end gently dipped down onto the ramp and they began to descend.

THE CZARS WERE COMING, but Major General Vasily Zamil decided they may well yet fit perfectly into the big picture.

The GRU Zenith base commander had been fearing their arrival anyway since his private countdown began thirty-four hours earlier, aware of the rumblings of treason reaching the ears of his GRU superiors in Moscow, but all of whom were, like himself, along for the same rocket ride, so to speak. Confirmation of a Czar encounter had become reality—and just as the hydraulic crane was loading the payload into the weapons bay—as he was informed the dreaded black ops had finally landed at Zenith Two, and were en route to Zenith One.

And that accelerated his own plans, complicating last-minute details.

No problem.

It had been a huge roll of the dice from the very beginning anyway, so why not step up to the table for the big gamble sooner than expected?

Zamil weighed the good news first, such as it was. As he watched the last of the thirty-foot-long missiles slowly extended through the hatch by the robotic arm, he ran an admiring eye down the length of the triple-decker 122-foot Delta-winged orbiter. Coated in black ferrite paint—with the latest in advanced stealth technology that was also stolen from the Americans through the cadre of gangster-groomed ESA operatives—its streamlined shape would be rendered virtually invisible to radar. That invisibility factor came complete with state-of-the-art blackout technology. The way he understood it, EMP could be hurled out while the space plane was in flight, the LOS—or loss of radio signal—simulated much like when the space shuttle reentered through the atmosphere, hammered as it was by shock waves, ionization, G-force. Supposedly, the screen was good for a ten- to twelve-mile window, and he knew the crew had already factored in the advanced navigational charting for the on-board computer avionics that would allow the safest and most arrow-straight line over international shipping lanes, steering clear of known U.S. and Russian military bases.

Second, and more important to mission parameters, it would be a horizontal takeoff—no elaborate checklist, either, to run down from the flight deck and through mission control—then a straight flight, using four of the new Starfire 1 after-burning turbofans to power the craft. The mobile launch platform, he saw, could remain right where it was in the far corner of the hangar, along with the two dead bodies of those soldiers not on his payroll and who had just attempted to question his authority when the nuclear rockets were removed from their vault.

As for the RLV's—main engines and solid rocket boosters, they weren't necessary for the purposes of his paymasters, nor would a seven-man crew be needed to carry out the mission. Space shuttles—any spacecraft for that matter, he knew—required a velocity of at least 17,500 mph to achieve low earth orbit, which meant thrust enough provided by liquid oxygen and liquid hydrogen to overcome their own weight, but the RLV was still several months away from fitting what would be reusable main engines and solid rocket boosters.

Besides, the four-man crew—commander, pilot, mission and payload specialists—would be going nowhere near a low earth orbit. In reality the craft was no more, no less, than a cutting-edge supersonic long-range bomber with all the high-tech trimmings and that only looked like a space shuttle.

All this in mind, he briefly recalled how he wanted to find some flaws initially with their plan, wishing to inform them it might be easier to use even scaled-down, solid-and-liquid propellant rockets where they could streak directly over the North Pole at supersonic speeds that could reach plus Mach 10, then…

Oh, well. He hadn't been paid, he knew, to quibble over their operational procedures. If it was martyrdom they sought, then that was their madness to contend with.

He had his own role to fulfill. He was in charge of mission control directly, and responsible indirectly for the special maintenance-engineer crew he had infiltrated into Zenith as of yesterday.

Zamil gave the final touch of the American flag on the fuselage an approving eye. It might not pass close inspection by a few American fighter jets, but by the time anybody figured out what was going on, what with the RLV's top speed of Mach 5, and with radar jamming and loss of radio signal activated for most of the flight…

It would be far too late in the game.

A check of his watch, striding for the elevator, and he plucked the handheld radio with secured frequency off his belt.

Zamil warned himself to not focus on the bad news,

but according to his chief of security, the Czars were already descending RampStar One. He knew he could have killed them where they sat in their vehicles—the flimsy ruse one of his men in Kazakhstan had alerted him to where they would truck in rocket fuel from Zenith Two—but ultimate success in battle nearly always resulted from swift and certain improvisation of tactics. Besides, their brazen approach signaled him the Czars suspected what was already in progress, and had come to fight. That, he determined, would work to his further advantage. With the Czar payloads, combined with his own rebel force now mining the aircraft in Zero Sector, the resulting conflagration would create two safety valves for himself.

One—mission control would have to flee into subzero safety uptop, allowing *Starfire* to roll out of the hangar, lift off, on its way then, with his own people to monitor incoming radio transmissions, work on screening its flight path from two military bases en route before it flew over the Sea of Okhotsk. Then it was out of his hands. Two—there would be no way to positively identify what would be vaporized puddles of goo left behind from the massive holocaust. By the time anyone from Moscow or the Czars, assuming there were any of the black ops left standing, figured it out, he would be sitting in Iran, collecting the other half of his ten-million-U.S.-dollar fee.

Zamil looked over his shoulder as they motored the ramp up to the open crew hatch. He slipped his access card into the magnetic slot of the service elevator, looked at his watch again. The four-man crew was in the process of locking in the last of the access codes for the avionics to their laptops, he knew, but it was time for them to leave their quarters, and board *Starfire*.

Takeoff minus now.

That was the go signal, and Zamil depressed the button on his tactical radio unit to let all hands know it was down to the dirty business of sabotage and mass murder.

As ZEKTI UVARDUZ DUMPED the twenty-five-pound nylon satchel onto the deck of the helicopter, reached inside and thumbed on the radio-remote signal, he stole a few moments to wonder about this madness he found himself submerged in. Two more Russian soldiers were now down and twitching out from sound-suppressed 9 mm rounds cored through their brains by his Makarov pistol, the AKM snug around his shoulder but ready to fill his hands in a moment's notice. The Chechen rebel knew—and heard the brief shouts and muffled chugs—that the other eighteen "engineers" were hard at it, rolling the large handcarts down the rows of aircraft, dropping Russian soldiers on the move when and where necessary, planting the loads of plastique into every other flying machine or tank.

How did this all come to pass? he briefly wondered, then allowed himself a grim chuckle. Well, he had been rotting—between beatings and electric shock to various parts of his anatomy while hanging, naked, upside down—in a prison in Dagestan, captured by an enemy he had soon, incredibly enough, joined in what would have previously been in his mind the most unholy of alliances. Yes, Colonel Shistoi's paid Russian contacts had been the reason he'd been freed, a list of charges that included murder, drug trafficking and rape to be expunged from a record that he had been sure would have been hung over his head during extradition to Moscow, where he would have been promptly marched—without any semblance of a fair trial—into a room and shot once in the back of the head. Shistoi, as it turned out, had his own strange collusion with a few Russians who were tied, in turn, to gangsters in Moscow. The Dagestani colonel had offered him a large sum of money and as many small arms of his choice, but when he'd outlined what most Chechen Muslims would view as the jihad opportunity of a lifetime, he had…

Well, he had thought it over. After all, he was being asked to place his life in the hands of the enemy who, it seemed, wanted the total destruction of a covert space base in Siberia, and what was to say the Russians wouldn't just kill him when he had completed his own task? In the end, Shistoi had left him with one of two choices. Fight, or go back to prison.

Some choice.

So there he was, one of a large fighting force of Muslim rebels from the lower republics, three or four from Iran, and who were now all cut loose by the pig-faced Russian who had slipped them onto the base.

Now for the end game.

What little he knew, though, on that matter was that his role in attacking the base had to do with the hijacking of a prototype space shuttle, which, he'd heard, was aboveground in one of the hangars. Perhaps to play on his own hatred of all things Russian, but Shistoi had implied that Muslim fighter pilots had been handpicked and specifically trained in a remote camp in Dagestan and solely for this mission. That alone made him wonder what more he could do to help them safely commandeer the shuttle. Did they intend to fly the space shuttle into the heart of Moscow? Plow it into the Kremlin? An overseas flight, perhaps, to strike at America? Was there some special ordnance aboard the space plane that was meant to wreak mass death and destruction, create a panic through the entire country that would see the authority of their hated enemies undermined?

The cosmonauts, or whatever they were called, he thought. They were the key. And he needed to find his way to that hangar. Besides, he wasn't looking to be incinerated by enough combined explosive power and subsequent blast waves where he couldn't see where one square yard of the immense vaulted airfield would not be seared and slammed to hellish obliteration. What with all the fuel trucks, rockets and small arms that would be cooked off in the fireballs…

A sudden change of plans certainly looked to be in order.

He was marching, swift and grim, pistol up and fanning for fresh enemy targets, whipping next around the tail end of the transport bird, when he found he was just in time to latch on to his ticket to Plan B.

Four men in black pressure suits emerged, single file, from a narrow steel door to the northeast, just beyond a ring of Hind-24 and Hokum helicopter gunships. Uvarduz noted the large black bags they carried, then smiled when he inspected them further.

How many cosmonauts, he thought, toted AKMs to board a space plane?

FRANJO BALAYKO HEARD the screaming madness brew like a bubbling caldron in the darkest cavities of his mind. As he listened to their bitter complaints he knew the lid on his rage was perhaps a few more bleating gripes from being blown off, and where they would be doused with the verbal venom of ten thousand-plus spitting cobras. Grateful, then, he had chosen not to arm himself for this gathering, he built another whiskey and water, only this round switched to a tall iced-tea glass and went easy on the ice.

From behind the white-marble bar trimmed in South African gold, he barked at the last of the scantily clad servant girls to leave the study and not come back unless ordered. The moment demanded all of their—and his—utmost concentration. Even still, he noted all six of the high-ranking aides to the UN General Assembly allow their gazes an extra few moments to linger on the women until two of his soldiers closed the floor-to-ceiling cedar doors behind them. Ah, but it seemed his special burden these days was to suffer spineless fools and pampered buffoons. However much he detested the UN lackeys, the three representatives of the European Space Agency were among the most agitated, and who—judging the sideways glances they threw at the late-arriving Russian party on the far side of the opposite couch—believed themselves too good to soil their image in the presence of such vile notoriety.

Bah! As if they weren't already made unclean, he thought, by their own hands, so deeply immersed in the sordid filth of their own greed and malice he judged them the worst of hypocrites.

But they were jackals, he knew, that needed close watching, and by lions, such as himself and the Russians.

Balayko drank deeply, then used a gold-plated lighter and torched a cigar. Puffing out gentle waves, he let them smoke, drink, stew in their own simmering anger and confusion, as he wandered a long narrowed gaze over the pack of hyenas then down the pride of Russians before he looked around the study. The room was, indeed, enormous, but he decided no amount of immense space and lavish setting could either contain their swollen egos or satisfy their grotesque vanity. These were truly some ugly, wicked men. They wore tailored suits made of the finest silk, shoes that were hand-tooled in Italian leather. They splashed their soft, flabby, unmortified flesh with obscenely expensive perfume made from scratch and on someone else's tab from the most famous stores in Paris. They drank only the best wine and liquor and consumed the richest, most sumptuous meals, craving only pleasure and instant gratification, as if the entire world owed them. Inside these bejeweled costumes of worldliness, he knew they were seething vats of shameless iniquity, and which he knew they did everything in their power to hide from the world as they whimpered on in quaking fear like the true cowards they really were.

Despicable.

On the other hand, he knew and accepted what he was—a greedy gangster who would seize upon any opportunity to make more money, which he didn't need to begin with, but wanted more of, and of everything he could consume in life before he died.

The hyenas, on the other hand—with the exception, of course, of Vladimir Yoravky and his lions—slithered and crawled about the earth like the vilest of worms, demanding like the most spoiled of children their fat cut of all the action while others took all the risk, did all the killing. In short, physically engineered on their behalf all of their ambitions they dreamed and schemed but wouldn't lift one manicured finger to plunge into the real dirty work that was necessary to build and maintain their shadow empire. Worst of all, men like these could be the most dangerous and cunning of animals when crisis arose, seeking their own safety nets, pointing fingers of blame and outrage elsewhere, the first to bail for the life rafts when the ship looked to be sinking.

Deplorable madmen! Detestable weaklings!

Admittedly, there was a crisis, but Balayko decided it was at just such times as this where reward—or punishment—was meted out by the fruits of each man's labor, and according to the lifelong habits of individual character that, in reality, walked Everyman to his ultimate destiny.

The German UN attaché, Pieter Grolerner, raised his voice yet another decibel, as he once again restated the obvious. Balayko winced at both his tone and the first words out of his mouth, thinking the man should be ashamed to call himself a German, and of warlike stock, no less. Or perhaps, like two of the three ESA cutouts from his country, he was merely looking at what he considered the new post-WWII German.

"We have heard about your problems in the country of what was to be our principal supplier. We warned you, did we not, about dealing with the extremist rabble to begin with! Now, we understand, our two key men in that horrid little country have up and disappeared. You are making deals within deals, going outside our original plan! I told my associates, and only days ago, we must wash our hands of any dealings with extremists who cannot be trusted, unless someone has them on a tight leash and within arm's reach! I could just scream over the liberties you have taken and at our expense!"

The Frenchman, Jacques Zafreu, picked up the whine ball. "He is correct! The tempestuous madness of what appears an endeavor in that wretched country, all but crushed now by an undetermined force, could very well jeopardize our own proposed mission for our United Nations Relief Sudan venture!"

Fellow Frenchman, Pierre Mambouti, a Camaroonian ex-patriot with suspicions of connections to his former country's heroin trade, jumped on the bandwagon. His normally bass voice of thunder was cut by more than half as the squealing note crackled in. "We are at great risk, and we can find no answers as to who may think they knew something about our operations in that abysmal little republic! We have faceless enemies, and we fear they are on the march and in our direction. And should we even proceed with a new contract through PetroBal, who is to say the same will not happen in the Sudan? A complete unraveling of all our hopes for a new source of oil!"

Jean-Claude Vries of Belgium chirped up. "And it was never our intention to become so deeply mired in some top-secret affair with the European Space Agency, I might add!"

"And what about our negotiations?"

Dead silence fell over the UN hyenas, as Balayko followed their nervous stares toward Yoravky. Yoravky, like himself, had plenty of blood on his hands, and wasn't opposed to sudden violence. Silently, Balayko urged him on to put these weaklings in their place.

The Russian boss filled his glass with more vodka, sipped, then leaned all the way back on the couch, crossing one leg over the other. "I have been supplying oil and gas from Siberia to your friends in Eastern Europe for three years now, and so that you and your comrades may enjoy the high life. I am wondering. Should some unforeseen circumstances befall myself, or Comrade Balayko, will you, then, run for cover like frightened children? Will you, then, wash your hands of me? Perhaps deny me altogether?"

Balayko felt the smile tug at the corner of his lips as he watched the UN flunkies squirm, glancing at one another, as if imploring the other guy to be the one to dare answer the big man first.

"Well?" Yoravky suddenly stormed. "Answer me!"

One of the ESA Germans, Schultz, cleared his throat. "If I may."

"By all means," the Russian boss said. "One of you show some spine before I become very angry."

"Our business together," Schultz said, "that was before separate and apart has now become entwined, mutual. And more dangerous. Technology and intelligence that we have passed on to both yourself and Herr Balayko has perhaps been discovered due to reports I have received about the destruction of the Zenith base in America. Operatives I had spent some time grooming—and at considerable expense and risk to myself and my comrades—have not reported in. There is suddenly too much mystery and too much disaster at every turn. And it makes me—and I sense I am speaking for the rest—very nervous."

"Is that a fact?" Balayko had heard enough. He stepped away from the bar, and blew a cloud of smoke, thick enough to drop a charging rhino, in the faces of the hyenas. "Listen to yourselves. You want reward and glory, but you are unwilling to struggle when the going gets tough. You have had it so easy and so comfortable for so long that you have lost any notion of what it is to be a man. To win the race, you must persevere, you must fight the giants. And even the ones who are not presently visible and causing you so much distress."

"Trust you?" Grolerner remarked. "Is that what you are telling us? That everything will be fine if we simply carry on?"

Balayko ran his scathing eye down the pack. "Let us be clear. Because of my connections in Dagestan and with Comrade Yoravky you have become rich men, which you would have never become on your own. You live like princes, your every whim and wish fulfilled at the snap of your fingers. Now that the moment demands some firm resolve, iron commitment, you come here, drink my wine, eat my food, use my whores, then have the gall to cry to me that one of us," he said, pointing at Yoravky with his cigar, "is letting you down, is not protecting your own kingdoms as you wish." He smoked, letting them cringe under his words. He was on a roll, feeling good, strong, when suddenly he found Zvit nearly running his way from the door. His lieutenant was holding the handheld radio to his face with knuckles so white, Balayko thought he would mash the instrument in his grasp.

"What?"

"There is a man out front…"

Balayko sensed the panic and fear rising like heat from a sauna around the room as he nearly shouted at Zvit when his lieutenant hesitated, "What man?"

"He is armed like some commando, and he is demanding we surrender for arrest."

"In the driveway?" Balayko bellowed, his lieutenant confirming as much, but he was already charging for the curtained windows at the far west corner. "One man?" He hurled the question over his shoulder as he saw the crush of bodies piling on in his wake, Yoravky and his soldiers producing pistols from inside their jackets. "Did he identify himself?" Balayko snarled at his lieutenant.

"He said he is Special Agent Frank Lemon from the United States Department of Justice."

As Balayko looked down at the motor pool, he saw a big man standing tall and ramrod-stiff in the outer sheen of the nightlights. He was wielding a massive autoshotgun, and weighted down in combat webbing that was hung with spare clips, grenades. Further, there was an HK subgun hung around his shoulder and what looked to be two very big stainless-steel handguns in shoulder rigging. Works enough, all around, Balayko thought, to turn himself into a one-man wrecking crew.

They were babbling in his ears, firing off their hysterical questions, two of the UN men bleating how they needed to get off the property when Balayko suddenly heard Zvit tell him, "Oh. And he told me we had thirty seconds to walk out front with our hands up. All of us."

Balayko gritted his teeth. Of all the impudence! Whoever it was—and he had friends in very high places of authority—he would know pain, disgrace, humiliation, American lawman or not. This was the lowest form of disrespect, albeit brazen, and...

The bedlam of panic then seemed to only further inflame Balayko's rage and fear, just as a worm of doubt began to creep into his own malice of heart. There might be something, after all, to this stranger showing up on his property, armed and making demands, perhaps even more to dread than...

He was about to throw open the window, when the big guy glanced at his watch, then looked up, raising the shotgun. There was a crazy look in those eyes, Balayko determined, as if the guy was committed to some wild-ass rampage, already knew, coming in, what he was all about and what he was going to do.

"That was about a good twenty or so seconds..."

And Zvit's warning was lost by the peal of thunder.

Balayko roared and hit the deck as the window was blasted out over his head in a wave of flying glass.

CHAPTER TWENTY-TWO

When they finally rolled out onto level ground, David McCarter's eyes adjusted back to near normal from the dazzling shock effect of what he could only think of as brilliant man-made starlight, but with no visible source of illumination. He began scanning the vast acreage of the walled-and-ceilinged airfield, and was momentarily shocked. The few available photos and word by way of Rushti's mouth proved a monstrous injustice to the stark reality.

First, McCarter couldn't dare begin to tally all the jumble of helicopter gunships and transports, the numerous tight groupings of T-72 tanks, BMP fighting vehicles, ZSU-23-4 batteries on mechanized platforms, the scattered dozen or more gargantuan twenty-four-wheeled fuel trucks. With this whole armada of hardware parked up and down near the north and west walls, the Phoenix Force leader was left wondering just how many Russian soldiers were actually on base, and how many pledged their dying breath to the Zenith commander? Forget Rushti, the man couldn't say if it was ten or a thousand guns ready to be unleashed on the lot of them. Going in—and blinded by the light, so to speak—wasn't the way McCarter would have normally handled such a precise, surgical undertaking, and what was intended to be a straight heist of a supertech space plane, under conditions of which he was virtually clueless.

Second on the list of X factors, they were all of three hundred feet, maybe more, below ground, all but sealed now inside a vault with walls so white—well, he couldn't tell the Alpha from the Omega. By bloody Mother infernal Russia! It was as if the halo of light was meant to keep any foot patrol plodding on, and getting nowhere fast, and as if the very expanse of it all was, indeed, stretching off into infinity, calling all armed souls to the nowhere of this white oblivion. Bottom line, though, they were stuck now, and forced to follow through with their quasi-defined role to seize the RLV.

McCarter spotted the commotion near the distant east edge of helicopter gunships, the flaming nozzles of assault rifles casting Russian soldiers to the ground in a flourish of twitching limbs and sharp cries of pain that were all but swallowed up into the seemingly eternal blinding shroud. Whatever answers he was searching for—well, the uncertain task he'd committed the team to was right then in the process of bringing the whole damn ugly truth, and blasting away right to their convoy.

And what was that business Rushti had remarked about timing? McCarter wondered, barreling out the door as the Czar braked the volatile behemoth to a sudden halt and shouldered his way out the other side, armed and as angry as a Stalin-enraged counterattack on the capital seat. Was all this a mere bloody coincidence? A clever plan? Duped into doing the black op's sordid bidding? Perfect timing, and on whose behalf?

Why worry now? he decided. In short order, brutal decisive action would reveal whatever the hydra.

The Phoenix Force leader found his commandos likewise streaking off the bench, to a man bounding from the cabs now, boots thudding down onto concrete and AK-47s up and tracking the enemy. Rushti was bulling out in front of the cab, McCarter next, spying more bullet-riddled bodies dumped to the deck down the line. Then he glimpsed a bulky package hurled into the belly of a Hokum by a hardman in the east vector.

Whoa!

Oh, but these raging mad marauders! Unless McCarter missed his guess, they were going to blow every piece of flying machine and tracked vehicle to flaming comets. And the enemy—maybe fifteen or so strong—was suddenly charging for what McCarter had been told was the sealed access door to the tunnel that would lead to mission control.

Which meant everyone's time was running out. Radio remote detonation or timed or...

Return fire began slashing the air, slugs whining off the concrete in a flurry of sparks and stone shrapnel just beyond the danger zone of the hard-charging Hawkins and James. The opposition hardforce, McCarter found, was suddenly bunching up while others shouted warnings to their brethren to the lightning arrival of the new combatants.

It was all ready to fly off the axis in a holocaust, and McCarter ordered his troops to advance for the tunnel door but leapfrog by way of cover, using the line of transports staggered down the south edge and head east. Little question they needed immediate and certain protection behind those steel barricades, but any measure of safe haven now seemed to the Stony Man warrior like an expanding universe none of them would ever see the end of.

"Get to the hangar!" Rushti shouted at McCarter, holding back on the trigger of his assault rifle, his line of tracking fire producing sparks that leaped off the hull of a chopper as four or five of their adversaries braked for cover behind that gunship, AKMs and AK-74s reaching around to pound out the firelit winking tempests of searing lead.

"Rufino! G-Man and Sea Wolf!" McCarter said as he fell in beside Hawkins on the backside of the closest vehicle, steel-jacketed hailstones drumming into the far door, canvas shredded above and just behind his six by the searching torrent of autofire. "Take that tunnel and secure mission control. T.J., you and me are going for the brass ring up top! Sea Wolf, give T.J. that sat link, just in case I need to phone home!" he told James, who slipped the nylon bag off his shoulder and handed it to the ex-Ranger. All of them were tied in with com links, backup tactical radios hooked on their belts, but no way would McCarter get caught short on his end as far as communication went. No, sir, not the way in which this particular Chinese fire drill was coming unraveled, and none of them, McCarter knew, could stay put but for a few moments longer. Any number of wild rounds, an RPG warhead plowing into their rocket fuel-plastique-mined convoy, and they would be turned into vapor and before they were even off the starting block.

"Ruf! Drop a couple of fifty-mil hellos into that rat pack!"

"I'm all over it, Commander!"

"I want you to get to Hangar A and secure that shuttle as we discussed!" Rushti roared over his shoulder at Phoenix Force, veering north and west to lead his Czars on vector where it looked as if he lived in hope to outflank the marauders.

As McCarter gauged the distance to the access door that led to the bank of elevators, Encizo dropped to a knee at the front bumper of the transport truck.

There!

One of the marauders, McCarter spotted, was bursting through the door in question, apparently abandoning his fighting brethren as he went in search of...

The shuttle!

Rearguard, McCarter wondered, or some loose cannon seeking his own safety net?

McCarter intended to find out.

The Phoenix Force leader looked toward Encizo, the tempests of scorching lead flying back and forth, walls and floor raked with sparking fingers and puked by ragged divots. He was hoping the tide was about to be turned in their favor by a quick 50 mm shellacking on the hardforce.

The Cuban warrior was bringing up the Steamroller

when the shrill and invisible knives of a doomsday Klaxon exploded in the air, signaling to McCarter that yet more hell was about to break loose.

SPECIAL AGENT TOM Bruce, aka Rosario Blancanales, figured his eagle's nest firepoint was as near perfect a component in the coming juggernaut in what was the most imperfect of battle strategies. But it was Ironman's call—and try telling their fearless leader it was the wrong one considering his state of hyperagitation and anger—thus it was their game to win or lose.

More often than not, sheer brazen, in Blancanales's combat experience, was enough to see Lady Luck give her nod of approval, if only in admiration for the pure audacity of the warrior spirit.

That would be Carl Lyons. Sneak up on the front gate, cold-cock the guard to then be cuffed and stuffed. Walk right up to the front door next, like a one-man army of Huns, announce himself and proclaim his intentions to the bad guys, then see what they were made of.

And Lyons had just signaled his own personal enemy contact, as the rolling thunder of the SPAS-12 washed up the cliffs and rang in the Able Team commando's ears.

Time to take the stage, and he was no bit player in the drama unfolding.

Blancanales gave the lay of the land another quick scouting, just the same, his opening act taking shape as he took in the action. He was about fifty yards higher than the roofline, and he figured his roost was situated an equal distance on the west side as he was elevated. That put him at what he could only call the sweet zone. He had an open line of fire with Little Bulldozer, coupled with a hawk-eye's view of both Lyons on the edge of the motor pool as he did the party crowd poolside and on to the Mi-26.

Away with sweet; this was near picture perfect as anything Michelangelo's brilliant hand could create.

Talk about sweet, however, nightslights had turned the compound into a gleaming bastion where the revelry around the pool was quickly increasing in decibels as the booze flowed and more security personnel made their way into the litter of beauties. To a gunsel they were way too involved and distracted in all their babe-trolling and helping themselves to a nip or two from the bar. Oddly enough, no one was jumping at the sound of the shotgun blast. But Blancanales figured between the loud music and all that pursuit of drunken debauchery…

Wrong!

He saw two of the hardmen near one of the bars squawking into handheld radios, fists filling with machine pistols in the next instant, angry voices of gunmen shouting out orders for the rest to get it in gear. He didn't need a psychic to read the air of rising panic, as the hardforce started en rush for the back patio doors—

And just as he heard the blistering retorts of autofire from Lyons's direction. A thunderclap rent the night from near the front of the mansion next, and Blancanales glimpsed the smoke ball billowing up where he suspected Lyons was right then bulling his way into the foyer.

And thus his own cue to get busy.

Blancanales squeezed the trigger on his squat hand-held rocket launcher. No sooner was a 40 mm HE round streaking for the deep end of the motor pool, locked on, it looked, to a limousine the size of a small cabin cruiser than the Stony Man warrior turned his sights poolward. Shifting the weapon, he aimed for the center of the sprawling customized waterland, tapped the trigger and directed another HE bomb that was meant to let all players and wannabe playboys know the party was, indeed, over.

IT WAS GUT-CHECK TIME, but McCarter knew his troops were ready, come what may.

There was near-perfect decimation of the first large gaggle of mystery adversaries, as Encizo's Steamroller dropped down three, then four big 50 mm asteroids into the ring of Hinds and Hokums. Gunmen became like rockets launched off personal platforms, sailing away in their mangled bloody lift-off, little more than ground slabs of beef. From what little the ex-SAS commando glimpsed of what remained of all that human flotsam, one of those hellbombs was a buckshot round. That particular warhead was packed with razor-sharp steel balls, and if they didn't kill a man outright, he would wish for the mercy of quick death after the fact.

Able now to advance on a weaving but swift course down the front bumpers of the troop transports, McCarter held back on the trigger of his AK-47, adding to Hawkins's blistering salvo as other streams of autofire pitched in to scythe the howling enemy off their feet. As wreckage winged into the back wall and more bodies cartwheeled from the boiling smoke and dragon sprays of fire, McCarter kept the steel door that led to the hangar in the periphery of his vision.

As the deafening wail of the Klaxon kept spiking his brain, McCarter fanned his left wing with a smoking muzzle. Just in time, he spotted Rushti and comrades clamp lead pincers on a few rabbits bolting their direction, all but skewering four or five fanatics off their feet.

How many more hardmen, though, were zipping all over the compound like raving suicidal madmen? What else was mined? Which doors?

Rushing up to the access door, magnetic swipe card in one hand and Hawkins covering his rear, McCarter briefly thought how he hated to split up the team. There was a dark cloud, it seemed, that hung over his every thought, some mocking voice that didn't seem to be his own but invading his mind, nonetheless, warning him to proceed with great caution.

McCarter felt the door unlatch, lifted his assault rifle. One last look at his troops, as James used his own access card and parted the big doors to their own tunnel and what would prove—he hoped—an ultimate barricade to the coming conflagration, and the ex-SAS commando kicked the door open with a thundering bootheel. Clear, or so it looked.

It was a narrow corridor, he found, gleaming white, with three cars marked in red stars midway down.

Just as Rushti had told them.

Only what hadn't the black op...

Never mind, McCarter told himself, reswiping the access card to lock the door shut behind them, as Rushti had instructed.

Phantom trouble could wait, McCarter decided. He flashed Hawkins a grim look, then moved swiftly for the lone Red Star, assault up and searching for live and infernal enemy.

IT WAS ALL Franjo Balayko could do to still the finger around the trigger of the Uzi submachine gun he had moments ago hauled out from the hidden armory in the study. Naturally—other than the Russians and his own roaming wolfpack of seven shooters—the VIPs were in a raging snit, flailing around like headless chickens in the second-floor hallway, eyes bulged with blind panic as they grabbed the arms of their own armed security guards and began blistering their ears with orders. Balayko shook his head in disgust. Unbelievable. A little bump in the road, one lion on the prowl— though there could be more, he knew—and the hyenas were openly displaying their true colors of pure yellow.

No question there was murderous trouble aplenty, as Balayko, heading for the landing of the winding staircase, heard the resounding and repeated thunderclaps of that massive autoshotgun, pounding out doom from what sounded directly below in the foyer. And the madman had apparently hurled a grenade at the frontline guard before invading the hallowed halls of his palace! No United States FBI or Justice man he'd ever heard of would dare act in such a reckless and audacious manner, he could be sure of that. Unless, that was, the rules of engagement had further changed, and unbeknownst to even his UN contacts who were always railing, both private and public, about brutal United States special ops tactics against their enemy combatants and that they shouted out for the whole world to hear all but violated every standard and code of the Geneva Convention.

Oh, but the outrage now! This show of force was no more, no less in his mind than utter blasphemy!

And the wild man below would make full accounting and restitution in great agony and spilled blood.

"Vlad!" Balayko shouted at the Russian boss, behind whom several doors down the hall were flying open and spilling forth ladies of the evening, their shrieks and cries of panic only hurling more fuel into the fiery rage the Serb felt ready to blow in his brain. "I will get you and your people to your cars!"

A stuttering fusillade of subgun fire suddenly replaced the cannon peal, and sounded near in his ears. Balayko swiveled his head, just in time to find two of his soldiers diced across the chest, their Uzis blazing out impotent rounds that scorched divots in the ceiling as they began tumbling down the stairs. Oh, but who was this wild man? He was wondering how many more armed raging bulls were on the premises, when his ears were pricked by what sounded yet more utter pandemonium in the direction of the pool. Disaster from the north!

That settled any lingering question about more rampaging human rhinos.

He needed to get this situation under control, and fast.

Yoravky, a stubby machine pistol in his hands, raced up to Balayko who couldn't right then say he cared much for what he read as a look of accusation in his eyes. "And what about those cowards?" the Russian boss snarled, spittle flying off his lips as he gestured with his weapon down the hall.

Balayko turned and spotted the VIPs. They were in full and hysterical stampede down the opposite end of the corridor, the pack heading in the direction of what would be the tropical-vegetation wrapped stairs that led to the pool's east deck. From there, Balayko knew the spineless worms would dash straight for their helicopter, thus leave him—and Yoravky—to hold the bag, take the blame. Only several of them were suddenly taking note of whatever the chaos descending from their proposed flight path, shuddering this way and that, clawing at their hired guns to shove them ahead before they fell in behind their human shields.

"They're useless," Balayko told Yoravky. "We must handle this ourselves."

Yoravky nodded. There was new fire in his eyes, and Balayko could tell the old street soldier was ready to rumble out of the closet.

"And when we do," Yoravky said, "those gutless jackals who bailed will be held accountable and in the strictest terms."

Balayko smiled. "It is true, then. Great minds think alike."

"Is there another way to the drive?"

"Only if you wish to jump about twenty feet from the balcony or perhaps climb down the trellis. And if this wild man got past the gate by force, there could be a small army waiting for us."

"Comrade Balayko, I have faced down far worse odds in my life than a mere small army of lawmen. More to the point, I am of former KGB stock. I know something about fighting, and even to the edge of death, if need be."

"Indeed."

"In that case, I will follow you."

Balayko hesitated a moment. He couldn't help but wonder what really waited when they made the driveway. Yes, the local authorities were buried deep in his pocket, and which only served to further inflame his doubt and anxiety as to why—if this was a legitimate United States Department of Justice raid—he hadn't been warned, and well in advance, considering how much money he paid his personal eyes and ears. All that aside, it was too late now to back out from a plan he himself just suggested. To do otherwise would brand him a coward, no better than the UN and ESA jellyfish on two legs.

Steeling himself, Balayko cradled the Uzi tight to his chest, mentally rekindled the old warrior instincts and desire to shed blood. He shouted the orders, loud and angry, for three of his soldiers to stay behind and occupy the invader, then swept past Yoravky, barreling back into the study for their escape route.

VASILY ZAMIL FEARED the big picture was in danger of being shattered. Or was it simply time to improvise?

If so, then how?

His assault rifle curling out wisps of smoke, Zamil fed his AK-74 a fresh clip, as the last of the four technicians who refused to leave mission control toppled to the floor, their computer terminals reduced to sparking rubbish where a few hasty rounds had chased down one who had chosen to run at the last second.

Half of his force was split, as he watched a large group of those scientists and control techs who wished to voluntarily leave the sprawling command room herded by his troops into an elevator at the far north corner under scathing curses and rough shoves. Of course, the remainder of the workforce would be promptly executed, he knew, once they were up top, then those soldiers would roll their military executive jet, fueled and ready to fly for Iran, out of the other hangar. The five remaining soldiers under his employ were now striding to the monitors, their grim expressions speaking volumes for what Zamil himself felt.

And, no, the GRU major general didn't like what he saw, not in the least.

Zero Sector was under siege by the Czars, as what appeared to be the last of the Muslim rebels fell, thrashing under long sweeps of autofire. So much for his hired fanatic help that he'd gone through so much money and risk to bring here. He figured he could have done better if he'd marched out a peasant village of old drunken hags with pitchforks to tackle the marauding enemy. Worse still, two key doors had been breached by the invaders, which meant the Czar in charge had somehow gotten his hands on top security clearance cards, and which burned to his mind that someone in Moscow was either on to him, had squeezed information out of his GRU and SVR associates...

Cursing, Zamil wandered his gaze down the bank of monitors that watched the hangar, and the access corridors that led to both mission control and the elevator that was now taking two of the invaders to the hangar. Yet even worse, the flight crew was only now boarding the shuttle, with assisting personnel only now trudging the rest of their gear up the ramp. Then he spotted one of the Muslim rabble roll on-screen, the sight merely compounding his agitation and anxiety. There was a brief exchange between the soldiers, one of the crew and the rebel—which he couldn't hear— but the fanatic looked to be pleading his case about something. The coward, he thought, had abandoned his role, opting, unless he missed his guess, to either fly on with the crew, as visions of jihad spurred him on, or to stand by, weapon ready, to help make sure the RLV made it safely out of the hangar.

The situation was beyond desperate, Zamil sensed.

It was out of control, building to critical mass.

Zamil hit the intercom button that would boom his voice throughout the hangar. "One of you! Stop whatever you are doing and open those hangar doors!" One of them acknowledged the order with a wave of his assault rifle, then bounded down the ramp. "Look alive! All of you! Two armed men are now coming up in Red Star One!"

That, he saw, encouraged them to pick up the pace. Would there be enough time? Yes, it would take only a matter of seconds to fire up those engines, but with two marauders now climbing...

Zamil pulled the cell unit from his coat pocket, thumbed on the red light that would allow him to begin punching in the access signal. He had been hoping to hold off until he was up top, the shuttle, at the very worst, already rolling down the runway, and further, preferably with him aboard his jet and streaking on behind its exhaust fumes. Yes, the walls around Zero Sector and the access doors were reinforced concrete, double-layered in titanium. Yes, the underground complex was meant to withstand any blast just this side of a full megaton. Yet...

Zamil couldn't be sure what would happen if he unleashed all that explosive energy now. On top of his extensive minefield—what would be close to five thousand pounds of plastic explosive—the Czars had rolled in five massive tankers which, he knew, were all brimmed to capacity with rocket propellant. Visions of EMP knocking out critical instruments, the ceiling cracking open into a gaping fissure with the hangar floors caving, dropping the shuttle down in one horrific earthquake-like swallow became like screaming demons in his mind. Then there was the payload aboard the craft to consider, and with nuclear explosives there was never any telling...

But those commandos were coming his way, as he saw the last of the Czars racing for the tunnel mouth. They would be the closest to the conflagration. And it would still be a few more seconds before those doors were sealed shut. Oh, but he would have loved nothing more at the moment than to be able to manually override the computerized electronic system and force those doors to remain open. Two problems in that regard, he knew. One—all doors and elevators were tied in to the same override code, and for the express purposes of lockdown, which meant his own elevator to freedom would be paralyzed. Two—lockdown was computer coded for a full forty-eight hours, with no accessing to reverse the process once initiated. To do so required direct and on-the-spot intervention from Moscow, and only after a full and thorough investigation as to why lockdown was implemented in the first place.

Zamil knew what he had to do.

It was his only option. That was, if he wanted to try to crush the invaders before they came blitzing into mission control.

Slowly, he felt his hand raise the cell unit. Then a finger, slightly trembling, reached out and began tapping in the series of numbers.

CHAPTER TWENTY-THREE

Special Agent Tim Hope, aka Hermann Schwarz, made swift headway through narrow gaps between the azaleas, then bulled through the hedgerow. As he gathered in his bearings, took in the pandemonium up and down both sides of the pool, he found the party had all but cycloned into high chaotic gear, but he'd expected as much after Blancanales deposited two instant mood deflaters onto the grounds. Party girls were to a screaming beauty flooding en masse to find the nearest available exit, which appeared to be one of two sets of French doors beyond the white-marble barbecue pit, gray-slate patio and gold-trimmed gazebo. Only the ruckus of weapons chatter from inside saw several of the women simply dart around to find the nearest cover, other palace playmates skidding off the patio in midflight like swans that had just been hit by a shotgun blast. Whether it was beneath a lounge chair, behind the pseudo-beach bars, or in the bushes, as long he could find his own clear firezone he didn't care where they hid, scurried, shrieked.

He spotted the cannibal herd on the far side of the pool as it emerged, stumbling and hollering, from the palm fronds and other Jurassic-era plants that appeared to conceal a stairwell leading to the second floor. As he scanned their faces, noting their slick suits but now all disheveled to cheap knockoffs only a street bum would don, their hundred-dollar coifs fairly sticking up in the air like fried electrical wires, he recognized their pasty mugs from Big Jo Jomanski's so-called J Files. Leading the harried bunch of UN jackals and ESA shadow men was what Schwarz could clearly tell was their combined security force.

Call it fifteen guns.

And looking to make a fast getaway in the Mi-26 chopper.

Ordinarily, Schwarz might question the legitimacy of gunning down such men. But he was in no normal frame of mind. Besides, whatever respectable face they presented to the world needed to be ripped off, expose the hidden demon for what it was.

Corruption. Graft. Extortion. Blackmail.

Now, there were those, he briefly pondered, who would wink, grin, shrug—nay, raise a toast over such transgressions, and as just the cost of doing business, or simply getting on in the world. The plain wicked truth was that money meant to serve the greater good—the poor, the oppressed, the downtrodden who so desperately needed aid and comfort as was their just due as part of suffering humanity—was siphoned off and swelled their black coffers so they could, simply put, live high and fat and at the expense of the very masses of misery and poverty and starvation that depended on them, and if only to get through another day.

In the bitter final end, Schwarz knew—since no man was above reproach and exemption—it was neither his place to judge nor to grant them absolution.

It was his duty, however, to bring justice down on their heads, swift and certain, and to let them make the call as to how they would receive it.

He gave the back palace face another search, heard withering autofire from inside the walls, but knew better than to interrupt Lyons who was hopefully in full angry mop-up mode.

First the fleeing hyenas, then check in with Special Agent Lemon.

Quickly, Schwarz replaced the HE round with a buckshot load, cocked it into firing mode. They were gathering steam, he noted, now that they believed themselves in the home stretch. He gave them some lead, letting the spearhead of security goons in black tux put some distance to the hyenas, then aimed for impact on a fat palm tree just beyond the last bar where all looked clear of noncombatants. No sooner did he tap the trigger and send the warhead streaking on then Schwarz broke cover. He was running hard and fast for the north edge of the pool, the shooters spotting him and swinging Uzi submachine guns his way, when the blast brought them all to a dead or shrieking halt.

Schwarz went cold inside at the sound of men belting out the agony of being chewed to crimson tatters. Gathering momentum, smelling blood, he strode around the pool, assault rifle up and blazing as mangled hardmen clambered to their feet, blinded and with faces chewed off to the bone and screaming for mercy they didn't receive, much less deserve. At first sweeping pan, the bulk of the conspirators was either down and hollering for what sounded like yet more mercy or help, or froze in their tracks, suits shredded to homeless seersucker, but none of them looking nowhere near as hideous as their former security shield.

Schwarz tuned out the shrill cries, blanked out the women blurring all over the deck downrange as he hit the surviving goon squad with a long anvil of autofire, stern to stem and back up. Somewhere beyond the sight and sound of his rattling spray of death, he made out the whining rhythm of chopper blades, but concentrated his wrath on the jackals in front of him. They were staggered down the line in mixed poses of surrender, as they knelt, hands behind their heads, to a filthy worm blubbering for mercy, help, demanding to know who he was in a babble that only further stoked the Able Team commando's rising fury.

Disgusted, turning and finding the Justice Department Bell JetRanger dropping down on a clearing just beyond the north edge of the pool, Schwarz looked back at the human serpents, then bellowed out the order for all of them to get on their faces and put their hands behind their backs. Four complied, whimpering on and bleating outrage and indignation, just the same, then Schwarz drilled a kick into the chests of two kneelers looking a little too defiant for his liking and sent them flying onto their backs.

"Anybody moves, anybody even whines once more," Schwarz growled, and began digging the plastic cuffs out of the small nylon bag hung from his shoulder, "I will shoot you dead."

That abruptly shut down the posturing of protest and outrage.

As he swiftly moved down the unholy rabble, fastening the cuffs tight and none too gently, eliciting a few cries of pain and anger, he listened to that eerie silence that came from within the bowels of the palace, and that sent him clear signals to wrap up and put this pack behind.

Dead or alive, Lyons needed backup.

He sensed them first, then heard their chuckling filter out of the rotor wash. Pivoting, cracking home a fresh magazine into his assault rifle and arming the bolt, Schwarz pinned Jomanski and Myers with a steely eye.

Jomanski, sporting a lopsided grin, said, "I've got to say, we really enjoyed your opening act there, Agent Hope."

One of the UN ghouls was right then blubbering out questions. Schwarz lifted him off his feet by the hair, producing a short but loud effeminate squeal.

"Here," the Able Team warrior said, hurling the sorry UN sack at Myers, and with rocket-powered thrust. "We promised you guys a piece of the action," he quickly added as the UN guy barreled into Myers. "I've got to go."

Schwarz was off and running for the palace, and what he knew was the main act. Whether the curtain had dropped, the cold bloody sickle of the Grim One had hooked Lyons.

The electronics wizard heard a fresh burst of subgun fire from deep in the bowels of the main house, followed by an explosion from out front. He broke into a sprint.

"COME ON!"

A fresh batch of angry questions wanted to burst through Manning's mind. Why weren't there any Russian soldiers on hand to greet the convoy when they made their way to the underground facility? Unless, that was, they'd all been executed by the alleged Muslim raiders. If that was the case, then why wouldn't a whole battalion of fresh troops descend on the airfield and engage the attackers? Unless, that was, the remainder of the "legitimate" soldiers belonged to the Zenith base commander, or maybe he'd sent most of the troops off for sudden R & R. And was the coming big bang remote or time-delayed? If radio-signal remote, why the delay? He was certain they were being watched from mission control, which, according to Rushti, doubled as the main command and control room.

Not now!

As one of the Czars hollered again at their comrades on the main floor, the big Canadian figured somebody had to do something, and fast. The doors were two feet of solid steel, most likely titanium reinforced to withstand bunker busters, even the smaller nukes that would be those fission bombs classed at under one hundred kilotons, but maybe more. Point being, he knew once they slammed shut there would be no hope for Rushti and the wounded teammate he dragged along to make it to cover. Beyond that slim and fading hope, Rushti was winging back one-handed autofire at two, maybe three or more shooters they'd either missed en route or who had bulled onto the scene from out of God only knew where.

Manning didn't know how much explosive or exactly what type was planted and where around what he could only consider an underground and endless concrete steppe. But he had to accept McCarter and Rushti at their word that it was enough to turn all of them into a pile of smoking ash, unless they were hunkered down in the tunnel, doors sealed tight.

There was maybe ten feet left to lockdown, Manning saw, nine…

"Cover me!" Manning roared at the others as he surged between the narrowing gap and out onto the main floor, holding back on the trigger of his AK-47 in a wild spray and pray that was directed from his one down to five o'clock.

Ten feet or so out and braking, Manning spied his line of autofire sweep down over three ragged figures who were hobbling themselves from various injuries, dark crimson splotches trailing their mummy-like advance. Manning grabbed the wounded Russian by the shoulder.

This was it! How much…

With Rushti's angry assistance, with all the adrenaline searing through his own blood, Manning nearly lifted the downed Czar as if he weighed no more than a small bag of groceries and slung him through the closing fissure. And—

His eyes then felt as if they'd pop from his skull as the gap narrowed to three—two feet—and the faces and shouts of his own teammates and the Russians cleaved his senses.

As Rushti dived through the doors, Manning pumped his legs for all he was worth, the scream of rage and frustration locked in his throat. He twisted sideways, AK-47 aimed out front and arrow-straight to avoid getting snagged, and leading his bull-rush for safety. He was almost there—another two or three feet—the thought that at worst he would lose a foot, maybe half of one leg crushed or snapped off—

The arms shot out and through the dwindling space, hands like steel talons bunching up in viselike grips, clamping down on his left shoulder and bicep. The wide-eyed and grim faces of Encizo and James blurred by somewhere in the corners of his eyes and the heel of his boot snagged but tore free when the steel barricade thudded shut. The sonic booms of the big bang rent the air.

He was on his face, skidding forward on his belly, as the seismic tremors rippled across the white concrete beneath, the walls seeming to shudder with each monstrous thunderclap. The doors were then assaulted with such raging force from the first tempest of fire, blast waves and steel asteroids that Manning grunted against the invisible knives slashing deep into his eardrums.

The big Canadian clambered to his feet, upon willing some steel into legs that were shaky with adrenaline overdrive. As what sounded nothing less than the infinite legions of the damned banging to break down the gates of Hell, the barricade appearing to cave from one huge drumroll after the other, the first sign of one then two dents pounded into their barrier, Manning found James, the team medic, crouched over the wounded Russian. All the thick arterial blood still pumping out of the Czar's thigh, and with what appeared his entire torso soaked where a dark scarlet finger quickly tapered down, Manning knew it was over for that soldier.

Rushti echoed as much. "He's gone!" he told James in a loud voice, and which was amped up a few more decibels higher with bitter anger. "We have to leave him."

Manning met Rushti's stare, the black op nodding as he closed on the big Canadian. "You didn't have to do what you did. But I won't forget, in case I need to return the favor to any of you."

"What next?" Encizo rasped as James walked to take point and the Czars stretched out against the opposite wall.

Manning followed Rushti's dark stare. The tunnel was more of the same gleaming white, he found, three stories high and as much across, and it appeared to run on forever. What little intel the black op had either deigned them worthy to know about the main tunnel, or had bare bones working knowledge himself, the big Canadian couldn't say. For all they knew there could be hidden valves to release tear, sleeping or nerve gas. There could be trapdoors, concealed panels, a running host of unknown factors. He was sure he could speak for his teammates as the thought screamed at him he didn't care to bull into one blind alley after the other. But, here they were...

"Maybe fifty yards. You cannot see it from here, but there is a bend to our left. If the door to mission control is closed, then we blow it. If not... Are there any suggestions?"

"Oh, yeah. I have one right here," Encizo said, and hefted the Steamroller.

"Then you take point on the far side across from the main door. Let's go," Rushti ordered.

And Manning fell in behind the Czar as the hard charge broke out. As the tidal wave of blasts hammered on at his back, Manning brought his assault rifle up to bear when a figure appeared to materialize out of the stark white wall and cut loose with autofire.

THE FIRST OF THREE explosions tore through the leading end of the motor pool, and just when he was sure they were beginning to see light at the end of their escape hatch. Only a split second ago something cold and angry in his gut had warned Franjo Balayko their march to freedom had all looked and felt too easy and now…

Yet another triburst of fireballs ripped apart more limos, about midway down. In front of his horrified eyes, they split open, gutted scrap, like oversize but flimsy beer cans stuffed with firecrackers. As the Serb boss felt the last of fading hope deflate as if his spirit was a pin-stuck balloon, it was all he could do to keep from screaming in primal rage. Then the thought ghosted through his head that perhaps it was time to flee, to vanish into the night, to survive, at any and all costs, to wait for the smoke of battle here to clear, sort through the wreckage and the bodies, get some answers from various cutouts before making whatever his next move. Only that wouldn't work, he knew. Not now. How would that look to not only his own soldiers, but his Russian partners? Especially as he recalled what Yoravky had stated about calling in the markers of all who chose this time to abandon ship.

He was no UN coward, no ESA weakling, but even still…

Balayko, screams of agony and shouts of fury whipped away by the sonic peals of a big handgun, nosedived to the concrete, shielding his head with his arms. In the process, he tore a gaping hole in his knee and elbow, the Uzi jarred from his grasp, skittering ahead as he banged down, grateful, if nothing else, there was ample enough belly to cushion the hard landing. As he crabbed ahead and hauled in the Israeli submachine gun with a one-handed sweep, a wall of sudden and inexplicable rage dropped over his spirit.

And turned him into ice and steel.

This was beyond wrong, he decided, beyond injustice. This was shameful, to run like a dog who had just been kicked in the tail.

He was rich. He was powerful. He was a man of the world to be reckoned with—nay, for heads and knees to bend before him, no matter who they were, since his wealth had been spread, far and wide, to make sure just such a blasphemous disaster didn't befall him.

And they were dying, he knew, all over the drive, as he glimpsed mangled figures carom off limo doors or sail over the hoods of vehicles that cost more than most men in his country made per year, only then to bounce down and flop away, bloody mannequins.

Enough.

Whether the Wild Man or a small army, Franjo Balayko didn't care which. If he was doomed to die a violent death this night, then he would make the enemy pay in blood and agony, and he would make a personal accounting of the roaring lion he now envisioned himself as being.

He decided the peals of weapons fire resounded from some point near the front steps. He heaved himself to his feet, Uzi in hand, and swung that direction. Snarling a curse, he blasted away at the tall shadow that seemed to float like a swift wraith from his line of fire, and just in time to vanish from sight behind a shower of wreckage and what looked severed limbs.

It was the Wild Man, no question.

Balayko looked down the row of luxury vehicles, searching for the safest and quickest vector to intercept or outflank his berserker adversary. He factored in the broken line of Russian shooters, all of them in a big hurry to herd Yoravky for a vehicle farther away from the mayhem, and figured they could provide him some moving cover. Then he listened for a moment to his own people, shouting and shooting, crying out and most likely dying where they stood, but at this point, he knew it was every man for himself.

If that was the way it had to be…

This was a night, he decided, where the wheat would truly be separated from the chaff, the lion from the hyena.

Franjo Balayko went in search of his Wild Man trophy.

RAFAEL ENCIZO WANTED to drop another HE round into the billowing cloud where the two shooters had just been hurtled into mission control, but Manning caught his attention with a shout from across the corridor. As he nodded at his teammate and watched Manning pull the stainless-steel object and radio-remote unit out of a small satchel, he took a knee, James and the Russians bunching up behind him. All weapons were held, he found, rock-steady, on the main and what Rushti claimed was the only entry to mission control.

Beyond the gargantuan war drums that turned the tunnel into a thundering echo chamber, Encizo strained his ears. He thought he heard coughing and growled oaths from somewhere in the room, bodies crashing around, but he wasn't about to take anything for granted, illusion hurled his way by the sound and fury or not. Steamroller smoking and extended to unload on more hardmen, he glimpsed Rushti in the corner of his eye. The black op appeared fascinated as he observed the battery-operated object crawl at roughly four knots for the thinning veil of smoke. It was shaped like a scorpion, its main body roughly the size of a softball. Encizo knew the miniature robot was both camera and moving explosive. It carried a half-pound load of C-4, and with the videocam as its eye Manning was able to receive both live and thermal images on his handheld monitor. Equipped with its own sensors, it was able to chart its own course as long as it was on a fairly straight line, but to navigate corners, chairs and other objects— bodies and wreckage at that point, Encizo knew—required Manning's careful watch on the monitor, the big Canadian adjusting the dial when necessary to keep it moving and penetrating.

It vanished beneath the floating smoke tendrils, and three seconds later Manning called, "Hey."

The big Canadian showed four fingers, signaling the enemy was now moving for the deep northeast corner.

Encizo didn't catch what he said next, but the smile breaking over Rushti's face and his nod of approval told him what to expect.

"Everybody hold up," Rushti ordered.

Encizo began mentally counting up the seconds, a bone in his knee cracking as he stood. He thought of Gadgets Schwarz, the Able Team commando's fondness for and proficiency with high-tech equipment. The Able Team warrior may or may not find the utter destruction of such a precision piece of cutting edge tech tool a sorry waste of what was nothing less than a labor of love. Then again, under these circumstances, Encizo could be sure Schwarz would give his grudging nod albeit with less than peaceful resignation.

At eight seconds Encizo heard the thunderclap, followed by the angry howls of men in pain and shock hurtled out into the tunnel, and he went racing for the door.

CARL LYONS BANGED ON with double-fisted .50-caliber Magnum thunder. He was down to six, maybe seven live ones as he tagged another Russian with twin sledge-hammers to the chest. The custom 250-grain boattails launched the man a few feet back before he came down, sprawled, a bloody hood ornament atop a white Rolls-Royce, and spraying around a gory paint job.

Lyons advanced, moving off to his left wing as survivors began ducking and weaving from one vehicle to the next on the far driveway side. Adrenaline kept him light on his feet, despite the added burden of the sub-gun and SPAS-12 hung down each shoulder. That, and he had them on the ropes, mauled, bloodied and scared, but a wounded animal, he knew, could be the most dangerous of predators. Another star in the plus column; the firelight and the vast array of large night eyes spread down the horseshoe-shaped driveway lent Lyons a near-perfect view, where he could detect shadows on the move behind the vehicular barricade even though he couldn't see them.

Two shooters lunged up, Uzis flaming briefly before Lyons tapped the hand cannons, showering vacant air with a glass hurricane as they dropped out of sight.

Hits or misses?

Tracking with the hand cannons, Lyons thought the gunners were a little slower on the trigger than he had originally anticipated, which accounted for his initial success where he took out nine or ten hardmen just inside the palace doors. Tossing two grenades had certainly loaded the lethal dice in his heavy favor.

Time to wrap it up, he knew, as he caught a sudden glimpse of both Vladimir Yoravky and Franjo Balayko.

How sweet it was!

They were linking up about three more fabulous joyrides down the line, squawking something at each other, but they were armed and dangerous.

That was all Lyons needed to know. The only question left to be answered was whether they would go out with a roar or a whimper.

Lyons was betting on the lion.

CHAPTER TWENTY-FOUR

They made quick work of three of the four Zenith conspirators, and Calvin James left Rushti and his ops to finish what was a brief run and gun through the deep northeast quad of the sprawling control room.

James ignored the blistering autofire, the shouts and curses slashing the air, the sparks leaping in his face, the smoke belching from demolished computer consoles and clinging to his nose, but spared the litter of murdered technicians—maybe twenty-plus—another angry look. Judging from the expressions of shock and outrage they wore as death masks, they never knew what hit them, and most likely never dared suspect the base commander was nothing other than a treacherous viper.

The monitor that framed the action under way in the shuttle hangar grabbing his eye, the black ex-SEAL was one step ahead of Manning and Encizo as he halted in front of the bank of security screens. James felt the rising fury and grim concern, as the three of them watched McCarter and Hawkins leap-frog toward the shuttle's on-ramp ladder, their assault rifles blazing on the silent screen. A pall of smoke drifting over two bodies down and a dozen or so yards beyond the elevator indicated a grenade had paved the way for the two-man juggernaut. It was something of a miracle—or good old-fashion auda-cious warrior spirit, he suspected—that had seen them even make it off the elevator, which could have just as easily proved their coffin. Guts aside, gain-ing access, though, to the crew hatch and whatever they intended to do beyond that, was another matter altogether.

One armed figure, he saw, was spraying autofire from the platform, feet away from the open crew hatch, but looked to be taking hits as he lurched upright, his face contorted in a snarl of pain and rage, then he went back to full-auto sweep of the hangar. Hawkins grabbed cover behind a steel bin, thrust his weapon around the corner, just beneath the fireflies of ricochets sparking overhead, and tagged another Russian hard-man with a precision burst to the chest, kicked him off his feet as if he'd been poleaxed.

They needed to get to that hangar, ASAP, James knew. But how? One look at a larger screen that seemed to swell in front of his eyes with roiling clouds of mul-ticolored fire, and he knew it would be minutes before all that rocket fuel burned itself out, wreckage stopped flying around like razoring asteroids, and other rock-ets and small arms blew and found someplace to bury themselves. And even after the firestorm died down, what was to say there would be any decent supply of oxygen left to breathe the whole stretch for the three of them to even charge for the elevator bank that would take them straight to their teammate's six?

As James couldn't decide if that conflagration on the screen looked like the big bang that had created the universe or the end of the world, two things tore his attention. The shooter was getting the final full touches of a converging stream of autofire from McCarter and Hawkins, spiraling now across the platform before he pitched forward and tumbled down the steps, when the turbofan engines on the delta-winged orbiter ignited.

Turbofan engines? Orbiter? James looked to stern—catching a bitter eyeful of the American flag and United States emblazoned on the fuselage in the process—and, sure enough, he made out the cone-shaped main and maneuvering engines, the aft control thrusters. It sure looked like a space shuttle, the wings slightly different from any American space plane, though, more tapered, something like an F-117, he thought, or maybe not.

Then the black ex-SEAL remembered this was not only Russia—where a lot of the country's hardware was either borrowed, copied or outright stolen—but the craft was, after all, a so-called reusable launch vehicle. A space truck, actually, in terms of cold, hard reality, but which was designed to fly both as airplane and rocket, takeoff and land—vertical and/or horizontal, only in this case he gathered it would be horizontal—everything to be used again and again. Simply refuel, basic ground maintenance, and off it went. There would be ailerons, rudder, high-octane jet fuel—not sure where to look for that—but which it was a safe bet the craft was topped out, with reserve tanks probably fitted somewhere. The sum total of which was all factored in to get the flying martyrs to wherever the target destination before redlining. Or maybe the missiles were programmed for long-range delivery, but without close-up inspection, without solid intel…

There would also be cutting-edge, on-board navigational computer avionics for autopilot, from radar altimeter to GPS to probably up-to-the-minute Doppler for oncoming frontal patterns, five on-board computers in all for data processing. But that, he recalled, was for the American shuttle. There was no telling what the Russian version carried as far as sophisticated electronics, supercomputers and such. Then, for the enemy's purposes, he suspected there were stolen coded access programs for its payload, and which, most likely, could be delivered to near bull's-eye precision in this day and age and where every major power on the global block was looking to shoot light-years ahead of the next competitor. No, this RLV was not fully finished to spec, he guessed, but this particular but bastardized version of a space bus with its twenty-megaton payload was set to fly. As Encizo pointed out, the hangar doors were wide open.

"If you are thinking what I think you are, there is only one way to help your friends."

Rushti, James saw, held his ground at the end of the aisle.

"That shuttle—or RLV or whatever you call it—can't be allowed to take off," Manning said.

"But you state the obvious, comrade."

James bared his teeth. "You got solutions, let's hear it and skip the clever-sounding crap."

"Look carefully at the fifth monitor down to your right and you will find we may have some trouble before—if—we reach the RLV in time."

James looked and found the problem. About ten armed problems, maybe more, depending on how many shooters were waiting in the other hangar, as small groups of four to six ran to join the main group, which was heading toward an entourage of figures in white labcoats. And the surviving work detail was surrounded by a force of five soldiers.

Long odds, James knew, and big problems.

"Just get us up top," James barked at Rushti, and fell in between his teammates.

IT WAS A STRANGE SENSATION, wading into the kill zone, armored in the spirit of Carl Lyons.

Hermann Schwarz still wasn't sure how he felt about that. He knew the Able Team leader wasn't tagged Ironman just because it sounded tough, like some Hollywood punk claiming false hero status and hanging his name up on the marquee.

Carl Lyons was the real deal.

And, even as he rolled down the opposite side of his partner's firepoint, Schwarz stole a second to admire the big man's brazen in-their-face moves, steeled and ready to imitate the Able Team leader's show of merciless force.

It looked like six savages were left to ring up. They were bobbing and weaving between shouts and growled curses down the line of vehicles, throwing Uzi subgun, pistol and machine pistol fire Lyons's way. But they were too hasty and either too angry and too fearful of losing their worlds to do anything other than annoy the Able Team leader with rounds that flew so high and wide all of one or two bullets slashed off the man's cover.

Lyons, though, was a whirlwind of thundering wrath, pounding out the double-fisted barrage of Magnum hell. The hand cannons blasted away at the pack, blowing out windows and windshields and gouging nasty swaths over pricey engine hoods, then Lyons hurled himself around the edge on the far side of the statue and resumed the wild gunslinger routine in what seemed the very next breath.

Time to rock and rumble!

Schwarz trained the assault rifle on the blindside of two goons who were both rising to their full height, madmen now hollering and blazing away with subguns in what looked utter defiance of death and ruin. They were stationary long enough for Lyons to catch one full in the chest and launch him back and several feet over the drive, then Schwarz cut loose with autofire. As he nailed one, then another hardman two vehicles farther downrange, hit another shooter whirling his way and flinging him into a shredded pirouette down the side of a stretch Mercedes limo, he discovered only the big boss men were left standing.

Or rather, one was seeking cover, bellowing out something about a deal. It was hard to tell who was who, what with fiery matériel showering the area and flames dancing shadows down the line, but Schwarz thought that was Yoravky offering Lyons the world to spare his life.

"Five million in cash, if you let us walk out of here!"

"Only five mil?"

"How much do you want?"

"You don't have enough money."

The Able Team leader stepped away from the statue, followed up the taunting and unloaded both massive handguns, as Yoravky lurched up between the space in the vehicles. The Russian Don's machine pistol flamed for a heartbeat or two as he was launched into the open.

One giant jackal down.

One to go.

Franjo Balayko was equally caught in the open air, but torn for a split second as to which threat to turn his Uzi on. He went for Lyons, and Schwarz stitched him with a rising burst up the ribs.

After a long three-sixty sweep, Schwarz decided the dead had gone to meet their eternal judge. He jogged forward to meet Lyons over the body of Balayko.

CHAPTER TWENTY-FIVE

As the commander and pilot of *Starfire One,* Jahbat Nafarazzi knew it was his task to get the space plane safely in the air, intact and online for the eight-thousand-mile-plus flight from Eastern Siberia down the Sea of Okhotsk and across the Pacific. First, that meant putting in the rest of the access codes for all the primary and secondary avionics software, and at the dire present that alone looked a giant leap for jihad. The one piece of good news was that he had just fired up the engines, switched the rotating hand controller to primary manual, just so he could roll them out of the hangar and onto the runway.

Only now…

The laptop's modem attached to the feeder system next to the radar altimeter on the upper left of the red-lighted instrument control panel—just about every-thing as far as digital reads, HUDs, the whole instrument panel, for that matter, was backward or, at best, slightly altered when compared to the American space shuttle as he had learned during four years of special training in Iran then Dagestan for this operation. He finished tapping in the sequence of number-letter encryption, just as the new round of autofire rattled up from middeck. Too late now, it occurred to him he should have closed and sealed the hatch, only up to then he couldn't be sure which—if any—of his crew was in or out of the craft, and how close their engagement with the enemy.

But he knew he had to do something about the threat, and lightning fast. Then the idea flared to mind. It would be a counterattack, and simply to bring them under control—mentally congratulating himself for having the foresight now—but he preferred to kill them outright. If they breached the middeck, any suicidal stand was the worst of all possible scenarios, and martyrdom was the last and least ambition for any of them. A trophy, better yet a human shield or two to be used as hostage leverage might also solidify any unforeseen stalling tactic in the event a crisis arose during the flight. Depending, though, on how the next few moments shaped up...

He had already seen the two black-clad shooters in action, evidence of their initial brutal success strewed around the hangar, and it was all he could do to concentrate, not look back out the flight deck's window where fear could grind away until despair shouted back at him all was lost. There was no time to wonder who they were, if the plan had been uncovered and if they were perhaps moments away from facing an entire army of Russian soldiers when he rolled them out of the hangar. The other bit of good news was that his payload specialist was safe and secure in the weapons bay—as far as he knew—and arming the missiles, but he needed a status report.

The bad news was that Zahadan Sandaj and the lone Chechen operative, Dirvit Aymon, were either down and dead near the crew hatch, or in the process of shooting it out with the two adversaries bounding up the ramp. By Allah, he desperately needed his brother Iranian now to fulfill his role as mission specialist. Then he determined he could carry out both duties, that crisis often simply tested the mettle of the true Islamic warrior, that success under fire and adverse conditions only served to elevate him to the status of superhuman. Thus he worked at an even more frenzied pace as he banged in the last sequence of numbers and letters that would lock in altitude and speed for every critical group of miles, linking them with the GPS software. Once that was done, there would be no way to override the program, short of shooting the flight deck to ruins. By chance, even if that was done, even if an American fighter jet launched a missile meant to blow them out of the sky...

Nafarazzi smiled.

Access Granted flashed in the upper right-hand corner of his laptop. Nafarazzi hit Enter.

Check.

Now the autopilot was preprogrammed once they were in the air and the wheels were retracted.

They were set for Mach 3, and at three times the speed of sound—2220 mph from indicated to true ground speed—but with westerly headwinds for most of the flight factored in, along with altitude and air pressure, then eventually descent and the gradual drop of speed to sub-Mach for their purposes, before the turbofans fired and propelled the space bus—

No matter.

Starfire's navigational avionics were locked in for the full journey now.

Nafarazzi grimaced at the sharp grunts and sustained bursts of autofire that tore up the access ladder. He grabbed the tac radio, hit the button. "Hammon! Report!" he demanded in Farsi, as he jumped out of his seat and tore down the zipper to his gear bag, his AKM assault rifle within a quick easy grab.

"The spears of God are armed! Praise be to God!" Hammon replied.

Nafarazzi gritted his teeth. He had no patience at that time for such vainglorious nonsense. "Two armed intruders have climbed the ramp!"

"Yes, I hear the shooting!"

Nafarazzi grabbed the small steel canister from his bag and told Hammon what to do.

"Throw down your weapons! If you know what is onboard this craft, then you know I can activate all four of those missiles from here!"

As McCarter stepped over the second body sprawled inside the crew hatch, aimed his AK-47 up the access ladder, he signaled Hawkins to lock them in. McCarter stared up the ladder, then took in the middeck, listening for any sound of movement. He strongly suspected there was one, maybe more fanatics either hunkered down in the weapons bay or en route through the tunnel access. As for his immediate problem, the invisible threat was close, the ex-SAS commando could feel him, just above, a few feet, if that, out of sight. For some strange reason he had spoken in Russian, then repeated himself in English, which left any number of questions hanging in McCarter's mind.

"Then you lose, too," McCarter said, as Hawkins closed and locked the hatch.

"So be it."

"This shuttle doesn't leave the hangar. I'm prepared to give up my life to keep that from happening."

"Then you are a fool."

McCarter indicated that Hawkins watch the middeck and airlock. It was now or never, a straight hard haul up the access ladder, spraying autofire the whole way. With luck, his armor would take any and all hits. But he could not, nay, *would not* let twenty megatons of suicidal Armageddon leave the ground. If he had to sacrifice his own life and the life of his friend and teammate in the process to spare a nuclear holocaust that would murder millions and shove the entire planet to the brink of World War Three...

He grabbed a rung. His finger began taking up slack on the AK's trigger when the object plunged through the hole, spewing out thick clouds of smoke.

A NUMBER OF FACTORS beyond their control warned Gary Manning they were too little, too late. By the time they surfaced in the elevator, not only were the Russian turncoats executing the work detail with long raking bursts of autofire near the closest—east end—hangar, but the shuttle was already taxiing onto the runway, nose aimed east. Distance to both aircraft and the standing enemy was factor number two.

As Manning fell in with the fighting force and charged on in a skirmish line, the big Canadian flanked by James and Encizo, with Rushti and his Czars on their right wing, he feared there was no chance—short of Encizo blasting the shuttle off the runway with the Steamroller—to stop the flying thermonuclear bomb. The turbofans, he saw, ignited into cones of fire, the space plane rapidly gathering momentum for takeoff as it rolled, harder and faster, and swept past their position. Any fading hope of shooting out the tires was gone in seconds flat as the craft tore off down the runway, seemingly swallowed into the misty white light near the far east end.

And since they couldn't reach McCarter and Hawkins, they assumed one of two worst-case scenarios. Their teammates either were lying dead in the hangar, or they were on board the RLV. As far as blasting to smithereens the shuttle with its nuclear payload went, that was a dicey proposition, at best, and may well prove a foolish fatal risk. On the off chance the payloads were touched off, there was still plain old radioactive contamination to fear. That aside, there was the dire concern that if McCarter and Hawkins were on board—and why—and in what kind of condition...

Cover became the next and most immediate concern.

There was none.

It was flat open ground to the hangar's east wall, maybe sixty yards and counting down, and the snow was about five to seven inches deep. Top it all off, they wore blacksuits, and against a pure white backdrop…

Which was why Encizo took the opportunity to drop to a knee and begin chugging out 50 mm bombs before the enemy could mark and start dropping them. The first two explosions ripped through a group of about fifteen to twenty traitors who were heading back into the open hangar door where Manning spied the nose end of an Mi-26 transport chopper. That bird could seat eighty troops, which gave some indication to the big Canadian that a small army within the army here had been part of the conspiracy.

Rotten…

Return fire was minimal at first, he next discovered, since the executioners were torn between chasing down several runners and shell-shocked by the sight of their fellows getting smashed and launched to broken rag dolls.

Rushti and his Czars, Manning saw, ran on, spreading out, angling for what appeared the agreed-upon charge for the back of the hangar. Rushti wanted a prisoner or two, and if that happened, so much the better, but Manning had more pressing matters to attend to, beyond waxing the surviving Zenith hardforce.

Fighting back any number of nightmare scenarios from distracting him, Manning began directing precision bursts at groups of twos and threes, as James shellacked more walking mangled on an advance with all grim purpose. Maybe eight or nine survivors began to flee for the relative safety of the hangar as a military-style VIP jet rolled through the opening.

Then two fireballs took out the sleek bird, reducing

it to flaming scrap, as nearby shredded hardmen flopped to the deck behind the cloud of flames and tempest of wreckage.

It was enough—barely—to tell Manning that mop-up was pretty much all that was left.

The big Canadian was almost afraid to look, but stood, turned and found he was in time to watch the space plane lift off, vanish altogether in the white shroud, and bitterly wonder, Now what?

"I WILL TAKE IT, then, that the good major general is either a prisoner or he is no longer among the living."

"Turn the craft around and bring it back to base or you will be shot down."

He heard two voices, floating to him from a great distance, but clawing through the thick veil of darkness. One sounded like Rushti, the other he recognized as the mystery adversary who had dropped the bomb on them.

Grenade?

He was alive! Sleeping gas, or whatever the concoction that had knocked him out cold in seconds flat…

And that was all David McCarter needed to know.

He cracked his eyes open, stifled off the groan as what struck him as harsh but somehow dark sunlight speared through the windshield. As he stared out at the vast sea of billowing white clouds, he flexed his hands and—

They were free! Why? And why was he even still alive? What about Hawkins? What in the name of…

His limbs felt like cement blocks, but adrenaline and ice-cold fear of the unknown quickly cleared away the cobwebs, drove the sludge out of his eyes. He found himself strapped into the right—the pilot's—seat, or maybe everything was ass backward since this was a Russian craft. Whatever the mystery and impending disaster, he was minus weapons, combat vest, harness, but he felt the cold steel handle on the underside of his right forearm, as he rolled the limb a little on the armrest. It was just inside the sleeve, sheathed right above the wrist, and how they had overlooked it was beyond him, but in all the excitement and their frenzy to get the RLV in the air...

"Ah, as we speak, one of your two comrades is now waking up."

"Mac? Are you and T.J. all right?"

McCarter was about to answer Manning when his nemesis swiveled some in his commander's chair and lifted the Makarov pistol.

"They are just fine—for the present—but never mind about them."

McCarter turned his head, found Hawkins coming alive in the mission specialist seat. "Say, mate. Can you hear me?" As Hawkins nodded, glanced at the AKM assault rifle aimed from the payload specialist's seat, McCarter quickly said, "How's that right arm holding up where you had that steel plate put in last year?"

"Silence!" the commander barked.

"Good to go, but that's the least of it. Or am I stating the obvious?" Hawkins said, acknowledging he was armed and dangerous a second before his captor jabbed him in the ribs with the assault rifle.

"Talk again and I will shoot you," Hawkins's seatmate snarled.

McCarter watched as the smile spread over the swarthy face next to him. The man was lean and wiry, hair closely cropped, with no beard, but the ex-SAS commando suspected the non-Muslim appearance, as far as facial hair went, was part of what had become a standard ruse by Islamic fanatics these days for infiltrating and maintaining sleeper cells. He had a thousand and one questions, but knew it was best to stay silent for the time being, and wait for what he hoped and silently prayed was the right moment, that one split second where his potential mark dropped his guard. He decided to let the fanatic gloat, enjoy whatever triumph he believed he was about to reap from his commandeering of the RLV. If he could make him think McCarter was a frightened, submissive captive, albeit a soldier who had failed…

"Whoever you are," the commander said, "let us be clear on the facts of life as I humbly give them to you. One, the radar sensors that shroud this craft can detect any bogey up to fifteen miles. Two, should a missile be launched at us, those sensors will transmit a signal that is tied in to the computer systems of the payload that, as you may or may not know, was specially engineered by the ESA in collusion with your country—that would be Russia, since I believe you used American commandos to help attack the base—in the event of a doomsday scenario as drawn by Moscow regarding this craft. Three, the missiles are coated in black ferrite paint, among other antiradar tracking and electronic countermeasures components. In other words, they are virtually invisible to radar. Moreover, they are rocket-driven warheads, which makes them far faster than any jet-propelled missile."

McCarter listened as Rushti snarled back from the radio box. "All of that may be true, but you would commit suicide. The system was not yet completed to launch those missiles on their own if the airspace monitored by its radar was breached. All that would happen is you blow yourselves up in midair, your mission a failure."

McCarter gauged the fanatic's reaction. There was just enough hesitation to tell him that much was most likely true.

The fanatic chuckled. "Perhaps. But you do not actually know that for certain, nor do you know what I know. And, being that I am aware how much Americans value the lives of their own—even two such unillustrious and failures as commandos such as I have here—I am betting you will not attempt such an attack. Further, I suspect, that since you are acting in some capacity in your own country's vested interest in this RLV, you cling to the false hope you may get the craft back in one working piece. Long live Islam! God is great!" he said, and snapped off the transmission just as Rushti launched into an angry reply.

McCarter watched for a moment as the fanatic commander worked the keyboard of his laptop. A radar screen flashed on, along with numbers scrolling in the top right-hand corner. The radar part of the monitor looked clear of air traffic.

Then the Briton stared out the windshield as they plunged into thick clouds, getting his bearings as best he could, as he noted the shafts of light spearing through in multicolored but dark-shrouded layers. Flying into—or rather under and past the sun—they had to be somewhere north of the equator, that was if he judged the foreshadowing of light and mixed shadow correct, but which meant they were heading east, nonetheless, and streaking on into yesterday once they crossed the international date line—or had they already soared into, theoretically speaking, the past?

How long he'd been under was impossible to say. If they were cruising at supersonic speed, and, he suspected, streaking over the Pacific the target—or targets—would either be the Hawaiian islands or the West Coast of the United States, his grim suspicion being the massive population of California. Consider four missiles, each packing enough mega-tonnage to wipe out…

He felt the ball of ice wedge in his twisting guts.

Could be that Los Angeles was marked for extinction. Or San Diego. Or San Francisco. Those were the most likely possibilities, but as for number four…

Well, Las Vegas was a short flight across the desert for the last missile, Portland just up the coast from San Francisco. That they were rocket-fueled instead of jet-engine-powered like the standard U.S. cruise missiles, then they were sacrificing range for speed. Then again, if the whole payload was intended as one flying bomb, assuming Rushti spoke the truth…

That meant the fanatics were hell-bent on plowing the RLV straight into the target.

"Since you let us live," McCarter said, "I assume you're probably itching to tell us what you plan to vaporize in your nuclear jihad?"

The commander chuckled. "I let you live so that you may bear final witness to the glory of Islam."

"No," Hawkins said. "You let us live because you didn't want us shooting up the ship before you went wheels up."

The commander nodded. "In a few short hours, gentlemen, four at the most, you will see the California coastline." Nafarazzi laughed. "Just look for the big sign that says 'Hollywood.'"

McCarter felt his heart skip a beat. The admission was all he needed to jump-start a new surge of adrenaline and fear. Twenty megatons was more than enough to incinerate all of Southern California. Four hours and counting, it would be what? he wondered. The dead of night on the other side of the ocean? Early morning? The infamous Los Angeles freeways choked with patented abysmal congestion as rush hour clogged at the starting gate?

Good news—good news?—he could count on their teammates back at Zenith to put in the SOS to the Farm. Then what? Brognola would alert the White House and then...

The Pacific Ocean was well traveled and monitored by a veritable fleet of American subs, carriers, battleships, Hawaii alone, serving as the midway point and major ring of surveillance and countersurveillance. And the lives of two men were less than nothing when weighed against the mass murder of countless millions.

They would be blown out of the sky, no matter what the fanatic or Rushti claimed in their exchange of saber-rattling. Why it hadn't already happened...

Well, chalk that up to either solid planning and state-of-the-art ECM and so forth or both…

"It's fitting, don't you think?"

McCarter looked at Nafarazzi, noticed how he released the web straps by depressing the steel catch around his sternum. "What's that?"

"That Los Angeles, your Hollywood, what is modern Babylon, or more fitting, Sodom and Gomorrah, is due to be vaporized in what I consider nothing less than the wrath of God, one giant fiery breath from Heaven that will cleanse the world of filth and immorality that you infidels attempt to contaminate and undermine the rest of the world with."

Which told McCarter one payload, one city, and that was no comfort at all.

Until then…

The Briton needed an opening, now, and quick. If this sack of living Evil beside him could be blinded, if only for an instant, by his own arrogance…

The pistol swung a few inches toward the Phoenix Force leader's face. The commander said, "Hammon, bring our parachutes. Disable those we won't be needing."

McCarter grunted. "So, you never intended to go down with the ship."

"Why? And that particular foolishness is better suited for mere foot soldiers, the cannon fodder, if you will. At any rate, the autopilot will take the craft to within one square mile of downtown Los Angeles, I am pleased to state. The very fact that no bogeys have yet shown up on my screen tells me that by the time our presence is known it will be way too late. Even if the ship is blown out of the sky within twenty-five miles of the coast, by then it will be so low, the blast alone could very well kill hundreds of thousands. Of course, you may be aware of fallout and the like. The prevailing winds blowing in from the Pacific will do just fine as far as my own Plan B goes. Naturally, whether ground zero is downtown Los Angeles or a mere few miles out to sea, there will be mass panic, nothing short of anarchy. Riots. Looting. Murder in the streets as the infidels come unhinged. Martial law. Complete meltdown of law and order. Perhaps even the White House will be overthrown by the panicked and terrified masses of armed savages in the streets and who will feel compelled to storm the gates, if only out of blind rage and horror. Yes. I can even now see it all clearly. The President, his family perhaps dragged out onto the White House lawns and executed in the most shameful and horrifying of ways and perhaps even filmed by the media who is always in search of a sensational story." He laughed and added, "Relax and enjoy the rest of the flight."

"SOUNDS LIKE YOU KNEW a whole lot more than you let on, Rushti."

Manning silently echoed Encizo's angry sentiments.

They were back in the abattoir of mission control. Maybe a dozen of the surviving traitors had thrown down their weapons and surrendered, and were currently under guard and interrogation by a few Czars up top. Only the battle to secure the grounds now seemed a minor skirmish with sticks when Manning considered the nightmare they were all faced with.

"What's this about the RLV doomsday scenario?" James demanded. "What all haven't you told us, comrade?"

"I think my teammate speaks for all of us," Encizo said, "when he says this is the final warning for you to come clean."

Rushti hardened his features, his jaw clenched as he stared down the bank of blank security monitors. "The fuel that powers the craft alone is of a highly classified nature, and which the Russian mafia—the Yoravky *kalorshniks*—in collusion with certain business partners and politicians in Moscow managed to stake claim to certain fields here in Siberia where this reserve was discovered. Aerodynamically speaking, it should not even fly at supersonic speeds, but it is made of, again, a highly classified alloy that only makes it appear to the naked eye as a huge lumbering space bus." Rushti cleared his throat. "Be that as it may, in the event of World War Three, my country's role in the Zenith Project—working with the ESA or rather its conspirators and on both sides, mind you—intended to build and place as many of these RLVs into low earth orbit as possible. From Earth stations, they could be programmed to become flying thermonuclear bombs, virtually undetectable by ground radar and other satellites. Even if they were shot down coming through the atmosphere there would be enough—"

"We have the picture," Manning cut in. "What we need now is to reach our people. Ruf?" the big Canadian said, locking stares with Encizo. "Please tell me you still have the buzz box?"

Encizo reached into a pouch on his combat vest and

produced the small black box. The instrument, Manning knew, was a state-of-the-art scrambler and signal relay device that would create ghost transmissions from an unsecured line. How secure their transmission would prove once they reached the Farm through a series of back channels...

Manning turned on Rushti. "We need a radio, sat link, anything to reach our people like five minutes ago! You can fill us in on anything you've forgotten or neglected to tell us while we dial up the SOS."

CHAPTER TWENTY-SIX

Stony Man Farm, Virginia

"That would make it—what?—almost three hours, give or take, since Phoenix said they took off."

Even as he said it, Hal Brognola knew Price and Kurtzman already knew as much, but just hearing his own voice...

Would do what? the big Fed thought. Delay the inevitable call?

"Hell," Brognola swore, "and with Rushti claiming a Russian radar and tracking station near Okhotsk coast told him it was clocked at Mach 3 and heading southeast and with the bearings we got..."

Neither the mission controller nor the cyberteam leader spoke, as Brognola let the statement trail off.

Kurtzman, he saw, brought up the digital map on the wall monitor. His laptop modem was hooked to the feeder mount at the base of the wall, and at the same time Tokaido was shooting up-to-the-second intel from the Computer Room. Oddly enough, despite the fact the oxygen seemed sucked out of the War Room and the walls had all but closed in, Brognola felt a steely calm. Then wondered if he was only clinging to hope, but what else could any of them do? This wasn't a business for the faint of heart.

As Kurtzman framed the area in question—from eastern Siberia and which encompassed the entire Pacific Ocean to the West Coast from Seattle to San Diego—Brognola knew he was seconds away from grabbing up the red phone and informing the President of the United States a thermonuclear bomb was God only knew how long from erupting on American soil.

"Hal, at this point it's all very bad news," Kurtzman stated. "The ship being marked as American is a cheap ruse, but it may buy them just enough time. And with stealth technology that may even be years ahead of what we have now…" Kurtzman hit a few keys and five red lines with numbers over each and running from about the 55th parallel to the 33rd appeared on the monitor. "Those are estimated impact times and targets—Seattle, Portland, San Francisco—"

"L.A. and San Diego," Brognola cut in. "What about Hawaii?"

"They've either hit it or they've sailed past. If past the islands, they would be far north and have another target or targets in mind," Kurtzman said. He tapped a few more keys and outlined a red area from what looked Vancouver to San Diego and a chunk of the Pacific Ocean off the coast.

"Mainland U.S.," Brognola said.

"Another problem is that there's no way we can

hack into any sat and park it or even steer it over the Pacific or find one…"

"I understand all that, Bear," Brognola said. "What you're showing us is pretty much an educated guess of its flight path, with projected distance, altitude, time to impact based on true ground speed."

"Hal," Price suddenly said, her voice solemn but edged with urgency. "We'll assume they have so far remained undetected. You're going to have to call the President."

"The best we can do with what little intel we have is track its path on educated guesses," Kurtzman said. "Basically, we're out of touch, totally blind at the moment. Under the circumstances we have to assume the worst of worst-case scenarios and make the preemptive call."

The big Fed felt his head nod ever so slightly. There was no choice. Fighter jets, or a missile launched from a submarine or a battleship, but either way the RLV had to be blown out of the sky. ASAP.

And, in the process, they would lose both McCarter and Hawkins. It was next to no consolation that Brognola knew that to a Stony Man operative they all understood and accepted the ultimate sacrifice. No questions, no pleas, no stalling for more time. Sudden death was part of the job description, but Brognola always lived in what was tenuous hope, at best, that the day would never come where they would lose another of their field operatives. It was something of a hollow hope always, considering the world in which they lived and fought, and how the stakes were so high, so volatile.

"Hal?" Price said. "Unless we hear from David or T.J., and even then…"

Brognola nodded and reached for the red phone.

THE RLV'S TERRORIST commander was grinning, bobbing his head, and McCarter knew it was now or never. He was hitting the delete key, rising from his chair when the ex-SAS commando depressed the release catch, and for a millisecond hoped to God they hadn't jammed it somehow.

He was free!

Hawkins was a blur of human lightning in the corner of his eye, but McCarter was locked in raging tempest himself, seizing his own initiative, sliding the blade out of its sheath and plunging the razor-sharp steel into the fanatic's throat. The pistol fell from his grasp as the terrorist staggered back a step, his eyes bulged in shock and horror, one hand reaching up to claw at the embedded steel. But McCarter held on—for his own life and the lives of millions—and tore the blade deep and across, through jugular, sinew, the final thin layer of flesh. The blade swept out behind a torrent of blood, the terrorist reeling back until he slammed into the bulkhead, gurgling, thrashing, his eyes rolling back in his head as he toppled to the deck.

McCarter was about to step over the convulsing body to help his teammate when he found he needn't bother. Another spreading pool of blood was all the grim testament the Briton needed that the ex-Ranger had delivered a near decapitating strike himself.

They were hardened professionals, used to dispensing violent death, but both of them held their ground for a moment—stunned by their own lightning kills, that it was over in less time than it took to blink—keeping the blades poised, as if fearing the dead would suddenly rise.

McCarter strode the few steps with Hawkins to the

pile of gear and parachute packs stacked near what he reckoned was the bank of payload controls. Hawkins held up two handfuls of shredded canopy, but showed the Phoenix Force leader the other packs were stuffed and ready. Another nylon bag contained helmets, oxygen bottles, gloves. Whether they would have enough time to check and repack the chutes, slip into the enemy's pressure suits for a jump in what he was sure was subzero, airless altitude was anybody's guess.

McCarter was turning to charge back for the main instrument panel, moving to radio his teammates when Hawkins shouted, "David."

And McCarter found that the terrorists, for whatever reason—arrogance and the now fatal conviction of their own invincibility—had decided not to throw their sat link overboard. McCarter hesitated, looked back out at the windshield as they shot from the cloud bank. Suddenly he felt the craft dip, the motion nearly rocking him off his heels. He'd logged more frequent flyer commando miles, he figured, than there were stars in the solar system. That was no turbulence.

They were losing altitude. Fast.

Another shudder, and he knew the speed was being cut back, and drastically.

"David, if you're thinking about looking at those missiles and maybe trying to disarm them…"

He was, in fact. Then he realized any second an American fighter jet or a Tomahawk missile could be launched from a sub. And, if it was true about the payload being touched off if the RLV's airspace was breached, they would never know what hit them.

"Get into one of those pressure suits, T.J., and go blow the hatch. I'll phone home."

"Hey, look at this."

McCarter found Hawkins holding up a flare gun. Rescue was hardly guaranteed, not by a longshot, but McCarter felt the tight smile tug at the corner of his mouth.

Stony Man Farm, Virginia

BROGNOLA PUT THE PHONE DOWN, felt their questions hanging in the air.

"The President's gone to the Situation Room," the big Fed told Price and Kurtzman. "They had a suspicion, once it breached airspace of a remote U.S. naval base on an island northwest of Hawaii that's not even found on any world map. But the Man told me that I only confirmed it."

They said nothing, but Brognola sensed they knew the bottom line.

"All hands, including British warships stationed in the Pacific, I understand, have been alerted. The works, people, have been scrambled."

And he knew he needn't bother running down the A and B list of fighters, subs, carriers.

Brognola felt his lips part as the mission controller and the cyberteam leader stared at a wall monitor that meant absolutely nothing in real time.

The Man knew the score. The Man knew who was on board. He had hard intel that the terrorists had been eliminated, what the package was, what the flight path and intended target.

All thanks, Brognola thought, to the efforts of five brave men.

Brognola clenched his fists. His knuckles popped, the sound echoing through the War Room like a pistol crack.

"Twenty minutes," Brognola said. "That's the proposed time frame he said was needed to try to pinpoint a 'reasonable' window of collateral damage, as far as shipping lanes, air traffic, while at the same time every control tower on the West Coast is being handed a presidential directive to reroute, bring back, keep grounded…well…"

"But they were jumping," Kurtzman said, a note of hope in his voice, "just as soon as David signed off."

Would it be enough time, enough clearance? Brognola wondered. He recalled the grim math Kurtzman had just done, minutes ago, and it was according to FEMA and NSA calculations of nuclear blasts.

One megaton, one city. That's what the brains in the U.S. intelligence think tanks called it. A one-megaton blast—a direct hit—in the average downtown American city would vomit out a crater two hundred feet deep, one thousand feet across. Within that first circle anywhere from one hundred thousand up to half a million people would be vaporized instantly, depending on population density, the lay of the urban landscape, while legions of other living creatures would be set ablaze. Buildings would literally melt, assuming a few were even still partially standing, or would be ignited into towering torches. Two miles beyond ground zero, and the blast waves were still going strong as they hurtled out 150 mph winds that were superheated like the core of the sun. Now…with twenty megatons, and simply multiply those numbers…

"Hal? What did he say about our people?"

Brognola looked at Price and answered. "He said he'd call back as soon as it was done."

AS A FORMER COMMANDO of the Special Air Service, and during his stint as a Stony Man warrior, David McCarter was no stranger to jumps at any height, HAHO, HALO or a straight six-hundred-foot combat plunge. Nor was Hawkins as an ex-Army Ranger unfamiliar with all the risks and any number of anticipated and unforeseen disasters that could strike at any time during a jump.

McCarter kept on plummeting toward the Pacific Ocean, and for the life of him he couldn't determine how high up, which direction he was tumbling…

The world rushed up at him in a maze of flying shadows and broken light. With the rapidly growing velvet expanse of a glassy surface and where only the smallest detail of whitecaps betrayed the swells…

And he knew the big bang was coming.

He twisted, one gloved hand reaching for the ripcord, his head swiveling in its oxygenated helmet. There was no sign of Hawkins, but the ex-Ranger had jumped first—and he had been a split second behind out the hatch—and it was a miracle all by itself they had even survived hitting the air and being blasted past the wings and tail at speeds that were close enough— or so it seemed—to Mach.

They had set their chronometers, roughly gauging descent, how far they would drift apart…

McCarter checked his watch.

One last look at the blackness below and he couldn't be sure if they were at twenty thousand or two thousand feet, but they needed as fast a plunge down as possible before opening the canopies. To get caught in the air, floating down while anywhere near what Kurtzman claimed had to be a fifty-mile relative safety zone from the twenty megaton airburst…

He kept waiting for the moment, braced for the worst, prepared for the end.

There was no sign of the RLV—not that he expected to see the flying nuclear space bus—but he'd been informed that the White House would be alerted, would have long since been told the terrible truth.

Which meant every available fighter jet scrambled, every nuke sub and battleship and carrier scouring every square mile, and he was surprised the sky—dark to the east—had not yet lit up.

The clock struck.

McCarter tugged on the steel pin. He was waiting for what seemed like an eternity for the familiar bone-jarring, gut-wrenching jolt that told him the canopy had opened when there was no mistaking the sudden burst of dazzling white light to the distant east for what it was.

EPILOGUE

They were dying.

The swells had been bouncing them around for close to six hours now, according to his last watch check, and that was just the beginning of all things to fear. Even with the pressure suits acting as another thermal layer over their formfitting blacksuits, the water this far north of the equator was bitter cold.

Like ice.

The sun became another infernal enemy. Not only did it further sap what little energy they had in reserve, but it nearly sucked out every last drop of life-sustaining water.

Which meant dehydration was fast setting in.

Which meant death wasn't far behind.

But they were still alive, still stroking, still clinging to whatever life they had left. And just when David McCarter didn't think he had any more left to give, a fire—dwindling, such as it was—flared on from deep inside, the silent warrior spirit urging him to take one more breath, thrust one more scissor kick to keep his head above water, endure one more angry swell rolling over his head or pounding him in the face.

Then there was yet another fear to consider.

Sharks, he reckoned, would soon enough be closing in, if they weren't already in the general vicinity. But with the current and the swells he suspected neither one of them would spot a dorsal fin until it was nearly right in front of eyes so tired, so bloodshot, and that felt as if the wind, the salty spray and the sun had sandpapered them to raw...

Strange, McCarter suddenly thought, how being eaten alive would seem like the most grotesque of all possible injustices, considering what the two of them had lived through—and what they had, indirectly, at least—as far as he knew—aborted.

No planes, no aircraft of any kind. No birds.

Nothing.

Alone, then, bobbing along with the current, the ocean would have been a vast soundless vault if not for the breaking swells. But just how alone were they? It was one thing to take in the invisible silent world for what it appeared, quite another to be aware...

Sharks.

There had still been some blood on his blade, he could be sure, when he'd used it to slice himself out of the harness since he had resheathed it in a hurry without wiping it off before jumping. Understandable, but under the circumstances suddenly unforgivable, and mighty damn foolish.

Sharks.

Something like thirty species out here, and how

many were man-eating he couldn't say, as he thought he spotted a dorsal fin.

It was. And it was a big one. From where he floated it looked the size of a standing surfboard, and knifing through the swells to the north, headed their way. With countless islands scattered all over the Pacific, any number of them were breeding grounds for seals and sea lions, though they were, generally speaking, farther north near the Bering Sea.

But which meant wherever there were those choice fat seal banquets there would be white sharks.

"David?"

Hawkins.

It was a miracle they were still close enough to shout and hear each other, a miracle, no less, they were still alive. If he'd hit the water like a falling asteroid, then gone under like a sinking stone before slicing himself free with his blade, he could be sure Hawkins was counting his blessings, too.

At least for the moment.

"I'm here!"

"We have company."

"I hope you mean by that a Search and Rescue chopper!"

"I have one flare left! I'm thinking…"

"Try and save it. But if that's what I think I just saw, use it. Go for the eyes!"

But he knew where there was one…

Something danced into his field of vision. The ocean, like the desert, he knew, could create its own illusions, so trusting eyes that were already battered by the elements…

But he would have sworn…

"David!"

McCarter squinted, bobbed up, rolled down, then was slammed full in the face by another and higher swell, his stomach knotting as he steeled himself for that bone-chilling scream that only a man who'd been chomped down on by a shark could emit. It didn't come, and McCarter thought he heard a note of urgency in his teammate's voice. Hawkins called out again, and McCarter stroked around, looking to the northwest. He grimaced as Hawkins shot the flare into the sky, wondering…

And the smile broke over McCarter's lips.

The flare was erupting high overhead in what was to him a sweet umbrella of blinding light. McCarter watched as the Sea Stallion banked hard, then came soaring their way.

"I'M SORRY, HAL. If there was anything humanly possible…"

"I understand, sir…"

He understood? What, exactly, did he understand? Hal Brognola wondered, as the brief conversation with the President filtered back through his mind, and like howling ghosts he knew would haunt him for a long time to come.

He understood that a twenty-megaton blast hadn't blown anywhere near the West Coast, the airburst, in fact, erupting over two hundred nautical miles out to sea the last he heard.

He understood that an unsuspecting Los Angeles had been saved.

And the big Fed wished to God he could tell the whole damn bunch out there in California why and who and how, and that they should be erecting monuments to two men by the names of David McCarter and Thomas Jackson Hawkins and putting their names on the Hollywood walk of fame and kissing the very ground on which those names were engraved and genuflecting and weeping so many tears of gratitude they would fill up the whole damn Pacific Ocean and...

But, he understood.

As far as saving L.A. and staving off World War Three for another day, the mission was a success.

And—true to Price's prophetic words that now bore bittersweet fruit—if Phoenix Force hadn't stumbled or bulled their way onto the Zenith plot and McCarter and Hawkins hadn't been captured and for whatever reason taken along for the ride...

Still, two of the best commandos on the planet were dead—or missing...

Or were they?

They had jumped, a good half hour or more by Kurtzman's reckoning, the RLV sailing on at what was guessed roughly Mach or sub-Mach. How high up was only a guess, but they were seasoned pros when it came to jumping, but under the circumstances...

And it stood to reason they didn't bother bailing with the sat link, and even if they hit the water with the high-tech thing in tow somehow...

Was he just holding on to hope?

He was alone in the War Room, and he was as alone as he'd felt in long bitter memory. It was all he could do to shut out what he could only call the screaming madness of anger and grief locked down. He stared at the wall monitor, at the area where Kurtzman had flagged where the space plane's thermonuclear payload had been touched off by a vertically launched Tomahawk from a new class of Seawolf-attack submarine.

"Hal."

He became aware of her presence, then realized Barbara Price had just walked in. For a second, as he started to look up, he wondered if she was coming to burden him with yet more ghosts or...

He wasn't sure what he saw on her face at first, as the ghosts retreated to their dark caverns of thought, but then reality gradually sank in as he stared at the mission controller's face.

Hal Brognola knew that look.

It was the smile of victory.

It was a wordless expression, of pure joy and relief.

And that told the big Fed all of their people had made it, if only to live to fight the good fight another day.

JAKE STRAIT

DAY OF JUDGMENT

BY FRANK RICH

INNER-CITY HELL JUST FOUND A NEW SAVIOR— THE BOGEYMAN

The damned, the dirty and the depraved all call the confines of inner-city hell home. And that's exactly where Jake Strait finds himself when a gorgeous blond angel hires him to infiltrate a religious sect to find her sister. But what he discovers instead is a wild-eyed prophet on the make, putting everyone at risk.

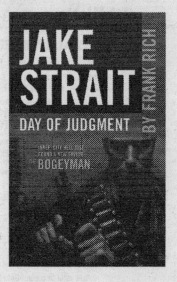

Available July 2007, wherever you buy books.

GOLD EAGLE®

GJS3

James Axler
Outlanders®

SKULL THRONE

RADIANT EVIL

Buried deep in the Mayan jungle amidst a civilization of lost survivors and emissaries of the dead, lies a relic that hides secrets to the prize— planet Earth. In sinister hands, it guarantees complete and absolute power. Kane and the rebels have just one chance to stop a rogue overlord from seizing glory, but must face an old enemy to stop him.

Available May 2007, wherever you buy books.

GOLD
EAGLE®

GOUT41

AleX Archer
THE LOST SCROLLS

In the right hands, ancient knowledge
can save a struggling planet...

Ancient scrolls recovered among the charred ruins of
the Library of Alexandria reveal astonishing knowledge
that could shatter the blueprint of world energy—and
archaeologist Annja Creed
finds herself an unwilling
conspirator in a bid for the
control of power.

**Available May 2007
wherever you buy books.**

GOLD
EAGLE®

GRA6